Promise Song

Linda Holeman

Published in Canada by Tundra Books, 481 University Avenue,
Toronto, Ontario M5G 2E9

Published in the United States by Tundra Books of Northern New York,
P.O. Box 1030, Plattsburgh, N.Y. 12901

Library of Congress Catalog Number: 96-61149

CANADIAN CATALOGUING IN PUBLICATION DATA
Holeman, Linda
    Promise song

ISBN 0-88776-387-1

I. Title

PS8565.06225P7 1997   jC813'.54   C96-931661-5
PZ7.H65Pr 1997

The publisher has applied funds from its Canada Council block grant for 1997
toward the editing and production of this book.

Cover design by Brian Bean
Cover illustration by Shelagh Armstrong

Printed and bound in Canada

01 00 99 98 97   5 4 3 2 1

For my daughter Zalie,
whose image helped me create Rosetta

The woods are lovely, dark and deep.
But I have promises to keep,
And miles to go before I sleep,
And miles to go before I sleep.

"Stopping by Woods on a Snowy Evening,"
Robert Frost

Acknowledgements

Special thanks to two people who helped ensure the authenticity of many details of this story – my mother, Donna Freeman, who so willingly shared her memories of life on a Canadian farm in the first part of this century, and Sigrid Johnson, at the Elizabeth Dafoe Library, University of Manitoba, who passed on invaluable information about the Icelandic people and their history. And, of course, thank you to my editor, Kathy Lowinger, for pushing me just a little further every time I thought there was no place left to go.

"Gudrun's Chain of Woes" and "Sayings of the High One" are both taken from *Poems of the Vikings* – the Elder Edda. Translated by Patricia Terry. Indianapolis and New York: The Bobbs-Merrill Company, Inc., 1969.

Preface

Between 1868 and 1925, over eighty thousand children from Britain were sent to Canada. All came from some sort of British "Home," or orphanage. Some were indeed orphans, placed into a Home when their parents died. Others had been street children, either abandoned or runaways from intolerable situations, living by begging and scavenging, and often more dead than alive. Still other children had one or both parents who, due to illness or poverty, had placed their children in a Home in the hopes that they would be better cared for.

Canada was a young country. It was in need of many hands to help develop it, especially in the rural areas.

It was to small, isolated farms, mainly in Eastern Canada, that the majority of British Home children were sent – to be "adopted" by Canadian families. From the British viewpoint, this was seen as a step-up in the world for the children. Instead of a childhood of institutional living with uncertain prospects, they would know family life, breathe clean, fresh air, and have a chance for a promising future in a new country.

Unfortunately, there were not enough employees of the plan to oversee the children once they arrived and were assigned a family. They were sent off, in good faith, to the people who requested them. Most had only a cursory follow-up as to their adjustment in their new life; some simply disappeared into the backwoods farms and secluded homesteads.

Some children found good homes, where they were treated as members of the family, working and playing alongside the family's own children, with the love and support of a mother and father. They received schooling, had an enjoyable social life, and often learned a trade as they grew into adulthood.

But others were not so fortunate, and their lives held nothing more than hard work, loneliness, and misery.

While all the above statements regarding the Home children are true and documented, Rosetta's story – *Promise Song* – comes strictly from my imagination.

Linda Holeman

Chapter One

The sea was flat, a dull slick of gray-blue paint, and for the first time in almost three weeks, the ship's growling engines were silenced.

Rosetta stared at the small wooden coffin, built by two of the ship's crew the evening before. The Union Jack draped over the rough box covered the chains wrapped around it to weigh it down, but Rosetta could still see the thick links, like rows of knuckles, gripping the container under the thin cloth.

As two sailors lifted the coffin onto a board near the port rail, the captain of the *Corsican* stepped forward.

"I have a few words to read," he said. "The Misses Watson and McLean here," he nodded to two middle-aged women standing in a group of young girls, "gave me what they knew about . . .," he looked down at the torn slip of paper in his hand, "about Ellen Morrison." At her name, there was a single, dry sob from somewhere in the group of girls. The captain cleared his throat. "Of course, being chaperons for so many girls is a hard duty. Miss Watson and Miss McLean have done a good job." Rosetta saw his eyes leave the two women and focus on the back row of girls on the deck, the taller, older ones. She lowered her own eyes. "So what I'm saying here," the captain continued, "is that this unfortunate accident is no fault of our chaperons." The water made soft kissing noises at the side of the ship.

The captain cleared his throat again, folded the paper in his hands, then opened it again and looked down at it. "Ellen Morrison was generally a good girl," he read. "Although high-spirited, she was kind to many of the younger girls. Ellen had lived at the Manchester Boys' and Girls' Refuge for the last two years. It is not known what past troubles she had before arriving at the Home. She was on her way to a new life in Canada, and sadly was taken only one day before she saw the shores of her next earthly home."

He folded the paper again, this time putting it in his pocket, and then nodded at the sailors holding the board. As the two men raised one end of the narrow plank, the captain said, "And so, on this twenty-second day of May 1900, we commit the body of Ellen Morrison to the deep."

Rosetta looked away as the box slid down the board. At the sound of the small, final splash, she thought, for once, how glad she was that Flora was too sick to come up on deck.

Rosetta closed her eyes, her lips automatically reciting along with the rest of the crowd, "The Lord is my shepherd, I shall not want," trying to find comfort in the words of the twenty-third Psalm. She kept her eyes closed, but the images behind her eyelids were not of green pastures, only of Ellen Morrison. At the orphanage, the Manchester Refuge, Ellen had often been scolded for her tricks and outspoken ways. Always grinning, a wide space between her two front teeth, Ellen had been a tall, wiry girl with hair like dried winter grass and eyes the color of hazelnuts. Now she lay, white and forever silent, in the unmarked box slowly drifting to the depths of the cold Atlantic Ocean.

Rosetta thought of Ellen as she had been only yesterday, the bright boldness of those eyes, with their pale, stubby lashes, blinking hard and fast as she dared the rest of the girls on deck to run under the rope one of the sailors had just put up across the end of the *Corsican's* deck.

"Don't none o' yous go under that rope," he'd said, tying the hairy brown twine in one of the final strange knots that all the sailors seemed to know. "Waves comin' up too high. Could make a mince o' you, against them iron railings. Best git down, inside now, young misses."

The stormy weather had blown up unexpectedly, and the swarm of older girls taking a morning walk around the deck headed back toward the door leading to the hold. They laughed and clutched each other as the sudden rough waves threw the *Corsican* up toward the sky, then down, down, as if it were reaching for the bottom of the ocean.

Rosetta hurried ahead; she wanted to make sure Flora wasn't seasick again. She turned back at Ellen's shouts.

"Come on, babies. Yer all scart. Watch me!"

A few of the girls had called after her, grabbing at the back of Ellen's coat as she ran toward the rope. But Ellen had nimbly dodged under the barrier and ran to the railing, touching it with her fingertips. As a wave dashed over the railing, she ran back under the rope.

Sliding on the wet deck, the girls squealed and covered their eyes with their hands as Ellen carried out her feat twice more, each time just escaping the roar of the waves.

"Come on!" Ellen yelled again. "Are none of you brave enough?"

Rosetta felt a smile twitching at the side of her mouth. Ellen looked so wild and free, racing up and down the deck. She waited a heartbeat more, then called over the wind and lashing of the water, "I'm not afraid, Ellen. Not me. I'll do it."

"No, Rosetta, don't," someone murmured.

But Rosetta raised her eyebrows at Ellen, then, as the ship rose up again, took off at a run. Her coat blew open, and the salty spray struck her cheeks and eyes. But it felt so good! So good to run, run hard. To not think of anything but reaching the end of the deck, of nothing but trying to grip the bottom of her hard leather boots onto the slippery deck. Not to think of Flora, or what they'd left behind, or what they were heading toward. Just to run and feel free. She ran back and forth once, then again, laughing the whole way the second time.

"So there you go, Miss Smart Ellen," she said, panting, wiping her wet hair back from her forehead. "I told you I could do it. I'm not scared."

"Yer all right, you are, Rosetta," Ellen said, her thin face cracked open with a delighted smile. "Come on, we'll do it together this time." She held out her hand.

Rosetta looked at the outstretched hand, and her smile faded. "No," she said. "I can't. I have to see to my sister."

Ellen shrugged. "Go on then. See if I care," she said, turning and starting up the deck again.

Rosetta stepped inside and went down the cramped stairway, balancing herself by placing her palms on the splintery boards that enclosed the stairs.

She was far below, in the cabins in steerage, wiping Flora's damp forehead as the little girl retched over the pail by her bunk, when the girls' laughter turned to screams of horror. It wasn't until lunchtime, when she went to the dining room to get cups of broth for herself and Flora, that she heard about Ellen and the final, crushing wall of water.

~

"Is Ellen in heaven, with her mama, Rosetta?"

"Yes, Ellen's in heaven now. But I don't know about her mother, whether she gave Ellen to the Home because she couldn't look after her, or if she died. Ellen never said."

"Tell me about our Mama, Rosetta."

"I've told you so many times, Flora."

"Please. Tell me how pretty she was. How much she loved us – loved me – before she went to Papa and the angels when I was a little baby. How happy she would be to know we were going to a new country. Tell me, Rosetta."

Rosetta looked down at her sister, lying beside her on the bunk. In the shadowy circle of light from the kerosene lamp hanging on one of the wooden poles, she saw that the little girl's face was thin and had a yellow cast. Her gray eyes looked enormous, and . . . old. Yes, thought Rosetta, that's what's so wrong. Flora looks much older than her six years.

With her hand, she tried to smooth Flora's fine brown hair. "All right, just this one more time." She took a deep breath. "Mama was very pretty. And that's why you are, too, Flora, because you look so much like her."

"How, Rosetta, how do I look like her?"

Rosetta closed her eyes, conjuring her mother's image. It frightened her sometime, how the picture in her mind kept shrinking, growing somehow fainter. She never imagined she could forget what her parents had looked like, and for the first three years she could remember them both clearly. But in this last year, something had started to happen. The pictures she carried in her head wouldn't come as easily any more.

"You're very small, like she was," Rosetta said. "You have the same curly hair and big gray eyes with thick dark lashes."

"You have eyes like mine, Rosetta."

"Yes. That's the only way I'm like Mama. She was so delicate. Even though I was only ten when she died, I can remember that when we held hands mine were almost as big as hers." Rosetta looked down at her own long fingers, with their square, strong nails. "I'm much more like Papa. He was very tall, with wavy dark hair. Chestnut colored, Mama used to say."

Flora giggled suddenly. "But you don't have a moustache, like you said Papa had."

Rosetta smiled at the sound of her little sister's laughter. She hadn't heard it for a long time. "No, thank goodness," she answered.

Flora snuggled deeper against her. "And you love adventures, like he did," she said, her voice growing softer, sleepy.

"Mmmm," Rosetta murmured, thinking that if her father hadn't loved adventures quite so much he wouldn't have gone away, that last time. It had been a few months before Flora was born. He'd promised, Mama told her later, to be back in time for the new baby.

But he hadn't been back, not when Flora was born, never again. And Rosetta had been with Mama when she received the letter, with its strange stamp and cramped, unfamiliar writing. The letter had been edged in black. It was her governess who had explained, gently, about the meaning of the black edges.

Her mother had become ill around the same time she received the letter. She grew more ill when she learned about the debts, and that all their money had been used to finance Rosetta's father's last journey. She never really got better, and became sicker and sicker, until finally . . .

But Rosetta always closed her mind, firmly, on that part. She couldn't bear to think about her mother, how she'd turned into someone Rosetta didn't know, hardly recognized. It was easier not to think about it, and she would never tell Flora. Flora hadn't even been two; she didn't remember their mother at all, anyway, or what had happened after she died.

She left her hand on Flora's head. "We'll be there tomorrow, Flora. By tomorrow, we'll be in Canada. Once we get off the boat you'll feel all better, and we'll go to a nice, new home. Won't you like that, Flora? A home, a real one. Not the Home, not the Manchester Refuge, but a house with a father and mother, and maybe even our own room."

"Just you and me? Not all the other girls?"

"That's what everyone's saying, Flora. That we'll be able to stay together." Rosetta pushed her back against the wall, trying to give Flora more room on the narrow mattress, lumpy and stained from many other sea voyages and many other bodies. "And I'll go to school, and be a teacher. Remember what Miss Hall always told me? That I could be a good teacher? So I'll finish school, in Canada, and become a teacher. You can be one of my students, Flora."

Flora's eyelids lowered. She rolled her head from side to side, her hair brushing against the front of Rosetta's dress.

"Promise, Rosetta," she said slowly. "Promise you'll stay with me. Always. Sing the Promise Song."

Rosetta looked around the tiny, dim cabin, automatically breathing through her mouth so she didn't have to smell the stale air that hung, like a permanent thick cloud, in the low, narrow room. The sleeping quarters were under the main deck and over the engine room. The room she shared with Flora and four other girls held three sets of stacked bunks covered with rough gray blankets. There were sixteen other rooms like it; the ship could hold almost one hundred bodies. On this trip, all the bunks were full of girls; the youngest was four, the oldest, fourteen, like Rosetta.

There was the constant thump of the ship's engines from the room under them. A heavy oily smell wafted up through the wooden floorboards, but it couldn't cover the other smells. The air was putrid with the odors of the three-week journey – the poor toilet and washing facilities and the often unemptied pails used when seasickness overtook many of the girls.

Rosetta shut her own burning eyes. "Go to sleep now, Flora," she whispered, stroking Flora's hair again. "You know that, no matter what, I'll always stay with you. I'll never leave you. Sisters have to be together, remember?"

Flora nodded.

"Listen to the song now, and go to sleep."

Rosetta thought for a moment, then, even though her throat ached with weariness, she started to sing, in a low voice, the song she'd made up when they had first gone to the Manchester Refuge. It was a song she used to soothe Flora to sleep when she was little more than a baby; a song whose words changed from season to season, from year to year, but with a tune that stayed the same. Flora had started calling it the Promise Song, because Rosetta sang about all the things they would do.

"I promise you, I promise you, I promise you,
dear Flora.
We've left the Home,
and off we go.
We'll stay together
in sun and snow.
And this is what I promise you."

She sung the stanza over and over, softer and softer, hoping Flora would fall asleep and stop asking questions. And even while she sang, she worried about the promises she was making. The only thing she knew for certain was that the next day everything would be different from the life Flora had always known, and the life she herself had lived for the last four years.

She thought of the way a whole crowd of them, the girls at the Refuge who were the most healthy, had been lined up and asked, "Who would like to go and live in Canada?" They were told that they wouldn't be living in an orphanage any more, but would have a proper home and family. They would be away from Manchester's damp, chilled city air, in the fresh sunshine of a Canadian countryside. And they wouldn't be Home children any more.

Of course, all the girls had put up their hands. Rosetta's heart had almost thumped out of her chest when Miss Hall had stopped in front of her and said, "You, Rosetta. You're fourteen, almost leaving age. And you're always reading about adventures. You take your sister and go. Go and have an adventure of your own."

And although the journey had been long and hard, Rosetta held on to one bright, glowing thought. It was with her when she woke, gritty-eyed and stiff, every morning and as she fell asleep every night.

And this night, the last one before she arrived in her new country, to her new life, Rosetta held the light even more tightly as she gently eased her body away from Flora's and climbed overhead to her own bunk.

"We won't be Home girls any more," she whispered, pulling the scratchy blanket over her shoulders. "No one will ever call me a Home girl again. We'll start a new life, the two of us. A new family. We won't be Home girls."

And in the swaying shadows, the rock and hum of the boat seemed to whisper back "Home girl, Home girl," until Rosetta's eyes finally closed.

Chapter Two

"This way, children, this way. Watch your step now."

Miss Watson stood at the bottom of the gangplank the next afternoon, waving her hand in a small circle, urging the girls toward her.

Rosetta squinted in the brilliant May sunshine that made the water alongside the dock wink and glitter. She rubbed Flora's hand between her own, noticing again how cold and almost boneless the little fingers felt.

They followed the pair of girls in front of them down the long sturdy plank onto the dock. When Rosetta stepped onto the hard stillness of land, she felt as if her legs were still locking and unlocking at the knee, bracing to keep her balance against the steady rocking of the waves that had tirelessly beat the *Corsican* for the last twenty days.

"Is this where we'll live, Rosetta?" Flora asked, giving Rosetta's hand one limp squeeze.

"I don't think so, Flora." Rosetta looked around at the crowded dockside, at the barrels and piled boxes on the roads. One of the shabby wooden buildings had a sign nailed on the front. Rosetta read it out loud. "Hal-i-fax. Halifax. No. This isn't where we'll live, Flora. I heard Miss McLean say that we're all going to somewhere called Belleville. There's a special place there, a house where we will stay for a while."

"Until we get our family?"

Rosetta looked down. There were deep, bruised pouches beneath Flora's eyes. "Yes, Flora, I would think so." She smiled what she hoped was a confident smile.

"How do we get there? To Bell . . . to that place. Not another ship, is it, Rosetta?"

At her little sister's fretful tone, Rosetta forced her smile wider, even though her whole face felt tight. "I don't think so. I don't think we have to do any more sailing." Rosetta hoped it was the truth. She had so many questions, but Miss McLean and Miss Watson, both with mouths like stitched seams, didn't like the girls bothering them.

They didn't come in sight of Canada until lunchtime. The country rose out of the sea, at first just a long dark hump, growing and growing until they could see buildings and even tiny moving figures.

As the *Corsican* drew closer, the girls stared at the wharves and wooden structures clustered along the waterfront. A number of church spires rose up behind the lower buildings.

Many of the girls had pushed up against the railing, their hands shielding their eyes against the dazzle of sun on water, trying to get a look at the new country.

"It looks small," one of the girls finally said.

"Well, silly, that's not *all* of Canada," someone answered.

They fell silent; nobody had been told anything about the country they were traveling to, except that one girl had heard from another girl whose brother had gone to Canada a few years before that it had orchards and orchards of apples, and lots of snow in the winter, and that the people spoke English, although a harsh, flat English, not like theirs at all.

It wasn't much to go on.

Rosetta stared at the city sprouting from the water, wondering if everyone's head felt like hers, throbbing with questions.

There was a sudden ragged cry just above her, and she tilted her head to see a black-backed gull, wheeling in wide, lazy rings above the ship. She watched it as it dipped and swung toward the land, looking back now and then, importantly, Rosetta thought, to see if the ship was still following.

Miss McLean's voice brought Rosetta back to the dock. "I want you all to stand behind your trunks and wait, with no talking." The metal trunks had been unloaded onto the dock. They sat, small and square, tied with a piece of rope, one trunk for each girl. Each girl's name, in black paint, was on the front. Each trunk held identical belongings – a nightdress, a change of clothing, a brush and comb, and a small Bible. The girls stood silently while the afternoon sunshine faded around them. Some of them shivered as the cool breeze off the water swept under their long cotton skirts or swirled their hair into winding tendrils.

Just when Rosetta could sense Flora starting to sway with exhaustion, a tall, spidery man came out of one of the bigger wooden shacks and, with a wave of his hand, signaled to Miss Watson and Miss McLean. They nodded at the first girl, and she followed them. Making an uneven, snaking line, the girls slowly filed into the building.

The furniture inside consisted of two long wooden tables and rows of low benches. By the time Rosetta came inside, the first girls were sitting on the benches. The two chaperons were holding thick stacks of papers and talking to the spidery man, who was sitting at the first table. Another man, much shorter and with much less hair, sat at the second.

The spidery man looked over the first few papers and then, with a sudden loud thump, stamped them. He passed one stack of papers to his partner, and each man looked at the top paper in front of him and called out a name.

Rosetta and Flora sat on the hard benches in the unheated room. The walls were a faded dirty green, and there was no ceiling covering the peaked roof, just wooden beams leading up to support the high eaves. The height of the room made the men's voices echo eerily as they called out the names in alphabetical order. As each girl rose from her place on the bench and walked across the room to the table, her footsteps had a hollow ring on the slanted planked floor. When the spidery man called Flora's name, the little girl jumped. Rosetta pried the small, cold fingers from her own.

"Go on, Flora," she whispered. "I'll be right after you. And stand up straight. Look bright. And strong, like I showed you. Lift your head."

When it was Rosetta's turn, she walked quickly to the second table. The short, balding man kept his head down, his finger on a line on the paper in front of him.

"Rosetta Westley?" he said, still looking down at the paper.

"Yes, sir," she answered, looking at his navy cap. CANADIAN IMMIGRATION was sewn in red letters across the top of the crown.

"Born January 26, 1886, Wolverhampton, England."

"Yes, sir," Rosetta repeated.

The man unexpectedly raised his head and looked up at her face. Then his eyes, cold and dark as old tea, traveled down the front of her dress, to her waist, at table height. "How old does that make you?"

Rosetta's eyes shifted slightly to the right. She didn't want to meet his eyes if he looked at her face again.

"Fourteen, sir," she said, "and a half." She quickly pressed her lips together. She didn't know why she had added that last part.

The man raised his stamp over the paper and brought it down with a bored whack. "Step to your left," he said, handing her the paper.

Rosetta took the edge of the paper and walked to the screened partition beside the table. A woman in a white uniform sat on a low stool. She was wearing an earpiece. From the earpiece ran a length of flexible tubing, and on the end of the tubing was a round metal disk. She reached out her hand, and Rosetta handed her the paper. The woman picked up the disk.

"Undo the top of your dress," she said.

Instinctively, Rosetta pressed her hands against the front buttons.

"Just going to listen to your heart and lungs, dear," the woman said. She didn't smile, but her face, although tired, wasn't unkind.

Keeping her eyes down, Rosetta undid the first three buttons of her dark-gray serge dress. The woman leaned forward and pressed the stethoscope's disk under the white cotton front of the girl's petticoat. The metal disk was cold on her skin.

"Take a breath," the woman said.

Rosetta's breath sounded shuddery, even to her own ears.

"And another," the woman said. She closed her eyes briefly, then took away the stethoscope.

"Open your mouth."

Rosetta did as she was told, and the woman leaned forward and peered inside. Then she made a check mark on the paper and gave a quick nod.

Rosetta stared at her.

"Go on then," she said.

Rosetta did up her dress and stepped out from behind the screen.

In front of her was an open door, allowing the last feeble rays of sunshine into the dreary room. Shaking back her hair, she walked out to join the silent row of girls standing on a board sidewalk at the back of the immigration building.

Rosetta gave a sigh of relief as she took her place in the line behind Flora. She was officially in Canada.

Chapter Three

Times of light and dark blended together. The hard wooden seats and backs offered no comfort, and the girls leaned against each other, trying to sleep as they jostled back and forth. The constant thunk *thunk*, thunk *thunk* of the wheels on the train tracks was only broken by arrivals and departures at stations. Bells would start clanging, followed by the almost unbearable screeching of metal on metal as the wheels ground to a halt. Clouds of steam gathered around the outside of the windows when the train sat still. But all too soon it would start up again, with its rhythmic chugging building and building until it was replaced by the familiar, monotonous thunk *thunk*.

The train ride on the Grand Trunk Railway lasted two days and two nights. The group of thirty girls that was destined for Belleville, Ontario, was exhausted and grimy as they climbed down the high wooden steps of the sooty black locomotive at the station. None of them spoke, or even looked around. They followed directions like rigid mannequins, climbing into the horse-drawn carts that took them to the Marchmont Home.

As the cart pulled in on the semi-circle of gravel that led from the main street to the front of the Home, Rosetta peered at the huge old house perched in the middle of the wide green yard. She reached up to rub the back of her neck, staring at the building but hardly seeing it. Her whole body was stiff and sore. All she could think about was resting on something soft.

A woman who introduced herself as Miss Cramer stood on the front step. She led the girls up the stairs, past the second floor, to the third. Rosetta kept her arm around Flora's shoulders, partly holding up the little girl. The big room at the top of the house, under the high, sloping roof, was filled with a double row of narrow beds covered with clean white sheets.

"Put your trunks at the foot of any bed," the woman said. "You'll only be here for a day or two, so don't take out your things. Have a wash in the room next door, and then come down for your supper."

"Supper, Rosetta? Shouldn't we be having our tea?"

"I expect things are a bit different here, Flora," Rosetta said, trying to put some enthusiasm into her voice. "And did you hear what she said? A day or two! That's all, just a day or two, and then we'll be with our family!"

"What do you promise now, Rosetta, what? Sing!" Flora's voice was almost sulky.

Rosetta was silent for a moment, then:

> "I promise you, I promise you, I promise you,
> dear Flora.
> We'll see apples growing
> under skies so blue.
> But no wormy apples
> for me and —"

She reached out and tickled Flora in the ribs. "You!"

Flora grabbed at Rosetta's hand and her opened lips turned up at the corners. A sound that was almost laughter slipped out as she tried to get at Rosetta to tickle her back. "And that is what you promise!" the little girl sang. Then, with the same tune, she carried on. "We're getting our family, our family, our family."

Our family, Rosetta thought, looking down at her sister. It had a nice sound.

~

"Throw me the ball, Flora, throw it," Rosetta called. The yard behind Marchmont was a broad expanse of grass surrounded by a high black wrought-iron fence. There were small trees along the fence, some with white flowers on them. As Rosetta was looking at them, wondering if they were apple trees, Flora threw the ball. It bounced past Rosetta and rolled along the side of the house. Rosetta ran to pick it up and looked at the traps lined up in the drive that ran beside the house. The two-wheeled carriages, each with one or two horses harnessed to it, hadn't been there when the girls had been sent out to the yard to play after breakfast.

As Rosetta scooped up the ball, she heard the short, hard blast of a whistle. Miss Cramer was standing in the middle of the yard, a whistle hanging around her neck.

"I want these girls to come with me," she called, holding a paper close to her nose. Her eyes squinting, she began the list of names. Rosetta edged closer to Flora.

Miss Cramer lowered the list. "And last, Flora Westley."

Flora looked up at Rosetta. "It's all right, Flora, go on," Rosetta said. Flora shook her head.

"Go, Flora," Rosetta repeated, giving her a little nudge.

"They probably want to fit you up for new clothes. Look," she said, pointing to the other girls falling into place in front of Miss Cramer, "it's all the littlest girls going." She gave Flora another gentle push. "I'll see you when you're done."

Flora started toward Miss Cramer, dragging one foot after the other, her head down. Rosetta noticed that the green ribbon she had tied in Flora's hair that morning had come partly undone, and she wondered if she should run after her and tie it properly.

But then Flora took her place at the end of the line, and as Miss Cramer turned and started toward the back door of the house, the girls trailing her like a line of ducklings, Flora turned one more time and stood staring at Rosetta. Rosetta clucked her tongue. Flora seemed to be so slow these days. It was quite irritating, really.

Once we're settled, in our new family, I'll get her moving, Rosetta thought. She'll eat and sleep properly, and perk up.

"Go *on*, Flora," she called in a harsh whisper. "Hurry along. You'll get left behind."

Later, all Rosetta could remember was how she pushed Flora away from her. How she'd shaken her head and clucked her tongue.

And that's what made her feel the worst. That she hadn't given Flora a hug or a kiss. She hadn't even smiled at her.

Chapter Four

It was all so jumbled, mixed up. Sitting on the seat of another train, listening to the same monotonous clacking of the wheels and staring out the window but seeing nothing, Rosetta kept trying to sort out the last six hours.

It was as if she was in a kind of terrible dream, except that she knew she was awake. This train was smaller than the one they'd taken from Halifax to Belleville. There was a card, tied with a piece of scratchy twine, hanging around her neck, like she was a sheep at an auction. She didn't even know where she was going. And Flora was gone.

She took a deep breath, forcing herself to think carefully. Maybe she could figure out what she should do, if she worked through it, step by step. She leaned her head against the rough horsehair back of the seat and closed her eyes.

She saw herself, in the yard at Belleville, sitting with some of the older girls.

"Do you think those are the apple trees?" she asked Isabel, the girl beside her on the soft green grass.

"Don't know," Isabel said. "They're not very big trees. I think of apple trees as big. Wonder when we'll get our dinner. I'm getting hungry."

Rosetta leaned back on her elbows and looked at the sky. A

few tattered pieces of misty white hung in the pale blue. It seemed as if the mist was waiting for something – a gentle breeze, or a sudden gust that might bring it together to form a true cloud. "It must be near dinnertime," she said, shielding her eyes from the sun, almost directly overhead. "Flora's been away a long time."

Nobody said anything. As the silence stretched, Rosetta thought about Flora. Thought about the way Flora had stared over her shoulder at Rosetta as she followed the other girls. About how tiny and helpless she had looked.

A small, cold lump started to form in the pit of Rosetta's stomach. "I'm going to see where the little girls are," she said, getting to her feet. The lump seemed to get bigger, harder.

Isabel stared up at her. "Miss Cramer said for us to wait here, Rosetta."

Rosetta pushed at her abdomen with her fist. The lump was hurting now. "I just want to see . . .," she started. "Flora . . . she gets very frightened if I'm not with her. . . ."

Isabel looked down at her skirt, tracing a seam with one finger. The girl near her, Nettie, plucked a stem of grass. She turned it this way and that, studying it.

Rosetta started walking toward the house, but suddenly the yard seemed so wide, the house so far away. She broke into a run. When she reached the back door, she shoved it open and looked around her, holding her hand flat against her chest. It felt as if the lump was moving upward, pushing against her lungs, crowding her heart, so that it was hard to breathe.

She started down the hallway. Clattering sounds on her left made her look into a room. It was the kitchen. A woman was sawing through a giant ham at a long wooden table. Another woman stood with her back to Rosetta, stirring something in a steaming cauldron on the stove. The woman at the table stopped her cutting and looked at her, but Rosetta hurried by, to the narrow back stairs.

She bounded up the steps two at a time, bunching her skirt at the front so she wouldn't trip. She arrived at the top floor, panting, and ran into the room she and Flora had slept in. Her trunk was still there, at the foot of the fourth bed.

But at the foot of the fifth bed, Flora's, there was nothing. Flora's trunk was gone.

Rosetta raced back down the stairs. She looked into the kitchen again, then ran along the hallway, past the dining room. She stopped at a large playroom, containing a box of balls, another of rag dolls, and a low shelf of books. There was no one in it. She ran by two closed doors, until she came to the front of the house, the large parlor. A man and woman sat on two of the straight chairs that ringed the perimeter of the room. The woman smiled.

The smile gave Rosetta confidence. "Excuse me," she said, trying to keep her voice normal, trying to hold down the panic that was rising up from the lump, up through her chest, into her throat. "Excuse me, I'm looking for my sister. She's just little, only six. Her name is Flora. Have you seen a little girl?"

The man and woman looked at each other. The woman's smile had faded as Rosetta spoke. "We're waiting for a little girl. Our little girl," the woman said. "But her name is Mildred, not Flora."

"Mildred? Mildred Knowles?" Rosetta asked. Mildred and Flora had been friends at the Refuge, and had played together on the *Corsican* when Flora felt well enough. Mildred had

23

been in the line of girls that had followed Miss Cramer into the house.

"She'll be Mildred McTavish now," the man said.

"We've just adopted her," the woman said. "I wanted a blonde girl, but my husband's always been partial to red-haired children. It was our lucky day when we saw Mildred."

Rosetta felt for the back of the nearest chair. "Have all the girls been adopted? All the little girls?"

The woman stood up. "We're just waiting to sign the papers. Should we call someone? You seem to be in a bit of a state."

"Where are they?" Rosetta said, no longer able to keep the tiny shriek out of her voice. "Where have they taken them? The girls. Where have they gone?"

"Well." The woman looked back to her husband. He was staring at the floor. "Well, I expect they've left by now. As soon as the papers are signed, and the belongings collected, each family goes on its way. I'm sure your sister was picked by a nice . . ."

Rosetta didn't wait for the rest of the sentence. She whirled around, hearing a thump as the chair she had been holding fell over on the patterned carpet, and ran out of the parlor and back down the hallway. She turned the knob of the first closed door, pushing it open. Miss Cramer was bending over a desk. Mildred Knowles was standing beside her trunk in the center of the office. They looked at Rosetta.

"Where is she?" Rosetta whispered. "Where's Flora?"

Miss Cramer came toward her. "She's been adopted, Rosetta. That's why she came to Canada, to find a family. You know that." Her voice was stern, but something around her eyes didn't suit the voice.

"But I thought we'd be together!" Rosetta's head turned in jerky movements, looking around the small room, her eyes darting into every corner as if she might find Flora hiding behind the potted plant or beneath the shiny brown horsehair settee near the window. "Nobody said we wouldn't be together. Nobody said!"

Miss Cramer just shook her head. "Now, Rosetta —" she started, but Rosetta interrupted her.

"But why didn't you say . . . I didn't even get a chance to tell her good-bye, to tell her . . . I promised her, you see, I . . ." Rosetta stopped as an elegant carriage rumbled by the window. A man sat up front, driving a pair of gleaming horses. On the back seat was a woman, her arm around someone beside her. As the carriage rolled out of view, Rosetta saw a flash of a green ribbon in curly pale-brown hair.

She raced from the room and down the hall again, past the parlor to the front door. Flinging it open, she leapt off the top step, landing in the gravel at the bottom. The hickory wheels of the carriage were slowing to a stop at the end of the drive, waiting for a cart piled with rags, pulled by a plodding old horse, to pass.

Rosetta sprinted down the drive. All she could see over the collapsible top of the carriage was the crown of the man's hat.

"Wait!" she screamed, waving her arms. "Oh please, wait."

She saw the long steel springs of the carriage jiggle, then a man appeared around the side of it.

"Miss?" he said. "Can I help you?"

Rosetta stopped. She had to tip her head back to look up at his face. He was very tall.

"It's Flora, sir. My sister. You have my sister. There." She pointed to the carriage, sitting down the drive.

The man studied her face. "Yes. Well, we do have Flora. We've adopted her."

"But she's my *sister*, sir." Rosetta started toward the carriage. "She needs me. You can't take her –"

The man stepped closer, blocking Rosetta from moving ahead. "But we can. We put our names in for a little girl over six months ago. We got notification from Miss Cramer, here at Marchmont, last week, that there was a new party of girls arriving. We made the trip to Belleville yesterday, and today we picked out Flora." His fingers brushed at his moustache.

Rosetta was shaking all over, as if she had a chill. "But you can't just *take* her. You don't know anything about her. You don't know what to do when she cries at night, or how milk makes her sick. You don't know –" She stopped as the woman from the carriage walked up and stood beside the man.

The woman was short and heavy. She carried a sunscreen that matched her dress, and she looked a good deal older than her husband. "What's going on, Harry?" she asked.

The man cleared his throat and patted his moustache again. "This young lady here," he said, not taking his hand away from his moustache, "this young lady claims to be Flora's sister, and is quite, well, upset, that we're taking her."

The woman looked at Rosetta's face, and at the waves of glossy dark-brown hair that had escaped from the ribbon at the back of Rosetta's neck. Her eyes moved down the girl's body, to her boots, the toes dusty in the gravel of the drive.

"It's all legal," she finally said. "We've signed the papers."

Rosetta grabbed the woman's hands in hers. "But she *needs* me, ma'am. I'm all she's known, since she was a baby. And I promised her. I promised her I'd never leave her."

The woman looked down at Rosetta's slender fingers, kneading her own short, thick ones.

"Couldn't you take me, too, ma'am?" Rosetta looked into the woman's narrowed eyes, then at the man. "Sir? Couldn't you? I'm very strong. I can work ever so hard, and I hardly eat anything. See? See how thin I am?"

The man pulled his eyes away from Rosetta's. He glanced over his shoulder, at the carriage, then looked back at his wife. "Margaret? It seems so cruel to separate them. And you're always saying you have too much work to handle. How you could use more help."

The woman twisted her fingers out of Rosetta's, brushing her hands together as if wiping something away.

"I wouldn't take any room, ma'am," Rosetta said. The woman's round face looked blurry, flattened by the tears brimming in Rosetta's eyes. She brushed at them with one short, angry swipe. "I would sleep anywhere – anywhere, and I'm ever so handy at baking. I can bake a pie. I can bake biscuits, light biscuits. I always helped in the kitchen in the Home, in Manchester. And I can read. I was a good pupil. I'm going to be a teacher. I can do anything!" Her voice had grown louder and louder.

The man touched his wife's arm. "What do you say, Margaret?" he said. His voice lowered. "You can see how it is."

The woman's lips were white. "I think not. We agreed on one little girl. And we already have Bess from next door to help with the housework. One child is all we can afford. We surely don't want a full-grown woman in the house as well." Her eyes trailed down Rosetta's body again. Then she raised her head, licked her lips, and looked straight into her husband's face.

"Come along, Harry. I don't want to leave Eliza alone in the carriage."

"Eliza?" Rosetta said.

"Eliza," the woman repeated. "I've always liked the sound of Eliza. The name Flora reminds me of a cow my family once had." She gave one short, hard tug on her husband's sleeve. "Come on now." Her eyes looked over the top of Rosetta's head, and Rosetta turned. Miss Cramer was hurrying down the drive.

"Is there a problem, Mr. and Mrs. Forsythe?" Miss Cramer called.

"No. Everything's fine, thank you," Mrs. Forsythe answered sharply, pulling on Mr. Forsythe's sleeve again.

In the moment of silence before Mr. Forsythe moved, Rosetta heard a faint voice. "Rosetta?" She leaned around Mr. Forsythe and saw Flora, half out of the carriage, one leg stretching toward the ground. "Come, Rosetta," Flora called. "Come. It's our family."

As Rosetta jerked forward, ready to run toward Flora, her wrist was gripped firmly. She looked down at it, trying to wrench it out of Miss Cramer's hand. "Don't cause a scene, Rosetta," the woman said. "Come back with me now."

Mrs. Forsythe dropped her husband's arm and hurried back to the carriage, her ample behind swaying from side to side.

Mr. Forsythe stepped in front of Rosetta again, blocking her view. She tried to look around him, able only to catch a glimpse of Mrs. Forsythe firmly setting Flora back into the carriage. Miss Cramer's fingers dug into Rosetta's wrist.

"Let me go!" Rosetta called, trying to pull her arm free.

"I'm so sorry," Mr. Forsythe said. "I am terribly, terribly sorry, young lady." He put his hands into his pockets and rocked back and forth, very slightly, on his heels and toes. "We'll treat your sister well. We'll be kind, I promise you."

At those words, Rosetta stopped pulling. Her breath came so fast she could hardly catch it. She felt as if she'd been running a very long time. "I promised, too," she said, the words coming out in gasps. She turned to pry at Miss Cramer's fingers. "I promised Flora."

Mr. Forsythe took his hands out of his pockets and gently took Rosetta's free hand. He pressed something cold into her palm and closed her fingers around it. "I'm so sorry," he repeated, then turned and ran toward the carriage.

Rosetta stared after him, starting to struggle again, jerking at her arm, but the woman's grip was surprisingly firm. As the carriage started with a jolt, Rosetta stood on her toes, stretching out her clenched fist.

"Flora!" she screamed. She saw a flurry of green ribbon trembling at the top of the shaking carriage, and over the rumbling of the wheels, she heard her name, one last time, a desperate, drawn-out wail in the final syllable.

And then the carriage, and Flora, were gone.

Rosetta swung around to face Miss Cramer, lifting her clenched hand. She brought it down, hard, on Miss Cramer's forearm. The woman's fingers finally loosened. Her mouth opened, looking at the spot where Rosetta had struck her. "There's no need for that," she said.

"You should have let me go," Rosetta whispered. "I told her I'd look after her. You should have let me go."

"You know I couldn't," Miss Cramer said, closing her eyes for a second. Then she opened them. "It's how things are done. Now come along, dear." Her voice returned to its normal matter-of-fact tone. "Come back to the house."

Rosetta opened her closed hand and looked at the strange coins Mr. Forsythe had put there, then at Miss Cramer.

"Put them in your pocket," the woman said. "Go on. They're yours. The gentleman gave them to you. Put them in the pocket of your dress," Miss Cramer said, then, hesitating for an instant, reached over to pat Rosetta's shoulder.

Rosetta did what she was told, in a shaky, uncoordinated gesture. She rubbed at her wrist, now turning a deep burgundy, in the same uncertain way. "She's frightened to be alone at night," she said, her voice so low that Miss Cramer leaned close to hear what she was saying. "You have to lay beside her until she falls asleep," Rosetta whispered. "And there's a song, a song she likes . . ."

A fine white powdering of dust from the departing carriage settled on Rosetta's hair. Miss Cramer put her arm around Rosetta's shoulders and started to lead her back to the house.

"Until she's asleep," Rosetta repeated, her face wet, "you have to sing it until she's completely asleep."

Chapter Five

Rosetta couldn't remember much about the next few hours. She knew she sat at the dining table, with a plate in front of her, but she didn't remember eating.

At one point she was aware that Isabel was brushing her long hair, retying the ribbon that held it in place, and wiping at her face with a damp cloth, but then she was in a buggy. There was noise, and smoke, and now here she was, on a train, with the cardboard sign hanging around her neck.

She ran her fingers over the edge of the cardboard, then picked it up and twisted it so she could read it. There were only two words, in big black letters.

"Thomson's Landing," Rosetta read, letting the words roll slowly off her tongue. "Thomson's Landing." She said it again, this time a little louder.

"Thomson's Landing!"

Rosetta jumped at the shouted words. For a minute she thought she was the one who had called them out so loudly, and glanced around, to see if anyone was looking at her. Then she heard them again.

They were closer, and louder, coming from somewhere behind her, and in a man's voice. She turned her head and, over the top of the seat, could see the conductor's cap and eyes.

He stopped beside Rosetta's seat. "You'll be getting off here," he said. "The stop is in about five minutes."

Rosetta nodded, fingering the edges of the cardboard. "Thank you," she said. Her throat hurt when she spoke.

As the conductor walked away, she looked out the window again, but it was nearly dark, and there seemed to be nothing but low bushes along the track.

As the train started to slow, Rosetta was able to make out rough wooden buildings to one side. There was a jerking and a loud, grinding noise, and Rosetta put her hand on the window to steady herself as the train finally stopped.

She stood up. There were only a few people in the car, and no one seemed to notice her. The conductor suddenly appeared in front of her, at the end of the car, and nodded. She started to walk down the aisle, but, feeling the slight sway of the cardboard against her chest, pulled the sign over her head, embarrassed at having anyone see her with it, as if she were a small child. She held the cardboard stiffly at her side.

"Watch it now," the conductor said, touching Rosetta lightly on her shoulder as she started down the step.

Rosetta looked at the toes of her boots on the black iron steps of the train. She saw them moving, but it was hard to believe that the boots belonged to her, that her feet were inside them, attached to her legs. Her whole body felt numb.

She saw the boots reach the bottom stair, then step onto the splintering planks of the platform. Finally she took a deep breath and lifted her head.

The station was a small whitewashed building. THOMSON'S LANDING had been painted along one side in large, neat letters. The building stood alone in the dusk, a row of budding trees just behind it. There was only one narrow door, and it was closed.

Rosetta turned her head to the right, then the left. There was no one on the platform.

"Your trunk's just there," the conductor said.

Rosetta followed his outstretched arm and saw the small metal trunk.

"Someone meetin' you?" the conductor asked.

Rosetta looked into his face. He was young, his cheeks ruddy and his eyes large and dark beneath the brim of his cap.

"I'm not sure," Rosetta said, trying to speak loudly, bravely. But the voice that came out was thin, pitiful. Rosetta cleared her throat, hating the unfamiliar tone.

"Well, the station shuts up after we go through," the conductor said. "I'm sure someone will be along for you soon." He looked behind him, at the waiting, puffing train.

"Thank you," Rosetta said, her chin high. She was glad to hear her usual voice. "Yes, I'm sure they'll be along." She thought of trying to smile, to show this young conductor that she was fine, that she could look after herself, and wasn't worried, but she couldn't trust her face just yet. She turned and walked to her trunk and sat down on it, facing the station's door, her back to the train. She knew the people inside the train were looking out the windows at her. She kept her shoulders back and her spine straight, even though she felt like lying down on the platform, curling into a small, tight ball, and disappearing.

Rosetta heard the conductor yell "All clear." There was a slamming of doors and a gust of wind that swirled dirt in her face and ruffled her skirt.

Then the train was gone, leaving Rosetta on her trunk, in the falling darkness, on the deserted platform of the Thomson's Landing station.

Rosetta waited. Eventually, a soft chirping began from the fields that spread out on the other side of the tracks. She didn't know what caused the slow, rhythmic sound, but it made her feel sadder and more alone than she had ever felt in her life.

"I'll find you, Flora," she said softly into the night. "I'll find you." She let her voice grow louder, bigger, out to the darkness beyond the tracks. "I promised you. Remember, I promised."

The chirping quieted, for just a moment, at the last and loudest word. Then, before the echo of "promised" could die down, the thrumming started up again, more persistent, as if determined to drown out Rosetta's words.

Chapter Six

"You the girl sent from the Home?"

Rosetta's eyelids flew open and her chin jerked up from her chest. She got to her feet so fast that for a minute the platform felt as if it were swaying, as if she might fall to one side.

It was completely dark, except for the lantern in front of her face. She couldn't see anything but the brilliant flickering of the flame.

"Yes," she said, putting up one hand to shield her eyes from the light. "Yes. I'm Rosetta Westley."

The lantern moved down, and Rosetta could just make out a tall, thin shape. "Come with me then," the deep voice said.

Rosetta started to follow the man. "Oh," she said, after a few steps. "Excuse me, but my trunk is back there. My things."

He kept walking. Rosetta hurried to his side, touched his arm. "Sir? Could you help me take my trunk?"

The man stopped, looking down at her hand on his arm.

"Get into the wagon first. I have to bring it around closer to the platform." He started walking again.

Rosetta matched her stride to his, and in a minute was stepping up onto a high wheel, climbing into the wagon. She heard the soft questioning snicker of a horse as she sat down on the straight wood bench that ran along the front of the wagon.

"Hold the lantern up high," the man said, handing it to her as he climbed up on the other side. He clucked to the horse, and they rolled around to the other side of the train platform, a few feet from Rosetta's trunk.

Rosetta heard a small grunt, then the wagon shook as the trunk was heaved over the side and landed with a thud on the boards. The man climbed up beside her again, and they started out into the darkness, Rosetta still holding the lantern as high as she could in front of her.

When her arm started aching, she changed hands. The man reached over and took the lantern from her and turned off the flame before he set it on the floor between them. At first Rosetta couldn't see anything, but in a few seconds she realized that everything was lightly washed with dull silver. She looked up at the sky; the moon was round and luminous. She slowly breathed out.

The moon, with its mysterious darker contours, wavered in and out with each breath Rosetta took, exactly like the English moon she had so often studied out the window at the Home. But this Canadian moon looked more radiant, closer, with no distracting light from the bright windows and sputtering gas lamps that lined the streets of Manchester.

She felt a little better, watching the moon.

They bumped along endlessly. Rosetta kept falling asleep, her head dropping forward. Then she'd awaken as the wagon hit a rock in the road, or the horse changed his pace. She knew much time had passed, and they must have come many miles. The man never said a word; the only sounds were the dull plopping of the horse's hooves on soft dirt and the rumble of the wagon's wheels. When she awoke the last time, and searched for the moon, it was gone. The sky had a disturbed, blown-apart look, in varying shades of black and gray, and Rosetta knew there were clouds, many of them, covering the moon.

"Is the place we're going far?" she finally asked. She assumed the man to be some sort of hired help; someone sent to pick her up from the train. "Are we going to the city, to this . . .," she searched her mind for the name that was printed on the cardboard in her pocket, "this Thomson's Landing?"

The man didn't answer for a minute. Then, "That stop was it. Thomson's Landing. Not much farther to the farm."

Farm. Rosetta had never seen a farm in England, but once, when she was much younger, she had gone out into the country, away from Wolverhampton. She remembered a carriage ride with her father and mother, before Flora had been born, before her father had gone away. She closed her eyes in the darkness, trying to bring back a picture of that ride, of the country.

There was the feel of her father's strong arms swinging her down from the carriage. Then a dim recollection of playing in a small copse, hiding behind the slender trees while her father looked for her, laughing and calling her name, and seeming to have a great deal of trouble finding her. She could see herself, like in a photograph, sitting on a blanket on soft grass covered with small white flowers growing wild all around.

"Snowdrops," she said out loud, then glanced at the man, but he didn't appear to have noticed that she'd spoken.

She thought of her mother's delicate, pale hands, showing

her how to braid long pieces of the grass together to make a thin, strong rope, and she thought she remembered seeing a black-faced lamb on one of the hills as they drove home. But the lamb might just be something one of the other girls at the Refuge had told her about. It was hard to keep her childhood memories clear now, after so much time had passed.

She had only been in the country once before, and now she was being taken to a farm to live. She turned to face the man.

"What are the people called?" she asked. "The people on the farm. They'll be my . . .," she hesitated, not sure if this man knew the situation. "Well, I'll be living there now. They asked for me," she said, a little more boldly, looking at the man's profile, trying to make out his features. He was so still and silent that Rosetta felt a stirring of irritation. She wanted him to talk to her, tell her about her new parents.

The man slapped the reins on the horse's back, clucked again, louder, and the speed of the wagon increased. Rosetta leaned to one side as the wagon turned, her upper arm pressing against the man's. When she straightened up, she shook her hair back.

"They're adopting me," she said, louder than necessary, still studying the side of the man's face. "And I'm going to have them adopt my little sister, as well," she said. There. It felt good to say it out loud. It made what she had been thinking about seem more real.

The man ignored her, pulling up on the reins. The horse immediately slowed. Rosetta saw light, like a small, square sun in the black that surrounded them.

"We're here," the man said. He jumped out of the wagon. Rosetta climbed down and stood beside it, twisting the hem of her jacket in her hands. The man lifted out the trunk and set it down.

"Go on up to the house," he said. He took out the lantern and lit it, then, carrying it, started to lead the horse through a set of open doors that Rosetta could make out in the lantern's flickering glow.

Rosetta looked at her trunk, then at the dark stretch between her and the bright window. She leaned over and grasped her trunk by both handles and, bracing her legs, lifted it. Its weight pulled Rosetta forward. She made her way across the darkness, moving toward the square of light, the trunk banging painfully against her knees with each step.

Chapter Seven

The soft *whump* of a door wakened Rosetta. She opened her eyes, but it took her a few minutes to sort out where she was. She had slept in so many places in the last month – ships, trains, strange rooms. But this was the strangest. It wasn't so much a room as a low space at the top of the house. The air in the room was already warm, although Rosetta could tell, by the sky outside the window beside her, that it was still very early. She got to her knees and looked out; it was a small window, with six panes of glass on top of the sash, and six panes under it.

There were a few pale streaks of coral-colored light just peeking over the top of a big wooden building not far from the house. When Rosetta looked at the set of open double doors on the building, she realized that it must be a sort of stable that the man had led the horse into last night.

Rosetta started to get to her feet, but immediately let out an "ouch" and crouched again, rubbing the top of her head. She looked up at the low, slanting roof. The only place she could stand up was in the very center. She hadn't been able to see the place when she'd climbed the narrow steps leading up here last night. She hadn't seen much of anything.

When she'd finally made it across the yard and set her

trunk down on the porch of the house, she'd knocked quietly on the door. After a long minute, she'd knocked again.

"The missus is sleeping," the man had said, appearing with the lantern. He'd opened the door and put the lantern inside, then came back and lifted Rosetta's trunk. She'd followed him, and he had gone across the room to a doorway. She'd heard the thumping of his feet on creaking stairs, the bang of the trunk being set down, and then the heavy footsteps again. She didn't even have time to look around before he was back. He stood at the bottom of the steps and pointed up.

"You can sleep up there," he'd said, then walked away, taking the glowing lamp off the table that stood in the middle of the room and disappearing through a door on another wall.

Rosetta stood in the dark for a minute, until her eyes adjusted to the gloom, then felt her way to the doorway leading to the steps. She started to climb them, her hands touching each side of the narrow stairway. When she got to the top, enough moonlight shone through the window for her to make out the square dark shadow that was her trunk, a long lighter shadow on the floor and, off to one side, a squat, small shadow that she thought must be a chamber pot.

She opened her trunk and felt around until she found her nightdress. Undressing quickly, looking back toward the stairway, she slipped the nightdress over her head and then leaned down and patted the long light shadow. There was a soft cover, and she pulled it back and lay down, then tugged it up over her.

It didn't feel exactly like a bed, more a lumpy mattress of some sort, with a smaller lumpy sack for her head.

"Where am I?" she whispered to the window, her eyes

wide. She wanted to try to sort it out, but her head throbbed and her throat was still sore.

"I'm too tired right now. I'll find out what this is all about tomorrow," she thought, and then closed her eyes. And before she could even begin to think about Flora, she was asleep.

~

In the subdued morning light she examined her surroundings more closely.

She'd slept on a pallet under a worn sheet and a thin quilt made of hundreds of tiny squares of faded material. Her pillow was just a smaller version of the pallet. She felt through the coarse cloth of the mattress and pillow and could make out many sharp ends. Straw, she decided, was the stuffing.

She had been right about the chamber pot in one corner, under the steeply sloping roof. Paper-thin shafts of light streamed through cracks where the slats of wood on the wall around the window didn't quite meet. On the wall opposite the window was a door. Rosetta went over to it and looked at the latch. She touched it, took her hand away, then took a breath and reached out again, moving it as soundlessly as she could. The door pulled open toward her.

A strong musty smell made Rosetta step back. She leaned forward and stared into the semi-darkness.

It was another room, exactly like hers, but the window had a piece of dark cloth nailed over it. Fingers of light showed a low form covered with old pieces of sacking. Rosetta stared at it; it had a vaguely familiar shape. She tiptoed a few steps into the room and lifted one edge of the rough sacking.

It was a hooded cradle, the maple smooth and gleaming, even in the faint light. Something about the still, dustless cradle and the musty smell of the room made a shiver start at the back of her neck. She dropped the sacking and edged out of the room, closing the door as quietly as she had opened it.

She lifted the lid of her trunk and took out her other dress, the good one. It was a satiny, soft brown, with a bit of ivory lace at the collar and cuffs. It had come to the Refuge in a box of clothes collected by the Manchester Ladies of Charitable Purposes. Miss Hall had brought it to Rosetta.

"This is the color for you, Rosetta," she'd said. "With your dark hair and that complexion, it will do just fine, although it may need some adjusting in certain areas."

But when Rosetta had put the dress on, Miss Hall's eye widened the tiniest bit. "I expect I was wrong about needing to alter it," she said. "You look very grown up, Rosetta."

Rosetta had picked up a handful of her long hair and pulled it up on the top of her head, smiling. Miss Hall had shaken her head. "But not old enough for putting your hair up, miss. Not until you're at least sixteen. It's not proper."

Rosetta thought about that day as she neatly folded her everyday dress into the trunk and took out her hairbrush. It had been one of the good days at the Refuge.

She started in at her hair, working at it until she felt she'd brushed out most of the dust from yesterday's train and wagon ride. She pulled the two side pieces back and tied them together with a length of ecru ribbon that Miss Hall had found to match the lace on the dress. The rest of her hair fell in soft waves down her back.

Twirling a strand of her own hair, Rosetta thought of Flora's hair. It was a mass of curls that tangled easily. She thought of the woman called Mrs. Forsythe, her pudgy, clutching fingers on her husband's arm, then those same fingers trying to brush Flora's hair. Rosetta felt a great ache wash over her. It was so strong that she had to sit down on the pallet.

"No," she whispered. "I won't let myself imagine what's happening to Flora. I'll only remember her when she was happy. When we were together. And think about how it will be when we're together again."

She rubbed at her eyes, wishing she had some water to wash her face. Then she pulled the sheet and quilt up neatly over the pallet and tried to puff up the flat pillow. When she was done, she sat down on her bed and waited for someone to come and tell her when she would be taken to her new home to meet her parents.

She had figured it out as she lay on the pallet, watching the morning light grow brighter.

This must be a stopping-place for the night. Because it was so late when the train got in last night, the man who had come to get her had decided that it was too far to go all the way to the farm, and so he had let her sleep here.

As she sat waiting, she thought again how, as she had told the man last night, once she was settled in with her new family, she would talk to them about Flora. Surely they would help her find her sister.

Rosetta's stomach rumbled, and she pressed both hands over it, trying to push away the hunger pains. From down-stairs she heard the scratching of a poker. The room got hotter and hotter. She got on her knees and looked at the window, then pushed up the sash. Fresh air swept into the room through the small opening.

Rosetta smelled the air. It was different than the air in Manchester; different, even, than Belleville. Warmer, and drier. And there was another, earthy smell. Rosetta guessed it was the smell of many animals.

As she leaned her face closer to the open window, Rosetta saw a man coming out of the big building. From his height, she assumed it was the man from last night. In the daylight she could see that he had black hair, thinning on top, and that he walked with a slight limp, favoring his left leg. His arms seemed very long; Rosetta saw that his hair-covered wrists protruded at least an inch from the cuffs of his dark-blue flannelette shirt. He was carrying a wooden bucket and heading toward the house.

Rosetta got up, this time remembering to duck her head so she wouldn't bang it. She went to the stairs and looked down. There was the sound of a door opening and closing and then a low rumble of words, followed by a higher, answering voice.

Rosetta stood still, looking at the crooked, narrow stairway. The man's head appeared around the end of the stairs unexpectedly. Both he and Rosetta jumped. Rosetta smiled; the man didn't. He was younger than Rosetta had thought he was in the darkness the night before. His eyes were like green marbles.

"You startled me," she called down. "I was wondering if I should come down."

The man nodded once, then his head disappeared.

Rosetta walked down the stairs and turned at the last step into the room she had walked across last night.

The man was sitting on a slat-backed chair at the end of a long, unpainted pine table. There was a matching chair at the opposite end, and a bench ran along each side. A woman stood at an iron stove along one wall of the room; her back toward the room. Rosetta smelled something warm and fragrant, and saliva rushed into her mouth.

"Good morning," she said. She tried to smile, but her mouth wouldn't work the way she wanted it to. She wondered when she would be able to smile again without the pain, without thinking about Flora.

The woman turned around and stared at Rosetta. Rosetta felt the trembling smile on her mouth fade.

It wasn't a woman after all, but she wasn't really a girl either. Rosetta couldn't tell how old she was. She was shorter than Rosetta, and her body held no curves to fill out the plain gray dress that hung limply on her slight, child-like frame. The skin on her face was stretched so tightly that her cheekbones stood out in high ridges. Her eyes were large, the blue of porcelain washed by wave after wave, but they were circled with dark rings, and her hair, so blonde it was almost white, was scraped back into such a small, angry knot at the back of her head that Rosetta thought it must hurt her temples.

Rosetta tried again. "Good morning," she said.

"Morning," the woman said. "Pour the mister his coffee." Her voice wasn't like the voices of the people Rosetta had heard at the Marchmont Home in Belleville; it wasn't like the conductor's or even the man sitting at the table. It had a lighter sound, a tiny up-and-down melody trying to sing out as she spoke.

Rosetta saw a tin pot with a spout and a handle on the stove. She walked over and reached toward the coffee pot.

The woman grabbed her arm. Rosetta looked at her, and the

woman handed Rosetta a rag and made a motion with her head toward the handle of the pot.

Rosetta wrapped the rag around the handle before lifting the coffee pot off the stove. She took it to the table and saw that the man was staring straight ahead, toward the door that led outside. He held his spoon in the curled fist of his right hand, resting on the table beside his empty bowl. There was no cup on the table.

Rosetta looked at the stove, but the woman had her back turned again and was scraping at something in a black pot. Glancing around the clean kitchen, with its patches of sunlight from the windows, Rosetta saw a large pine dish dresser, painted red-brown. The top two shelves had molding running across them, and leaning against the molding were china plates, decorated in blue flowers. The third shelf had an assortment of delicate china cups and saucers, some in the same blue floral pattern and some painted with pretty scenes. Under the shelf was a row of heavy crockery mugs hanging on iron hooks.

She hurried to the dish dresser and took down a mug, then set it on the table. She slowly and carefully poured the steaming black coffee to the top, and stepped back.

The woman came up beside her with the heavy black pot and plopped a big ladleful of oatmeal into the man's bowl. Almost before she had a chance to move the pot out of the way, the man started in on the hot porridge, shoving one large spoonful after another into his mouth.

Rosetta watched the woman, but she kept her blonde head down and returned the pot to the stove. Rosetta followed her, setting the coffee pot back in its place beside the black pot.

There were a few long slurps and then the sound of a chair scraping across the wooden floor. Rosetta turned to see the man standing, draining the coffee mug.

He set it on the table and started toward the door leading outside, picking up a broad-brimmed hat, stained around the band, from the other end of the table.

Rosetta watched him, then called, "Sir?"

He stopped and turned around, putting on his hat.

Rosetta walked up to him. "Sir? I'm wondering when I'll be going."

"Going?" the man repeated.

"To my new home. My family. Will you be taking me there, or will they come here to fetch me?"

The man's eyes flickered to a spot behind Rosetta.

Rosetta waited, trying to ignore the dull ache in her stomach. It's hunger, she told herself. But it didn't feel like hunger. It felt as if she couldn't eat a thing, ever again, and suddenly, just as she'd had the feeling about Flora, when she'd been taken away at Marchmont, Rosetta was overwhelmed by a horrible sensation. She knew what the man was about to say.

Then he said it. "This is where you'll be staying."

"Here?" Rosetta said, the word coming out like a bark. She'd been right. "For how long?"

"Depends. Depends on how hard you work, girl."

Rosetta shook her head. "No," she said. "No, you don't understand. I'm to be adopted. I'm to have a new family, a new –"

"No, girl," he interrupted, "*you* don't understand. We got a letter from that place, the place in Belleville we found out about from the preacher in Peterborough. He told us we could get help from there. A girl to help the wife with the work." His eyes moved behind Rosetta again. "That's what it said, didn't it?"

Rosetta felt everything around her go perfectly still. She didn't hear an answer from the woman behind her, but the man continued.

"According to the letter," he said, his eyes coming back to Rosetta's face, "it's only the young ones gets adopted. The ones what's almost growed up, like you, gets a contract of indenture." He dragged out the word, slowly, in-den-chur. "That means we hired you, to work for us. You live here, with us, and help the missus," he said. "She's been poorly over the winter. And you'll help me, too, when I need it, with the outside chores."

Rosetta didn't move.

"And as long as you do your job, you stay. If you don't, we can send you back, and they send us someone better." He settled his hat firmly on his head. "So you best mind yourself, girl, and do what the missus tells you."

Finally, Rosetta turned her head. The woman was still standing at the stove, still holding the ladle in her hand. Her eyes were flat, but her mouth worked in a constant, small chewing motion.

As Rosetta watched the curious movement of the woman's mouth, a sudden gust of warm air swirled around her. Before she could look back at the man, he was gone, closing the door with a quiet thud that sounded as loud as the sky crashing down through the ceiling, falling in pieces at her feet.

Chapter Eight

"Here," the woman said, pouring a mug of coffee and handing it to Rosetta. "Drink."

Rosetta took the mug from her and looked into the steaming blackness. She raised it to her mouth and let the liquid touch her lips. It was scalding, and bitter.

"I've never had coffee before," she said, still staring at the drink.

The woman carried the dirty bowl and mug from the table and put them in a big tin pan sitting in a low zinc sink under a window. She took a huge kettle off the stove and poured hot water over the dirty dishes, then pumped cold into the pan from the small pump on the counter beside the sink.

"It's not real coffee. Dandelion root," she said. "Now we will start the noon meal."

Rosetta finally looked at her.

"Is it true?" she asked. "Is this really where I'm to live?"

The woman crossed to a sideboard in one corner of the kitchen and opened a drawer. She took out a long, wrinkled envelope and handed it to Rosetta. Rosetta put the mug on the table and sat down, taking out the single sheet. After she had read what was written there, she folded the paper and slid it back into the envelope.

"I'm hired help," she said to the envelope in her hands.

"Yes," the woman answered, and set a slab of meat, a wooden board, and a long knife on the table in front of Rosetta. Then she looked at Rosetta's dress, her eyes lingering on the satiny dark-brown material. She took off her own apron and set it on Rosetta's lap, picking the envelope out of Rosetta's hand, running her fingers along one edge of it.

"Cut the meat," she said, "small pieces." Then she returned the envelope to its place in the drawer.

~

Rosetta stayed in the house with the woman until dinnertime. She helped her make a thick stew, and mixed flour and water for dumplings to drop on top of the boiling mixture. She washed dishes and swept the kitchen with a strange, long-whisked broom, and then sewed two buttons on a big shirt that she knew belonged to the man. Not a word was spoken.

As she worked, Rosetta looked around the house. As well as the table and chairs and benches and stove and dish dresser and sideboard, there was a dark-red spool couch with a wool-filled mattress against one of the walls. There were two rocking chairs, also with slat backs, pushed away from the stove. A pine clock ticked quietly on the top shelf of the sideboard. There was a large, square trapdoor near the enclosed stairway that led to the room Rosetta had slept in. The walls of the kitchen, unlike the unadorned wooden boards upstairs, were covered with a thick white plaster.

Rosetta stole glances of the other rooms on the main floor as she swept. Off the kitchen to one side was a door just slightly ajar. Rosetta could see a darkened parlor with a stiff, horsehair settle, two Windsor chairs, and a number of small tables covered with lacy white doilies. The two windows were covered with drawn blinds; long, heavy curtains hung down at the sides. A handwoven rag carpet covered the middle of the wooden floor.

To the other side of the kitchen was a bedroom. It held a low-slung double bed covered with a patchwork quilt similar to the one on her pallet. A big trunk stood at its foot. She could also see a small bureau, its top covered with a damask linen, beside the bed. An oval photograph of an elderly man and woman hung on the wall over the bureau. A rocking chair with a cane seat was in the corner on the other side of the bed.

As well as the front door of the kitchen, leading into the yard and the lane that went to the main road, there was a smaller back door. When the woman opened it and returned with an armload of wood to keep the fire hot and the stew bubbling, Rosetta realized it was a woodshed.

Eventually, the woman went out on the porch with a wooden spoon and the big black pot she'd cooked the porridge in and banged on the bottom of the pot three times. Within five minutes Rosetta heard footsteps and a faint splashing of water on the porch, then the door opened. The man and another, much older man, stooped and hobbling, his cheeks and chin covered with grizzled white stubble, trooped in. Both men hung their hats on nails beside the door and sat down at the table. The younger man looked at his wife, dishing four bowls of stew at the stove.

"The girl working?" he said, although Rosetta was right there, at the stove, too.

The woman set a bowl down in front of him, and Rosetta saw her nod once. She set another bowl in front of the other man, then turned back to Rosetta and dipped her head at the two bowls still sitting on the stove.

Rosetta carried them over, and after the woman sat down opposite her husband, she took a seat on the bench across from the old man. When the men started to eat, she saw the woman pick up her spoon, so she took hers and picked up one of the chunks of meat she had cut hours earlier. She started chewing, and although she knew the meat had boiled for hours, and she had chopped onions and cut limp, whiskery carrots into rounds and put them in the bubbling pot and had seen the woman add salt and some other small, dry seeds, she couldn't taste anything. It was like opening and closing her teeth on a thick piece of paper.

There was no sound except for the men's chewing and swallowing and the tiny clinks of their spoons against the crockery.

Finally, Rosetta managed to swallow the meat. Then she put her spoon down neatly beside her bowl. "My name is Rosetta," she said. "My father was very interested in Egypt, and named me after an ancient stone, covered with writing that was discovered to be both Egyptian and Greek."

The old man lifted his head and stared at her across the table. A tiny shred of wet carrot hung, trembling, in the whiskers on his chin.

"A stone?" the woman said. She looked at Rosetta, then at her husband. "Her father called her after a stone?"

"It's called the Rosetta Stone, and it's very famous," Rosetta said. "It was found near Rosetta, in Egypt, in 1799."

The woman looked back at her. "I am named after my grandmother. It is a popular name from one of the sagas —"

She was interrupted as the man pushed back his bowl and got to his feet. "No call for talk at table," he said, giving Rosetta one quick, angry look. "Come on, Ben. We aim to finish up that harrowing in the back field by supper." He took his hat and left, the old man following him.

The woman and Rosetta stayed at their spots at the table. "Ben is our hired man. My husband's name is Albert," the woman said. "Albert Thomas. I am Gudrun. Gudrun Thomas. But I have always been known as Runa."

Rosetta held her hand out to the woman. "Rosetta Westley," she said.

Runa looked at the girl's hand, then stretched her own smaller one toward it. As Rosetta closed her fingers around Runa's, she thought, suddenly, of the cold, still body of a bird she had once discovered under a leaf, in the garden at Manchester Refuge.

~

Later in the afternoon, Runa gave Rosetta a pail and told her to wash down the porch.

"There is a big pump in the yard," she said.

Rosetta took the pail and stepped outside. The sunlight was clear and bright.

On the bottom step of the narrow porch that ran along the front of the house, Rosetta turned to study the place that she'd been brought to. The house was clapboard, but the wood had never been painted and had been turned a silvery gray by the sun and wind and rain. The door she had come out of, in the center of the house, was low and wide. The porch faced south, and the two windows on either side of the door had sashes of eight panes over eight.

In the half-storey upstairs was a smaller window, and Rosetta realized it was the window of the musty, closed-off room. She noticed some of the shingles on the roof lifting and curling in the sun.

There was nothing pretty about the house; it stood, square and unimaginative, in the middle of the mud yard. A few tired clumps of daisies grew around the porch, and one forlorn morning glory twined up a porch support.

Rosetta stepped backward into the yard, still looking up at the house. She stood for a long time, blinking back the hot tears that had crouched, burning, behind her eyes all day, since the morning, when the man had told her what she was to them. Simply hired help.

This wasn't a home for Flora. She would never be allowed to bring Flora here. The man had made that perfectly obvious.

"And neither shall I stay here," Rosetta said out loud. But she still had to get through today.

Then she turned and looked for the pump. It was halfway between the house and another very small, low house, built of round, roughly hewn logs. It wasn't much more than a shanty, with dried mud between the logs. The sloping roof was made of weathered wooden shingles, black with age.

Rosetta put the bucket down beside the pump and used the privy that stood in a cluster of elderberry bushes beside the house. As she came out, she saw, behind the house and off to one side, a large garden. There were neatly hoed rows of green growth of various height.

Besides the large barn, with an open door near the peaked roof, which was probably the loft, there were a number of other outbuildings. Rosetta could make out moving animals inside an area surrounded by low cedar rails, and heard the sudden cranky *plok plok* of a chicken that came scratching out from behind the privy.

She went back to the pump and started moving the iron handle up and down. Soon a cold, clear stream of water splashed out, and she filled the bucket. As she looked up from the sparkling water, she saw Mr. Thomas coming toward her.

Bent over with the effort, he was pushing a wooden wheelbarrow filled with what looked to be some sort of dark soil.

"Mr. Thomas?" Rosetta called, letting the pump handle go. She rubbed her upper arm with her left hand. Mr. Thomas stopped, setting down the wheelbarrow and pushing back his hat, wiping at his forehead with his forearm.

"I was just wondering," Rosetta said, "if you have any apple trees."

The man stared at her. "Apple trees?"

"Yes. I heard that there are ever so many apple trees in Canada."

Mr. Thomas picked up the wooden handles of the wheelbarrow and looked straight ahead. He made a sound of disgust in his throat. "You see anything looks like apple trees around here?"

Rosetta looked to one side of the farmyard, at the bushes that surrounded the privy and hung over one side of the cedar fence. On the other side was a small stand of trees, but they were rustling poplars and lacy willows, with taller, straighter oak interspersed throughout them. She didn't know what apple trees looked like, how tall they were, or what shape of leaves they would have. She turned and looked behind her, to the open field that spread out behind the house. In the far distance she could see a dark ridge of trees, and one huge old tree at the far edge of the field. Its branches were gnarled and black against the cerulean sky. Somehow it didn't give Rosetta the impression of being an apple tree. She looked at the field in front of the house, cut by the narrow ribbon of dirt that ran up to it from the main road.

By the time she looked back at Mr. Thomas, he was already struggling along with the wheelbarrow again. She thought she saw him shake his head once, in a rapid, irritated way, but it was hard to tell, the way the wheelbarrow rumbled and bumped along across the yard.

She'd have to ask Runa if there were any apple trees on the farm. She planned to find Flora soon, and she would want to tell her what apple trees looked like.

~

Supper was as quick and silent as dinner had been. It was more of the same, the stew heated up and biscuits Runa had baked after dinner, hard and flat now that they'd sat in the pan all afternoon.

"Would you like another biscuit, Runa?" Rosetta asked, picking up the plate and holding it out to the woman.

Mr. Thomas lifted his head from over his bowl. "What you say?" he asked, his mouth full. His green eyes blazed.

Rosetta put the plate down. "I asked Runa if she'd –"

She jumped as Mr. Thomas slammed his spoon down into the stew. Greasy droplets splashed the front of his sweat-stained shirt.

"Who do you think you are?" he said, his eyes narrowing.

Rosetta licked her lips, glancing at Runa, but the woman's head was lowered, and she was picking tiny pieces off her biscuit and dropping them onto the table in front of her. Ben kept chewing, his eyes fixed on a spot on the table in front of him, but his spoon was still, poised over his bowl.

"You think you can just waltz around here, in your fancy dress, with your hair all prettied up like you was going to a party, and call your missus," he tossed his head in Runa's direction, "call her by her Christian name? You'll call her Mrs. Thomas. You work for her, and for me, and don't you forget it. Don't you be getting any put-on ideas to go along with that voice of yours. One step out of line and you'll be gone from here. Remember that."

He picked up his spoon and dug it into his stew again. Rosetta picked hers up, too, but just sat there, holding it, her fingers clenched around it. Her cheeks burned, and she longed to raise her arm and throw her spoon at Mr. Thomas, hit him right in the face with it. She imagined him sitting stunned, bits of stew stuck onto his forehead and nose. But she stayed still, thinking – just today, get through today – holding her spoon tightly, until Runa had finished crumbling her biscuit, and Mr. Thomas and Ben had cleaned their bowls and gone outside again.

Then she got up and poured warm water from the kettle on the stove into the dishpan, and took the bowls from the table and put them into the water. When she turned around to wipe Runa's pile of crumbs off the table, the woman was gone.

She finished washing and drying the dishes and the stew pot and put them on the open shelves, folded the wet rag and the drying towel neatly and hung them on the nails beside the stove. Then she pushed the chairs and benches in around the table, and smoothed her hair with her hands.

She looked around the slowly darkening room. There were no pictures on the walls, no small ornaments anywhere.

Rosetta glanced toward the stairs. It was too early to go to bed, and she didn't want to spend any more time than she had to in the low, hot space under the roof. She looked out the front window.

Mr. Thomas was sitting on the top stair of the porch, smoking a pipe. Rosetta stepped back. If she went out, she'd have to step around him, or ask him to move. She didn't want to do either.

She took a drink of water from the dipper in the pail near the sink. As she drank, she stared out the window to the field with the old tree. She thought she saw something moving near it. She put the dipper back in the pail and leaned forward, for a better look. There *was* someone under the tree, swaying back and forth in the falling darkness.

Rosetta could tell it wasn't old Ben. It was someone young, and small. Runa, Rosetta thought, but it looked too short even for Runa. "Oh," Rosetta said, as the person stood up. It was Runa after all; she had been on her knees. Rosetta could recognize her round head, her hair so pale that she looked bald from this distance.

Just then the door opened, and Rosetta whirled around as if she had been doing something she shouldn't have.

It was Mr. Thomas. He closed the door behind him.

"Go to bed," he said. "We let you lie in today, this being your first day and all, but tomorrow you get up with the sun. First cockcrow, you get down here and have the breakfast laid out. Then you'll go out and milk the cows. There's six of 'em, and a couple have calves. You can slop the pigs, and collect the eggs. Once you do those morning chores, you come back in and help Mrs. Thomas."

Rosetta stared at him. How could she be expected to know how to milk a cow or slop a pig? Whatever slopping meant. Or even approach a chicken? She was from Manchester, from England. A big city in England. She opened her mouth to tell him, to ask him what he thought she knew, ask him who he thought she was. But seeing the puzzling anger burning behind his eyes, in the set of his mouth, she closed her own. It didn't matter what he thought, or if she knew how to do all those things. She wouldn't be here long enough for it to matter.

"Git, then," Mr. Thomas said, and Rosetta walked across the room to the stairs, forcing herself not to hurry, but feeling Mr. Thomas's eyes on her all the way.

She walked up the stairs slowly, too, not giving him the satisfaction of knowing she was in a hurry to get away from him. In her stuffy room she sat on the pallet until she heard the kitchen door opening and closing and the murmur of Runa's voice.

Listening to the man and woman below her, a bitter smile twisted her lips. "My new parents," she whispered, then let out a croak. "Ha." It was almost laughable. To think she had imagined a jolly, elderly couple who would open their arms to her and make her feel that she had, at long last, a home. Who would immediately set about helping her find Flora. Who would love her.

The couple downstairs – well. There seemed to be no love at all between them, or if there was, it was well hidden beneath gruff, short words and strange, nervous glances. No extra love, that was certain. And this place, this place . . . Rosetta looked at the rough wooden walls . . . even this house felt like it had no love in it. No. This was not a place for her. This was not a place she would stay.

~

When the house was completely quiet and her own room dark but for a small, growing patch of moonlight on the quilt, Rosetta undressed and put on her nightdress. She neatly folded up her good dress, and then opened her trunk and took out the gray serge dress she had packed away that morning.

She put her hand into one of its pockets. The cardboard sign was still there. She took it out and set it on the windowsill. In the other pocket she found what she was looking for.

She examined the coins in the moonlight. She didn't know how much they were; they were so different from the crowns and shillings she was used to. But surely they were enough for the train ride back to Belleville. She would get up early, before anyone was up, and set out on the road. Once she started walking someone would come along in a wagon and give her a ride to – she looked at the cardboard – to Thomson's Landing. And then she'd get on the train and go back to Marchmont. Tell them how it had been a mistake, how she couldn't stay at the desolate farm, in the middle of nowhere, and milk cows and feed chickens and do – what was that thing? – slop to pigs. How she would work in a house in a city, cooking and cleaning, as long as she had Flora with her. She would get Miss Cramer, yes, Miss Cramer had seemed kind, get her to talk to the Forsythes.

I'll work it all out, Rosetta thought, laying back on top of the thin quilt, the coins in her hand, I will. She drew her lips into a hard, determined line.

But still, when she closed her eyes, her chin began to quiver, and the stinging tears she had held in all day started to roll down the sides of her face in blistering, snaking trails, into her ears and onto her neck. Rosetta sat up, both hands over her mouth so the Thomases couldn't hear her sobs. She wouldn't give *him* the satisfaction of knowing she was crying.

She shook her head, trying to will away her sadness by conjuring up the man's glowering face, by trying to bring back her anger from the supper table. Being angry made her feel strong. She wiped at her eyes with the heels of her hands, squeezed the coins tightly for a minute, then slipped them under the pillow.

"All right," she whispered. "All right. Tomorrow." And she started humming, humming the tune to the Promise Song, thinking of the words she would use if Flora were lying beside her.

Chapter Nine

The sky was starting to lighten, and the morning birds were already shouting their early messages when Rosetta realized how hungry she was. She stooped by the side of the road and pulled some of the tender new grass out of the soil and chewed on it, shifting her bundle – the sheet containing the contents of her trunk – to the other hand. She had hesitated for a moment, before taking the sheet off the pallet, but she couldn't carry her trunk, and there was no other way to take her belongings with her.

She had tried not to let herself fall asleep the night before, afraid that if she did she wouldn't awaken in time to slip out before Mr. and Mrs. Thomas got up. She had kept awake through the long black hours by going over multiplication tables, reciting memorized poems, and making up new verses to the Promise Song, verses she would sing to Flora as soon as they were together. At one point she had been aware of the soft patter of rain on the low roof over her head, and, listening to the gentle rhythm, let her aching eyes close, for just a moment. She realized she must have dozed, because there was a time when she had been trying to remember the next line of a poem she had learned at the Manchester Refuge and then suddenly found herself doing the eleven times table. After that she made herself sit up, so she wouldn't be so comfortable and be tempted to close her eyes again.

Rosetta had told herself at first, still trying to stifle her sobs, that she should leave right after she was sure Mr. and Mrs. Thomas were asleep and have the whole night to travel. But she wasn't sure she'd be able to see her way in the pitch black. Like on her first night at the farm, the moon had disappeared shortly after it had made its appearance, and the thought of wandering out in the strange countryside for hours, without knowing where she was going, or what she might encounter, seemed too huge and frightening an idea.

So she waited for as long as she could, until she knew the deepest hours of the night were past, and then bundled up her things and slowly made her way downstairs and out the door without a sound. She wasn't sure when Mr. Thomas got up, but felt she had at least a few hours before actual daylight. After silently pulling the kitchen door closed behind her, she hurried down the long dark lane. At the end, where it met the road, she stopped, then remembered how her left arm had pressed against the man's as they turned into the yard two nights ago. So she turned right and started off.

Now she had been walking for what felt like over an hour. The sky was starting to glow pinker and pinker in the distance ahead. She walked faster, looking over her shoulder now and then. Her quick footsteps created a steady rhythm on the hard dirt of the road. The sound was soon accompanied by the nervous scolding of squirrels and the foraging of small animals in the bordering underbrush. She passed a few farms, set far back like the Thomas farm, but she didn't see anyone moving about.

As she rounded a bend, a cart pulled by an ox came into

view. Rosetta's first instinct was to dart into the low bushes, but she realized that the cart was coming from the wrong direction. Mr. Thomas, if he was looking for her, would come up from behind. And besides, no one else knew her.

The roughly built cart slowly rolled by. Rosetta kept her head down. She heard a "How do" come from above her – a man's voice – and she raised her hand in greeting without lifting her head.

After walking for what felt like another hour, she heard the welcome sound of trickling water, and pushed through the long grass and bushes off the road, toward the sound. She found a small stream, and, kneeling, cupped her hands and drank, letting the water run down her neck, wetting the front of her dress. Still kneeling, she reached into her pocket and closed her fingers around the coins there.

Please let these be enough, she thought. Enough to get to Belleville, or at least some place close to there.

As she started to make her way to the road, she heard the rumble of wheels again. Pulling back into the bushes, she peeked in the direction she'd just traveled. She breathed a sigh of relief as she saw it was only the same cart that had passed her earlier, the cart with the ox. Suddenly she realized she should ask for a ride. The faster and farther she got away from Albert Thomas, the better.

She hurried up to the road and waved at the man. He slowed down, touching the brim of his straw hat.

"Could you give me a ride, please, sir?" she called.

The cart stopped. "Surely. Hop up," the man said.

Rosetta climbed in, throwing her bundle behind the rough plank that served as a seat and sitting down beside the man.

"Ain't going too far," he said. "Only on to my place, 'nother half-mile up the road." He made a clucking sound, and the ox returned to its lumbering pace.

"Oh," Rosetta said, disappointed. She felt the man's eyes on her, but looked straight ahead. "That will be fine."

"You visiting someone?" he asked.

Rosetta nodded. "Uh, yes. Yes, I've been visiting. And now I'm going . . ." she stopped. "I'm going back."

"Back where?"

Rosetta wished she knew the names of some other places; she didn't want to tell this man anything. But Belleville was a big city. Thousands of people must live there. "To Belleville."

"The wife's got a sister up Belleville way," the man said.

"How nice," Rosetta murmured, hoping he wouldn't ask her any more questions. She took the coins out of her pocket. "Will this be enough?" she asked. "To take the train from Thomson's Landing to Belleville?" She held her breath while the man leaned over to look at her palm.

"Don't know the fare, but I do believe that'll be more'n enough," he said, raising his eyes to study her face as Rosetta let her breath out in a long, relieved whoosh. "But you got yourself a long ways to get to Thomson's Landing. You plannin' on walking? Take you most of the day. An' likely you'll have missed the train. Best if you go on over to Magrath Corners, just around the next bend, and turn left at the fork, see if anyone from there is going to Thomson's Landing."

She put the money back in her pocket. "Perhaps I'll do that."

"Well, here's where I turn off to my place," the man said, pulling on the reins. The ox obediently slowed.

Rosetta saw they were at a crossroads, where the road

widened. The trees were far back from the road here. "Thank you very much," she said. "I—" she stopped as the man turned in his seat and looked behind him.

"Who the blazes can that be, traveling at such a speed so early of a morning?" he said.

Rosetta followed his gaze. All she could see was a huge cloud of dust on the road. But within seconds, as the dust ball grew closer, she could see that it was Mr. Thomas, standing up in his wagon and slapping the reins so hard his arms flew out at the elbows, urging the horse on at a full gallop. Her head swiveled, looking for a place to run. She grabbed her bundle and jumped out of the cart, but one edge of the bulging sheet caught on a nail holding the plank seat in place and ripped it wide open. Rosetta's good dress, her nightdress, brush and comb, and Bible all scattered in the dust. She stopped for half a second, eyeing everything she owned lying at her feet, then turned from it to run off the road, toward the trees.

But there wasn't time. The horse's hooves pounded up in front of her, and Rosetta shrank back from the rolling eyes and foaming mouth of the huge, panting animal and was forced up against the cart behind her.

Mr. Thomas leapt out of his wagon and strode toward her.

"Knew you wouldn't a got too far," he said. "Not on foot." He looked at the other man, whose mouth was hanging open as he leaned forward, staring at the pair on the road. "Morning, Reg."

Reg pointed one long finger at Rosetta. "That girl been visiting with you, Albert?"

Mr. Thomas gave a snort. "Visitin'? Hardly likely. She's just a Home girl we got sent. Sent to work. And after one day she decided she don't like it. Decided she could find some place better to work, is that it?" He glared at Rosetta.

"No. It was just a mistake. That's all. It wouldn't have worked out. And now I need to find my sister. I'm going back to look for her."

"Weren't no mistake, girl," Mr. Thomas said, taking her by the top of her arm. "Now you get in the wagon. You ain't goin' nowheres except back to the farm. Besides, how far you think you could walk?"

"She got money, Albert," Reg said. "Showed it to me. Musta stole it from you, eh? Soons you turn your back. And here I was thinkin' of asking her up to the house for a meal. Bet she woulda stole me and the missus blind, too."

Mr. Thomas's face had paled under his wind-burn. "You found my money?" he said, tightening his hand around Rosetta's arm.

"No," Rosetta said, dropping her shoulder to relieve the pressure on the soft skin on her arm. "No. It's mine. It's my money."

"Show it to me."

When Rosetta didn't move, Reg called down, "It's in her pocket, Albert. She has it in her pocket."

Mr. Thomas reached over and dug in one and then the other of Rosetta's pockets. He pulled out the coins and looked at them, then stuck them deep down into his own trouser pocket.

"Mr. Thomas. That's mine. You can't take it," Rosetta said from between her teeth.

"Much obliged, Reg," Mr. Thomas called to the other man. "You go on now. I can handle this."

Reg shook his head. "Seems like you got yourself trouble, Albert. I heard you can't trust them kids." He didn't move, but sat watching, his eyes round, his hat pushed to the back of his head, obviously enjoying the unexpected early-morning drama.

Mr. Thomas kept his grip on Rosetta's arm. "Get your things. Pick them up." Rosetta gathered everything up as best she could, holding it all against her chest. Then Mr. Thomas pushed her into the wagon and climbed in after her. "Good day now, Reg," he said and, without waiting to hear the other man's reply, slapped the back of the horse hard with the reins and then pulled them to one side sharply, so the horse turned around on the wide road.

"You work for me, and that means I have to feed you and buy you clothes," Mr. Thomas said, yelling to make himself heard over the rumbling of the wheels, the pounding of the horse's hooves. "Where d'you think I'm gonna get that extra money, the money to buy you decent work clothes? You think you gonna muck out the barn in them boots?" He pointed his chin toward Rosetta's thin leather boots. "Come winter, you think they're gonna keep you warm? Hmmm? You don't think you're gonna cost me money? And look at this day already. Wasted good working time coming out to find you and bring you back. Good working time. You costing me money already."

Rosetta sat as still as she could on the rocking seat. "Please, Mr. Thomas. I think you can see that this won't work out." She had to yell, too. Her bonnet was blown back off her head but still tied around her throat. Long strands of hair swirled around her face. "Please give me back my money. I'll stay for a

69

while. I will. But only for a while, until you can find someone else. And then I have to go to my sister."

"Your sister! Pah!" Mr. Thomas finally turned his head to look at her. "Don't you let me hear no more about no sister. You hear me?" His voice had risen to a roar. "I don't want to hear no story about a sister!"

For the first time, Rosetta was afraid. There was such a bitter sound in Mr. Thomas's voice, such a hateful look on his face, that she thought he might do something awful, right then, strike her, or throw her out of the wagon, jump out after her and beat her.

She knew he was angry at her for running away, but why was he so furious at her talk about Flora? Why would he grow so enraged because she wanted to be with her sister?

She turned her face away from his, so he wouldn't see the fear she knew was in her eyes, and looked out at the blur of green countryside that rushed by them. She kept her back stiff, closed her mouth and kept it closed, in a firm, straight line, all the way back to the farm.

Chapter Ten

"May I know what's in that contract, please? The contract that says I'm hired help?" Rosetta chose her words carefully, so that Mr. Thomas wouldn't know that his wife had already shown her the contract once before. She was starting to realize that Runa was afraid of her husband, afraid, as Rosetta had been early this morning in the wagon. She didn't want to get the thin, little woman into trouble.

Runa glanced at her husband. She and Rosetta were doing the supper dishes while Mr. Thomas drank another cup of coffee at the table before returning to the barn.

Mr. Thomas set his cup down on the table and glared at Rosetta. She looked back at him, no longer frightened. All day, since he had brought her back that morning, she had been thinking about what she could do next – when she could leave, go and look for Flora. Mr. Thomas had taken his anger away with him, out to the fields. When he came in for his noon dinner with Ben, he hadn't looked at Rosetta or said a word about the episode. Runa had avoided Rosetta most of the day, only speaking to her when it was necessary to tell her what she needed her to do.

As Rosetta did the simple chores Runa abruptly assigned her, she tried to remember the words she had read in the contract, that first morning. Yesterday morning. Only yesterday. She felt as if weeks had gone by. She had been too shocked to remember much of what the contract said, but she was sure, now, that there was some mention of wages.

"May I?" she asked again.

Mr. Thomas gave one nod, and Runa took out the envelope. "You read it out loud to us," Mr. Thomas said, just as his wife was about to hand it to Rosetta. The woman pulled her arm back and took the paper out of the envelope. Rosetta anxiously watched as Runa's eyes scanned the paper.

"Well, go on. Read it out, wife."

Rosetta glanced back at him, wondering why he didn't read it himself.

"It says," Runa read, "that as well as room and board, the sum of two dollars shall be paid twice yearly. Schooling shall be provided until the age of fifteen." She quickly put the paper down on the table, as if it was burning her hand, and timidly looked at her husband.

Mr. Thomas half rose out of his chair, and Runa stepped away from the table and the paper. "You sure you're speaking the truth, Runa?" he asked. "You're sure you're right about the amount, there?" He sat back down.

As Rosetta watched him, she suddenly realized why he didn't pick it up and check it for himself. Mr. Thomas couldn't read.

"Yes, Albert. "Two dollars, twice yearly."

Rosetta licked her lips. "That would be in November, then, Mr. Thomas. November, when I get my wages." She closed her eyes for a moment. November. Six long months before she had any money again, before she could leave. Unless she tried getting away before that. But with no money, and especially now that she had tried it once . . . she knew that Mr. Thomas would be keeping a close eye on her.

"I suppose," Mr. Thomas said, getting up and walking out. As the door slammed behind him, Rosetta saw Runa's shoulders slump and an expression of relief pass over her face. Rosetta looked away; it was hard to watch the woman's worry over saying and doing exactly the right things, things that wouldn't anger her husband.

Six months, Rosetta thought again, bringing Mr. Thomas's cup to the dishpan. Well, maybe this was the only way it could be. She might have to stay here, but that didn't mean she had to like it. It didn't mean she had to be afraid of Mr. Thomas, like Runa was. And it didn't mean she couldn't find out where Flora was. She would write a letter to Belleville and ask for Flora's address.

She felt better as she rinsed and dried the cup and hung it back on its hook. She would wait a day or two, for things to settle down, and then she would ask Runa to help her get a letter off to Belleville. Rosetta watched the woman slowly wiping the table. In spite of her hesitant movements, her silence and fearful expression, there was something about her that Rosetta recognized, something that was familiar. As Rosetta continued to watch her, she felt a slow, sad, but warm nudge begin to push under her ribs.

~

For Rosetta's first few weeks on the farm, Runa told her what to do and showed her how to carry out tasks in an almost apologetic tone. Unlike her husband, she showed no irritation or anger when Rosetta didn't understand her new jobs.

73

She was glad it was Runa who showed her how to milk the cows – how to avoid the switching tails that slapped her face as she struggled to draw milk from the rubbery teats. Runa demonstrated how to gently slip a hand under a roosting hen and how to be firm with the pigs. Rosetta hated the pigs, with their coarse, bristled backs and rooting snouts and wicked little eyes.

But apart from her instructions, Runa was silent, and dodged Rosetta whenever they didn't have to work closely. A few times Rosetta tried to start a conversation with her, by chatting about the job they were doing or the weather, hoping to bring up the topic of Flora. But the woman only responded in terse, one-word answers. Finally, Rosetta fell silent, too, no longer trying to talk to her unless it was to ask questions about how to complete some unfamiliar job. She would be leaving as soon as she could anyway. She would do her job, and when she got paid, she would leave.

The only remotely friendly thing Runa said to her was about what to call her. Sometime in the second week, as the two of them scrubbed clothes with lye soap in a big galvanized tub, Rosetta said, "Please pass me that shirt, Mrs. Thomas." The woman handed it to her, saying, "When he's not here, you don't have to call me that. You can call me Runa."

Rosetta nodded. Although it was only eight in the morning, the air was hot and humid. Insects flew into the open door of the added-on room beside the woodshed. There was an older, smaller woodstove there, in this room called the summer kitchen. Runa told Rosetta that on the hot days they would cook there, and heat the water for washing clothes, to try to keep the house kitchen cool for eating.

The daylight hours passed quickly; there was so much hard work to do, so much to learn, that although Rosetta thought, every hour, about Flora, wondering where she was and how she was making out, she rarely had time to dwell on her sadness. Still, she waited, waited and watched for the right time to tell Runa about Flora. It never seemed to come. In her heart Rosetta knew now that the woman couldn't possibly speak to her husband for her, or help her in any big way, but all she needed was a piece of paper, a pencil, and an envelope and stamp.

Each evening, after the supper dishes were dried and the floor swept and her outside chores finally done, there was a bit of daylight left before Rosetta climbed the stairs to her bed. The June evenings were warm and still, with the slowly lowering sun creating long, cool shadows that almost glowed with a purple cast. But even the beauty of the closing of day couldn't lift the heavy curtain of sorrow that fell over Rosetta. It was the loneliest time, when she missed Flora the most. Sometimes she wandered outside the yard, and had discovered a little clearing in the wooded area not far from the house. There, among the trees, she wrote letters in her head to Flora, telling her about the things that had happened that day. What the woody rhubarb stalk she had broken off in the garden and crunched between her teeth tasted like. The warm smoothness of a freshly laid egg. The look of newborn kittens, discovered hidden in the hay in the loft. The quiet of a farm at night, so different than the noise she and Flora had been used to at the Manchester Refuge. There they fell asleep to the clatter of the carriage wheels on cobblestone, the calls of people out for the evening, the barking and snarling of the stray dogs that fought amongst themselves over a scrap of bread. But here – only the wild cacophony of romantic bullfrogs as they sang their courting songs, and the never-ending sawing of the cicadas. There was so much to tell Flora!

This was also the hour when Runa disappeared. Rosetta never seemed to catch her leaving the house or yard. She would just turn or look up and Runa would be gone.

Then, one evening, as Rosetta worked to finish pulling the suckers off the final row of tomato plants in the garden, Mr. Thomas hollered for her. She looked up, resting the handle of the hoe against her cheek.

"Bring her back in, quick, afore she starts eating that wild onion and bloats up," Mr. Thomas called, pointing at the small dark figure of a calf halfway across the field of waving oats. "Musta slipped out where that rail at the back is loose. Take this here rope."

Rosetta put down the hoe between the rows of curling cabbage leaves and hurried over to take the noosed rope Mr. Thomas held out to her. Then she took off at a run.

The calf stayed still until she was within a few feet of it, then, with a kick of its hind legs, scampered away.

"You come back, you naughty thing," Rosetta called, running after it again. The game kept up for the next ten minutes, with the calf letting Rosetta get a few feet away each time, then running off on its splayed, knobby legs.

Rosetta finally managed to grab the calf's tail and hold firm, panting, brushing a strand of hair off her sweating cheek and then tossing the rope around the calf's neck. She tightened it, and as her breathing slowed, she looked to see how far she'd come, and there was the huge old tree. Under it was a small plot, enclosed by a rotting picket fence. Inside the fence were three gray, leaning wooden crosses. Rosetta saw, in the scattered shade thrown by the branches of a young birch, a bent figure. Runa.

She was on her knees, weeding an area covered by beautiful flowers. Beside her was a bucket of water, with a dipper floating on top.

As Rosetta walked closer, pulling the now-docile calf along with her, she could hear Runa saying something. It was in a melodic singsong tone, as if she were reciting something to herself, or perhaps it was poetry. But it was in a language Rosetta didn't recognize. Then she saw Runa lift the dipper and tenderly sprinkle water over the vibrant blooms. Rosetta opened her mouth to call out to her, but at that moment the woman leaned forward to reach the farthest flowers.

Rosetta closed her mouth. The shifting of Runa's body had disclosed two crudely squared granite headstones.

As Runa sat back on her heels, she suddenly looked in the direction of the farmhouse and saw Rosetta. Her pale face remained expressionless, although Rosetta saw the muscles of her throat working.

"I'm sorry," Rosetta said quietly, although she didn't know what she was sorry about – for creeping up on Runa, for discovering her secret, or for the graves. The noisy shrilling of the cicadas grew louder in Rosetta's ears, filling her whole head.

Runa stared at Rosetta's face, as if searching for something there, then looked back at the headstones. "My babies," she said.

Chapter Eleven

The cicadas finished their last long trill, and silence fell for an instant. Then suddenly the calf jerked on the rope and let out one low, bawling cry. Rosetta took a deep breath.

"These are my babies," Runa repeated.

Rosetta came closer. She stood behind Runa and looked at the upright stones, while Runa remained on her knees, her hands with their dirt-encrusted nails lying limply in her aproned lap. Over the woman's head, Rosetta read the words chipped into the first stone.

> "Asleep in Jesus' Blessed Sleep
> From which none ever wake to weep"
> Sacred to the memory of Charles Albert
> Beloved son of Albert and Runa
> Born February 27, 1897
> Died March 13, 1897

The second stone was similar.

> "Of Such is the Kingdom of Heaven"
> Sacred to the memory of Robert Jacob
> Beloved son of Albert and Runa
> Born August 20, 1899
> Died August 28, 1899

Rosetta dug her fingers into the soft hair of the calf's neck. There didn't seem to be anything to say. Finally, Runa spoke.

"My little boys," she said in the same expressionless way she'd said my babies. "These two are the only ones of the babies that lived. The rest came too soon." She kept looking straight ahead, at the graves. "The last time was just before you came. It seems I am not to have a living child."

"You've made this a beautiful place, Runa," Rosetta said quietly. She had wondered why there were no children on the Thomas farm, and her mind suddenly went to the covered cradle in the attic room next to hers.

"Yes," Runa said. "Albert made the stones. He worked on them all last winter. Before that, all we had were the wooden crosses, like those." She inclined her head to the old crosses in the little square. "Those are Albert's parents, and his uncle. They owned this farm, and it passed on to Albert. The crosses are all right, but these," she swept her hand in front of her, "these are," she paused, searching for the right word, "important looking." She twisted her head up toward Rosetta. "Even though they were so tiny, my boys, these stones make them seem important. They *were* important." Then she tightened her apron strings and picked up the bucket. She emptied what was left of it around the base of the birch tree. "The calf run away again?" she said and, not waiting for an answer, started toward the house, the empty bucket banging against the side of her leg.

Rosetta followed her, keeping a firm grip on the rope.

∼

After that evening, something in Runa seemed to open up. She talked, cautiously at first, to Rosetta as they worked around the kitchen. She continued to go out to the graves each evening. Rosetta never tried to go with her, or asked if she could.

A week later Runa brought back a small bouquet of purple jack-in-the-pulpit from her evening visit. She put it in a chipped white china milk pitcher and set it in the middle of the table.

"Oh!" Rosetta cried spontaneously, smiling and clasping her hands. "That looks so pretty!"

"Yes," Runa said, standing back and looking at the pitcher. "It does." She smiled at the flowers. Rosetta looked at her out of the corner of her eye, not wanting to stare, in case she scared away the first smile she had seen on the woman's face.

Rosetta didn't realize that it had been a month and a half since she had smiled, as well.

~

Little by little, day by day, Runa spoke more to Rosetta. On a rainy July morning, when it was too wet to work in the garden, Runa asked Rosetta to help her give the bedroom a good cleaning. "I want to move that, so I can clean the floor under it," she said, pointing to the chest at the foot of the bed.

Rosetta stood on one side of the chest and gripped a twisted horsehair handle. The chest was reinforced with iron at the corners and had a rounded lid.

"Ready?" Runa asked, gripping the other handle.

Rosetta nodded, and with a fair amount of pushing and pulling, and grunts from both of them, they managed to half lift, half drag the chest out into the middle of the room.

"It's so heavy," Rosetta said, wiping her forehead with the back of her sleeve.

"It's from home," Runa said.

"Home?" Rosetta repeated. She ran her hand over the humped lid. "Where is your home, Runa?"

Runa brushed her palms together, as if the horsehair handle had left dust on her hands. "This is my home," she said. "This house, this farm," she waved toward the window, "and the fields, the big maple, and the birch tree out there. Albert. It's my home now."

"But you came from somewhere else," Rosetta said. "Like me." She looked at the side of Runa's face, the slump of her thin shoulders.

Runa turned to face Rosetta, then looked down at the chest. "The place I come from is called Lydveldidh Island," she said, looking up again. Then, seeing the puzzled look on the girl's face, translated the name to English. "Iceland," she said. "I come from Iceland."

"Iceland," Rosetta breathed. She tried to visualize the tattered world map that had hung on one wall of the classroom at the Manchester Refuge.

Runa glanced toward the window again. "It's very far from here." She looked down at the chest, and suddenly knelt in front of it and threw open the lid.

"These are some of the things I brought." She lifted out a heavy quilt, the design one of circles and starbursts, and handed it to Rosetta. "I made this quilt the year before I came to Canada. When I was twelve. And this shawl," she said, pulling up a thick square of brown and gray and white, "is from wool of the sheep we had on our farm. Feel it," she said, and Rosetta reached out and ran her fingers over the soft, hairy wool. "The sheep have a different wool in Iceland. Thicker. We call it Lopi."

Rosetta nodded and kept looking at the items Runa pulled out of the chest. An intricately carved wooden candleholder. A small, round picture of a man and woman, with hair light like Runa's, in a heavy oak frame. Books with unfamiliar letters.

When Runa had finished, she stood up. Rosetta fingered the edge of the quilt, studying the intricate pattern. "Runa? Could I ask you something?" She looked up from the quilt, to Runa.

The woman nodded.

"I would like to write a letter, to find my sister. She came with me, from England. But she was taken somewhere else."

"You have a sister?" Runa asked slowly.

"Yes. She's only a little girl, six years old. I need to find her, Runa, but I have to write to the Marchmont Home, in Belleville. Surely they'll tell me where she is, so I can write to her, and make sure she's all right. Can you help me send a letter to try and find her?"

Runa took the quilt from Rosetta's arms without meeting her eyes. "We have no paper, or envelopes," Runa said. She folded the quilt carefully. "And I have no money for a stamp." Her voice grew softer as she folded the quilt into a smaller and smaller square. "Mr. Thomas looks after all the buying, and all the money. I don't have any to give you."

Rosetta looked at the folded quilt hanging over the woman's arm. "Runa? Were you sent here? Like I was?"

"No," Runa answered shortly, putting the quilt back in the chest.

By the determined thud of the closing lid, and the tightening of Runa's lips, Rosetta knew the conversation was over.

~

The rain stopped by evening.

"Would you like to come with me, to the tree?" Runa said, pausing at the door while Rosetta scrubbed the tabletop with salt.

"Yes," Rosetta said, smiling and wiping her hands on her apron.

The ground was wet and soggy around the graves, and many of the flowers had been beaten down by the heavy rainfall. At first, Runa and Rosetta just stood and looked at the small area. Then Rosetta stooped and began to pick up some of the bruised blossoms on the ground. "There are so many different flowers here," she said. "You don't have any flowers like these around the house."

"No," Runa said. "Mrs. Fergusson, Ada, on the next farm, she gave most of them to me. Cuttings and roots from her own flowers. She has a beautiful flower garden."

Rosetta studied one of the plants. "Do you know their names?"

Runa squatted beside the girl. "Oh yes. Ada taught me all the names. She taught me many things, when I first came here. She has been a good friend." She looked up and into the distance. "She has been like a mother." Then she began pointing. "That plant is a peony, and those are iris, but they're finished blossoming now. These little blue ones are chimney bellflowers, and that's love-in-a-mist. That's nicotine, and some four o'clocks. The pretty red one is Flora's paintbrush."

"Flora's paintbrush?" Rosetta said, standing. "That's its name?"

"Yes. Why?" Runa asked, rising to stand beside Rosetta, brushing off her skirt.

"That's my sister's name. Flora. I didn't know there was a flower with her name. I'll have to tell her."

Runa moved away and ran her fingertips over the top of one of the granite headstones.

"They were even going to change her name. Flora's," Rosetta said, looking down at the Flora's paintbrush. "Did I tell you that?"

"No. You didn't," Runa answered.

Rosetta stepped up to the birch and leaned over. She pulled at a piece of bindweed that was twining around the slender trunk of the young tree. "The people who adopted her weren't going to call her Flora. They were going to change her name to Eliza. Eliza. Imagine changing someone's name."

Runa pointed to the first headstone. "Charles," she said. "Mr. Thomas called him Charles, but in my heart my first living son was named Hjalmar. And Robert," she continued, pointing to the second stone, "he was my little Mattias. Both were names of great Icelandic poets." Her eyes had a far-away look. "I always planned that I would name my children after famous people, artists and writers. It's what I dreamed of. Writing poetry."

"The first time I saw you here, you were saying something. Was it poetry?"

"Yes," Runa answered. "We have many sagas, many poems. It was our custom to sit by the fire at night and have one member of the family recite these sagas and poems to the rest. And so we learned our history. When I'm here I often remember the old poems. Here, I am at peace."

"I love poetry, too," Rosetta said. "Could you . . . would you tell me one?"

Runa thought for a moment. "There is one I say most often, here." She looked toward the headstones. "It's about a very powerful queen, whose name was also Gudrun, like mine. Gudrun's last two sons die as heroes, and this is what she says when she hears of their deaths. The poem is called," she stopped, her mouth moving silently as she translated, "is called 'Gudrun's Chain of Woes.' I will have to translate everything, so it will be slow. And it might not be the kind of poetry you know."

"That's all right. Please, go on." Rosetta sat down on the grass, looking up at the woman.

Runa stood straighter. Her eyes grew even lighter, and her face became calm. Her voice soft and hesitant, she recited:

"I am all alone like an aspen in a forest
bereft of kinsmen like a fir-tree stripped of branches
all my joy lost like the leaves of a tree
when flames seize them on a summer day."

When she stopped, she bit her lip shyly. "It's hard to find the right English words."

Rosetta blinked her eyes rapidly. "Oh, Runa," she finally said. "How beautiful. But how sad."

Runa nodded. "But it somehow comforts me, to know other women feel alone. Lose the children they loved."

She stooped and picked up a bruised flower, then shook her head, as if annoyed with herself. "Imagine me, dreaming of writing my own poems. But that was when I was a foolish girl, full of silly dreams by the fire at night. Now I am happy to simply remember the great poems."

"I don't think it's a silly idea," Rosetta said. "I plan to be a teacher. I've always planned to be a teacher." She gave the bindweed a final yank and cocked her head, looking at the small birch. "This little tree is growing full and nice," she said.

Runa nodded. "Once, long ago," she said, "there were many, many birch trees covering Iceland. But as more and more people came to be on the land, most of the trees were cut down for building, and now very few remain. Before we left, I took a tiny cutting from a birch on our land. Even on the ship coming here, I dampened the soil with my drinking water and kept it alive. I planted it at the first settlement we stayed in, and the roots took. Then, when I came to this farm, I brought another cutting from the rooted sapling." She brushed her fingertips over the feathery leaves. "And now it grows here, to shade my babies."

Rosetta waited for a few heartbeats. "Could I take some of these flowers to my room? The Flora's paintbrush. Just one or two; I could put them in a jar on my windowsill."

"If they help you, then yes. Take them. Take as many as you want," Runa said. She turned away sharply and walked back toward the house, not waiting for Rosetta.

Chapter Twelve

Late July's air was hot and heavy. Even the birds perching in the trees around the yard chirped listlessly. There was no rain, no cooling breeze.

Rosetta spent long hours in the garden, weeding and digging at the vegetables, the beets and turnips and onions and carrots that would be kept through the winter in the root cellar under the kitchen floor. The endless *scritch*, *scritch* of the hoe in the dry ground was a lonely sound. As she worked, mosquitoes attacked, feasting on her sweating hairline and neck. When she paused to swat at them, and wipe her wet face with her apron, Rosetta would look at the too-blue sky, seeing enormous cumulus clouds scudding across it. Was Flora looking up at these same clouds? The work seemed never-ending and monotonous; there was nothing to break the routine of every day.

Rosetta hadn't been out of the yard, except to go to the big tree with Runa, for close to two months. Neither had Runa, although Mr. Thomas would drive off some afternoons and come back with a box of dry foods from Magrath Corners – sugar, flour, oats, tea, salt, and tobacco for his pipe.

Rosetta was still wearing the gray serge dress she'd arrived in. It was hot and scratchy for summer. Every second Monday she put on her good dress, and washed and dried and ironed the patched and stained dress. Strangely, Rosetta thought, that while the dress was far too short in the sleeves and at the hem, it was looser on her than it had been when she'd left Manchester. Her leather boots were worn almost clear through at the bottom, and pinched her big toes painfully. She waited for Mr. Thomas to mention buying her new boots with the money he'd taken from her, but so far he hadn't.

One afternoon, when Mr. Thomas had gone to Magrath Corners, Runa came out to the garden and called to Rosetta. "Come. We will go and see the Fergussons."

Rosetta pushed back her bonnet and patted at her thick hair. "Shall I put on my good dress?" she asked.

"No. We have to walk through the fields. No need to dress up for Ada," Runa said, putting a small woven basket of eggs, packed in straw, over her arm.

They walked first across a field of pale-green oats and then one of rough, bearded barley that scratched at Rosetta's bare hands. As they came upon a pleasant stone house, the front yard alive with playing children, Rosetta saw a large, red-faced woman. She was vigorously soaping a naked, squirming child of about two in a big wood tub that sat in the soft dirt in the shade created by the front porch.

The woman's dark-red hair, streaked with gray, was untidily pulled into a bun at the nape of her neck. It reminded Rosetta of a flattened cow pat.

"Well, hello, Runa," the woman called. She wrapped the wet child in a big piece of flannel and laughed. Her laugh boomed across the yard, as deep as a man's. "This laddie got into the pig pen and smelled to high heaven. Didn't you, Geordie?" Rosetta recognized the woman's thick accent as

Scottish. Some of the women who had worked at the Refuge had been from Scotland.

The child in Mrs. Fergusson's arms gave Runa and Rosetta a big smile, showing a neat row of pearly baby teeth.

"Shelagh!" the woman called to a girl in the yard who looked about eight or nine, "take young master Fergusson inside and dress him in clean clothes." The girl came running, and the woman transferred the toddler to her arms.

Mrs. Fergusson rolled her sleeves down over her strong arms. "And I've missed ye, lass, not seeing you all the summer long." Her eyes moved over Runa from top to bottom. Watching the older woman's face, Rosetta's breath caught in her throat in an unexpected rush of longing. When had anyone last looked at her like that, with concern and love?

"This is Rosetta, Ada. Rosetta, Mrs. Fergusson."

Mrs. Fergusson gave Rosetta an open smile identical to that of the wet little boy, although unlike her son's, the woman's teeth were crooked and darkening. Her face, with its large features, was decidedly plain, but there was something comforting in the smile that radiated up to her eyes.

"About time you had some help over there. All alone and working so hard with no one to have a word with. Every time I've seen Albert in town I've told him to tell you to come over for a wee chat. But he said you weren't up to it, nor to having visitors, so I stayed away." She kept on studying Runa. "Was he right? Have you been poorly?"

Runa looked down. "He never told me he'd seen you, Ada."

"Well, I guess it slipped his mind," the older woman said kindly, but Rosetta saw a quick flash of anger in her wide, gold-flecked brown eyes. "You just remember that you're always welcome here. And don't wait for an invitation ever again." She shook her head and made a tsking noise. "Come on now, up to the porch, and set yourself down for a wee spell. You look all bothered, after walking in so hot a sun."

They went up onto the shaded porch and stood watching two little boys rolling over each other in the dust of the yard.

"I expect those boys will be crying over the end of summer before long," Mrs. Fergusson said. "Going back to school isn't something most youngsters look forward to."

Rosetta watched the children. "Is it very far? The school?"

"Well, not too bad," the woman answered. "About two miles up toward Magrath Corners way."

"Two miles from here," Rosetta said, thinking out loud, "and then about another mile and a half farther to our farm. It shouldn't take too long to walk."

Runa stood, silent and still, by the wooden rocker. Mrs. Fergusson looked away from the boys to Rosetta. "You thinking of going to school, then?"

Rosetta's eyes flicked toward the woman. "Oh, yes. At least for as long as I'm here. For a few months, anyway. I'm planning on being a teacher so I need to go to school as much as I can. Why?"

"Oh, no reason," Mrs. Fergusson said, "just that you being as old as you are. I reckoned you might be finished with all your schooling. But then my Iain is about your age, or maybe a mite older. He's aiming to go for one last year." She hollered into the yard. "William! You quit that now. You'll rip Samuel's shirt. Mind what I tell you, boys." She shook her head. "Those two won't be happy until their clothes are in shreds."

"I still had a year to complete before leaving time in the

Manchester Refuge School," Rosetta said. She looked at Runa. "I love school."

When Runa didn't answer, Mrs. Fergusson said, "Well, this is thirsty weather. Come, young lady," she said, looking at Rosetta, "you can help me get something cool to drink. But first, Runa, I have something for you."

Runa had started to sit down in the rocker at the end of the porch, but she leapt up before she was all the way down. "Is it the puppy?" she cried.

"All weaned now," Mrs. Fergusson said.

Runa clapped her hands together, and her face broke into a loose, natural smile. Rosetta was surprised at the difference it made to Runa's pale, flat face.

She looks almost pretty, Rosetta thought. Suddenly she could see what Runa might have been like, before the hard work on the farm, before Albert, before the tiny graves under the birch tree.

Mrs. Fergusson went down the porch steps and a few feet into the yard. Rosetta saw her bend over a shaggy dog lying on its side in the sun. The big dog raised its head, thumping its tail once on the ground and sending up a small puff of yellow dust.

When Mrs. Fergusson straightened up, she was cradling something against her large bosom, and as she came back up the steps, Runa held out her arms.

"A little male. Gave the other one over to the Markhams." She glanced back at the big dog, who was still stretched out on her side in the sun. "I expect this'll be the last litter for old Bonnie. Only two pups this time, and it was hard on her." She put the puppy in Runa's arms, and Runa buried her face in the furry brown back.

"You sure about that man of yours now?" Mrs. Fergusson said, watching Runa. "That he'll let you keep it?"

Runa raised her head. Her eyes were pink-rimmed and damp. "He said I could, Ada. He said, after . . ." she stopped. "He said next summer I could get a dog. And it's next summer." She lowered her face to the puppy's back again. "As long as I don't let it in the house, he said I could have one."

"Good," Mrs. Fergusson said. "Good," she repeated, patting Runa's arm. "Oh, there's our Iain now," she said, as a tall, well-built boy with hair the color of old honey came out of the barn carrying a set of harnesses. A balding man whose face was seamed as old leather, but with a wiry, strong-looking body, stayed behind, closing up the barn doors.

Rosetta watched the easy way the boy strode across the yard. He glanced at the porch, looked away, then back.

"Iain," Mrs. Fergusson called. "It's Mrs. Thomas and her girl, Rosetta, here for a visit."

Iain nodded at the porch. Rosetta could see his fine, straight features; he hadn't inherited any of his mother's looks except for the large brown eyes. Rosetta wasn't close enough to see if they, too, were flecked with gold. The sun glinted on his hair, giving it a burnished glow. She smiled at him, and he quickly glanced down at the harness, fiddling with one of the straps.

"Archie? Archie!" Mrs. Fergusson called out to the old man, but he didn't appear to hear her and went in the opposite direction. "I swear he's getting deafer every month," she said, then, to Iain, "Go tell your pa I've made some lemonade when he feels like a glass."

Rosetta was surprised that the man was Mrs. Fergusson's

husband. He was a great deal older than her, and especially old to be a father to such young children.

Mrs. Fergusson's voice interrupted her thoughts. "Come in, Rosetta," she said, opening the door. "Come and help me while Runa gets to know her new dog."

Rosetta followed the woman into the cool dimness of the house. The big, spotless room was so different than the Thomas kitchen. The walls were washed with a pale-blue color, and there were pictures and beautifully painted plates hanging on all of them. A low set of shelves in one corner held a jumbled assortment of books, and starched white muslin curtains danced in the breeze at the open windows. On the table, much longer than the Thomases, was a huge blue and white vase, filled with Queen Anne's lace, bright-orange day lilies, and even brighter, smaller marigolds.

"This is a lovely house, Mrs. Fergusson," Rosetta said. "The flowers, and the curtains, and," she swept her arm out in front of her, "and the plates on the wall, well, everything is so . . . so charming."

Mrs. Fergusson set three glasses on the scrubbed tabletop, took a cloth-covered jug from inside a cupboard with slatted sides and a similar slatted door. She smiled. "Charming, is it? Why, I don't suppose there's a soul in this country has ever told me my house was charming." As Rosetta walked over to the vase of flowers, Mrs. Fergusson studied the girl's face, taking in her smooth, flushed cheeks and thick, shining hair, neatly pulled back into a long braid that hung almost to her waist. Her eyes traveled down to Rosetta's red, chapped hands and lingered on the angry slashes on her forearms, burns from reaching into the cantankerous old woodstove. She looked at the patched, shapeless dress and the scuffed boots molded to the girl's feet.

"You making out all right, over there with Albert and Runa?" she asked, uncovering the jug and beginning to pour lemonade into the glasses.

Rosetta stared at the tight orange head of one of the marigolds. "Runa and I get along well," she said, then lifted her eyes to the window, watching the curtain flutter in the warm breeze.

"I suspected you did," she said. She set the heavy jug down with a quiet thump. "Runa's a good wee girl. A real gentle soul." She sighed. "But she's not the same as when Albert first brought her down here." She picked up a rag and wiped at an imaginary spot on the table. "Losing what means so much to you, well, it can do strange things to a person."

Rosetta reached out toward the flower, running the tip of her finger over it. "I know," she said so softly that Mrs. Fergusson didn't seem to hear.

Mrs. Fergusson shook her head. "But here I am, rattling on again," she said. She pushed a big tin toward Rosetta. "You put some of these oatmeal cookies on a plate while I carry out the lemonade." She started toward the door, then stopped. "I think that little dog will cheer Runa up some. A woman just seems to need something small to look after, something that needs her."

"I know," Rosetta said again, but this time her lips didn't even move.

~

"What do you plan to call him, Runa?" Rosetta asked, as they trudged along the road toward the farm. Runa was afraid to go through the fields again, in case the puppy ran off between the rows and got lost.

"Sigi," Runa said. She looked down at the puppy in her arms. "Sigi, short for Sigurjon." The pup squirmed and whimpered. Runa put it down, and she and Rosetta watched as the dog sniffed Runa's feet, then scampered over to Rosetta's shoes and snuffled at them. Then it stood in the middle of the road and looked back, south, in the direction of the Fergussons' farm, turned his head and looked north, up the empty road that led to the Thomases'. Lifting his tiny black nose, he gave a short, saucy bark, and then, without any warning, turned and started racing north. He looked like a ball of fur on four tiny sticks.

Rosetta and Runa watched him for a second, looked at each other, and smiled. Then, without a word, they both hitched up their skirts and started chasing the little dog, the thick yellow dust of the road billowing behind them like a ruffled cloud. Their peals of laughter echoed through the green and gold fields on either side of the road, bouncing back and forth around them in the warm air.

~

"Sigi! Come, Sigi!" Rosetta called, putting down the basket of wet clothes she had been carrying and giving one high, sharp whistle. The brown dog raced toward her, its tongue flapping out of one side of its mouth. "Look," Rosetta said to Runa, hanging damp sheets on the ropes strung between two posts behind the house. "Look, Runa," Rosetta repeated. "He already knows his name. And he comes when I whistle."

Runa pushed a wooden peg firmly over the white cotton sheet. "All Bonnie's pups are smart. Everyone in the area wants one."

Rosetta picked up a pair of Mr. Thomas's heavy denim

overalls and shook them. She hung them over the rope that ran parallel to Runa's. "Why did you call him Sigi?"

Runa picked another peg out of her apron pocket. "I once had a dog, back in Iceland," she said. "His name was Sigi. But, of course, I had to leave him behind when we came." She put the clothespin on the last corner of the sheet and bent over the wash basket.

"What was it like? Iceland?" Rosetta asked.

Runa shaded her eyes with her hand and looked across the field, golden in the morning sun. She sighed and put her hands on the rope in front of her, studying her knuckles. "I came here, to Canada, seven years ago. I was just a little younger than you then. I was thirteen."

She kept looking at her knuckles. Rosetta didn't move, even when Sigi pounced on the toe of her boot, his baby growls squeaky as his tiny, pointed teeth wrestled with the rough leather.

After a moment Runa continued, as if telling the story to her hands. "Several hundred of us came to Canada. We were all sick, and very tired, when we got here. There had been hard times in Iceland, and we had been hungry for some years. We were told life was rich in Canada. When we arrived, we all went to Kinmount, up north of here. We were promised a settlement farther west, in the place they call Manitoba, but it wasn't ready; no homes or supplies for the winter. So the whole group was to stay in Kinmount for a year. The men were given work, building the Victoria railroad. One of my country-men who had lived in Canada for a while organized a school for us all to learn the English language. And it was there that Albert," she swallowed, "that my father met Mr. Thomas. He was also working on the railroad that winter, laying the tracks to make extra money. His parents had died, and his uncle was running this place, but he was old and sickly. He needed Albert here. Albert fell in love with my older sister, Gerdur, that winter. They planned to marry. It was arranged. But then . . ."

Rosetta saw the woman's knuckles grow white on the rope.

Runa continued, "Gerdur changed her mind, and ran off with someone else, someone Papa hated. We were all shocked, especially, of course, Albert. So my father told me I should marry him instead. He thought it would be good for me. My mother died long before we came here. I was the youngest, and I was . . . different. Different than my brothers, different than Gerdur. Papa never knew what to do with me. So he told Albert to take me, instead of Gerdur. I think now that Albert was still in shock. He agreed, and when everyone moved to Gimli, to the place in Manitoba, I came here. I was fifteen."

She stopped talking. Rosetta tried to imagine coming to this farm with Albert. She thought of Runa's face when she'd held the puppy. How she'd looked so young, and almost pretty.

"And your sister?" she finally said. "What happened to her?"

Runa's eyes fluttered, as if she'd been thinking about something else. "Gerdur? She found she'd made a mistake, with the other man. She had a child with him, but he never married her. She had to go with the baby to Gimli, back to our father. Poor Gerdur! What life must have been for her! I heard all this from my aunt. She once wrote me a letter, before she moved farther west."

"Have you ever heard from her? Your sister?"

Runa looked around the yard, at the fields and the dusky trees in the distance. "Gerdur would have been happy here.

She would have made Albert happy. She didn't care about books; she cared about the land. She was strong, and had a loud laugh, and could tell a wonderful story. Albert was so happy when he was with Gerdur. I saw that." Runa stooped and picked up another sheet. "He didn't know me. But I guess he hoped I might be like my sister. He needed someone like Gerdur, not like me. Someone who would give him many children." Runa smoothed a crease in the sheet. "I wrote to her in Gimli, more than once, but she never answered. I thought it must be because she was ashamed of what she'd done, to Albert. And maybe she was mad at me, too. I don't know." She clamped the sheet on the line, but it was hanging crooked, and Rosetta saw that one side dragged in the dirt. "She hurt Albert so badly. He will never forgive her. And I know he will never forgive me either. For not being Gerdur."

"But it wasn't your fault!" Rosetta said. "You didn't want to marry him, did you? Your father made you!" Her voice rose.

Runa turned and faced her. Her eyes had turned dark, a dull, deep cloud hanging over the pale blue. "I was afraid of my father. He was a cruel man. When I was a very little girl, I learned to always do as he wished, to stay quiet, invisible, and he left me alone. But Gerdur spoke back to him and wouldn't obey. She was beaten often, and still she fought. But not me. I was too afraid. Do you know what it feels like to be afraid, really afraid?"

Rosetta thought of her mother's death, and being taken, carrying Flora in her arms, to the Manchester Refuge and left there. She thought of the carriage, rumbling out of the driveway, carrying Flora away from her. "Yes," she said.

"I was, what's the word, paralyzed at times. Too afraid to

even move. How I longed to be like Gerdur! She protected me as best she could, when I couldn't get out of Papa's way fast enough. But I knew she thought I was weak, weak and useless.

"I could have said no to Papa, that last time," she said, her voice louder than Rosetta had ever heard. "When he said I had to marry Albert, I could have done something. I could have screamed and kicked. I could have run away. But I didn't." The last word came out as close to a shout as seemed possible for Runa. She put her one hand over her mouth, as if she had shocked herself, then shaded her eyes again with the other hand, this time looking toward the old tree. She took her hand away from her mouth and spoke more softly again. "But I wasn't strong enough. I wasn't like Gerdur, and I'm not like you, Rosetta." Her eyes looked into Rosetta's. "I'm not like you," she said again. "And now it's too late. It's too late for me to run anywhere, or to fight about anything." She picked up the empty basket, turned and started back toward the house, ignoring the puppy that scampered beside her, grabbing at the hem of her swishing skirt.

Rosetta hurried after her. "You could try again. You could write to her again, couldn't you? She's your big sister. A long time has passed – over five years. I'm sure she would want to talk to you now." She reached out and touched Runa's sleeve.

The woman stopped and turned her head so Rosetta could hear her almost whispered words. Her head hung forward on her thin neck. It seemed that the tiny display of passion Rosetta had seen so briefly had been buried again. "She knows where I am," Runa said. "It is not her that is searching for her little sister."

99

Chapter Thirteen

"Hurry, Rosetta, take off your apron and fix your hair. We're going to town."

Rosetta looked up from the potato plants she was working on. She'd been at it all afternoon and had come out after supper to finish up. She'd been going up and down the rows, sprinkling the plants with Paris Green. First she had to wet the leaves, throwing a bit of water on them from the pail she carried with one hand, then, with the other hand she'd give the big tobacco tin with holes punched in the lid a shake over each dampened plant. The tin contained the Paris Green, a brilliant-green powder that would poison the potato bugs who loved to eat the leaves.

"I'll get to do a bit of shopping," Runa said, smoothing down her hair with her hands. Rosetta followed her out of the potato patch.

"I knew Albert was going in tonight. He has to get more bailing twine for the binder. When I asked him if you and I could come, I didn't think he'd say yes. But this time he did!" Runa's cheeks had a tiny flush, and even though she tried to fix her hair, a few long strands kept slipping out of the tight knot. She looked younger, excited. She had on a different dress, one that Rosetta had never seen her wear; it was a faded sprig, but it had a pretty collar and cuffs. Rosetta thought about putting her good dress on, but then remembered that the last time she had worn it on a Monday washday, it had split under the arm as she reached for something. She had stitched the seam, but it had ripped again immediately. It was just too tight now. She took off her apron and brushed her gray serge dress down with a damp rag.

In a few minutes the wagon pulled up, and Runa climbed into the front, beside Albert. Rosetta sat in the back, her legs hanging over the open end, and they rolled through the peaceful July evening and into the town.

As they drove down the main street, Rosetta looked around her in amazement. When Runa had said town, Rosetta had imagined a bustling, noisy place with many people and fine carriages, similar to what she had caught glimpses of in Belleville. But here everything was unfinished-looking. The wood on the low, plain buildings was almost raw, and there was nothing extra – no shutters or windowboxes, nothing decorative. The street that ran through the center of the sleepy town was simply an extension of the dusty country road. A few rough wagons, like the Thomases', sat in front of some of the buildings. It was a new town, in the middle of the country. Compared to the centuries-old streets and buildings of Manchester, it was plain and unexciting to Rosetta. She sighed. But at least, she told herself, I'm away from the farm.

Mr. Thomas let them off in front of a low building with high, wide steps and a porch running along its whole front. MAGRATH CORNERS POST OFFICE AND GENERAL STORE, announced a bold sign over the square top of the building. A small knot of people stood talking on the broad porch.

"I'll be back after I stop at the livery," Mr. Thomas said. "You get any supplies we're short on."

Runa nodded, and as she and Rosetta went into the store, Rosetta stopped at the doorway. She'd been in many small, individual shops in England – the greengrocer's, sweet shops, milliners, but this place! Although the inside, like the outside, was plain and practical, it was far bigger than any of those cramped shops that lined the narrow streets of Manchester. And it held so many different items that Rosetta didn't know where to look first.

In the center was a potbellied stove, ringed by worn Windsor chairs. A few men sat in the chairs, chewing plugs of tobacco and spitting long strings of dark saliva into cans beside their chairs. Nearby was a large wooden barrel with a lid, PICKLES marked across the side in big black letters.

In the aisles, Rosetta saw bolts of muslin, calico, damask, Irish linen, denim, and cotton. There were bins of supplies of sugar, salt, tea, flour, and spices. The shelves were packed with floral-painted tins, linen-wrapped cheeses, thimbles, lanterns, and harness oil. Along the wooden counter was a seemingly endless row of glass jars of penny candy, from licorice whips and saltwater taffy to jawbreakers and striped peppermints. Craning her neck back to look at the ceiling, Rosetta let her eyes linger over copper kettles and pots, wicker baskets, lengths of rope, and leaf tobacco hanging from the beams. The walls were covered with hooks that supported all sorts of farm tools, harnesses, fruit molds, and carved hickory ax handles.

But it was the post office wicket that Rosetta went toward. On a shelf beside the barred wicket was a stack of smooth, velvety looking paper. Rosetta lightly ran her fingertips over the top sheet, then touched the envelopes beside the paper.

She stood and looked at the wooden slots behind the wicket. A short, bald man, making entries in an account book at the end of the counter, looked up at her.

"Are you needing something?" he asked, then looked back at the page, writing a line with a steel pen.

Rosetta watched him. "No," she said. "I was just wondering about the price of mailing a letter to Belleville."

The man put his index finger on a line on the page in front of him. "You want to post a letter?"

"Not today," Rosetta said. "But I wanted to know the cost."

"Two cents," the man said. "Regular letter anywhere in Canada is two cents." He began writing again.

"Thank you," Rosetta said. Only two cents. But it might as well have been two dollars.

The man looked up again and frowned. "You the Home girl I heard was working up to the Thomas place?"

Rosetta nodded grimly at the hated name. The man half stood and looked beyond the wicket. "Miz Thomas?" he called. "Miz Thomas, you keep an eye on this girl of yours now. Don't want no trouble."

Rosetta turned away from the wicket, the trip spoiled.

～

"Do you know who the school teacher is?" Rosetta asked the next evening, as she and Runa stood side by side, chopping cabbage to make sauerkraut.

"I heard it's someone new. A woman. The last few years it was a man, Mr. Leland. But he moved on. This new one boards with Mr. and Mrs. Magrath, behind the store."

Rosetta reached for another head of cabbage and started to work on it. "Did you like school?"

"It is not the same in Iceland. There are no schools, but a teacher will come to different homes, and stay there for some time, teaching all the family to read and write. This way everyone knows how to do these things."

"That's how I was taught, at first, in England. Someone came to my house. But afterwards, in the Manchester Refuge, there was a classroom. I loved it!"

Runa glanced over at Rosetta. The girl had stopped cutting and was smiling to herself.

"It was so wonderful. Everything seemed so, I don't know how to describe it, but everything always followed everything else. The numbers, working in rows, and if you use them correctly, they will always create the same right answer. The words, always the right words, creating stories and poems where there is an ending that is complete. Everything works out in stories. It made me feel," Rosetta thought for a moment, "calm. It made me feel calm. Everything had order; everything always made sense in the classroom." She started chopping again. "When will I start school?"

"I don't know."

"But surely, when summer is over, school will begin. Mrs. Fergusson would know. I could run over and ask her, tonight, after chores. I wouldn't want to miss any school time."

Runa continued to cut the cabbage, but some tiny change, a slowing in the rhythm of her knife, made Rosetta stop.

"I *can* go, can't I? I will be going to school, won't I? You read it out, in the contract. That I can go to school."

Nothing about Runa moved except the hand holding the

knife. *Chink, clunk, chink, clunk.* Rosetta listened to the noise of the knife chopping through the firm head of the vegetable and then hitting the wooden table.

"Runa. Please answer. I have to go to school. I have to. I plan to be a teacher, remember? I have it worked out. If I'm a teacher, I'll be able to make enough money to support Flora and me. We'll live together, and she can be a student in my school. I've been planning and planning. So please, please, don't tell me I can't go to school, even for the few months until I leave." She put her hand on the woman's arm and gave it a slight shake.

Runa stopped chopping and looked down at Rosetta's hand on her arm. "Mr. Thomas told me you'll have to stay home and help out until the fall wheat is planted and all the vegetables canned for winter. The corn will have to be shucked, and the potatoes dug up and stored." She raised her eyes to Rosetta's. "I told him I could manage it. But he says no, you're to stay and help. It will be October before he'll let you go."

She started chopping again. Rosetta watched her busy hands, then picked up another cabbage. Ignoring the sting of disappointment behind her eyes, she slowly started cutting the round head into long, narrow slices.

Outside she heard Mr. Thomas sharpening his scythe, and the raspy, filing *zooop* of the blade on the whetstone made her back teeth ache.

~

August was a hard month. Mr. Thomas and Ben were harvesting the fields, and Runa and Rosetta worked from early morning to late at night getting in all the vegetables that hadn't already been dried or pickled or canned.

One evening, when Rosetta and Runa were wiping out the big kettle they'd been sealing jars of tomatoes in, they heard pounding footsteps. As they both looked to the open door, Mr. Thomas came running into the house.

"Quick! Come and help me get old Josie hitched to the wagon and get it out to the field. Ben's been taken real bad." Mr. Thomas's face was running with sweat, and his hat was gone, the untanned strip of skin on his forehead as bright as a white bandage against the rest of his dark-brown face and neck.

Without stopping to ask questions, Runa followed her husband out the door. Rosetta ran along, too, and in a few minutes all three of them were bouncing over the half-threshed field to Ben's mower, hitched to a team of two horses.

The old man lay a few yards from the machine, in a pile of cut wheat. He was perfectly still, his eyes closed. One hand clutched the top of his shirt. Mr. Thomas jumped out and motioned to Runa and Rosetta. "Open the back of the wagon, then help me lift him in." He already had his hands under the man's shoulders. "We'll go careful now." As he started to lift him, the man's head moved slightly, and he mumbled something.

"Did he get cut, Albert?" Runa asked, her hands running gently over Ben's sweat-stained shirt and trouser legs.

"No. Weren't no accident. I just looked over from my mower and saw he weren't on his. I came over and found him like this. He musta climbed down and dropped here. He hasn't moved since I come for you."

"Should we take him to the house, and you see if you can get word to the doctor?"

"No," Ben uttered weakly, and they all looked down. He

106

opened his eyes. "Don't need no doctor. Take me back to my girl's place. Just take me back home. I'll be right as rain after I rested. Right as rain," he said, his voice still feeble, his right hand coming up to rub at his left arm. "Just felt a might dizzy, and had me some pain in my chest and shoulder for a spell." He attempted to pull himself up, but let out a groan and dropped back into Mr. Thomas's hands.

"All right now, Ben, you rest easy. I'll take you on home to your daughter. Runa, Rosetta, you each take a leg." The three of them managed to get the old man into the back of the wagon, and then Mr. Thomas jumped into the front and picked up the reins. He looked up at the fading sky, then at Rosetta.

"Run on over to the Fergussons'. See if Archie has any extra men. Tell him I need a man for tomorrow, to finish up this field." Then he slapped the reins and was gone.

～

Rosetta was out of breath when she arrived at the Fergusson farm. Sigi had come with her, running through the fields. She stepped up on the porch and knocked on the door frame. The door, like at the Thomas farm, stood wide open. Mrs. Fergusson and Shelagh looked up from the table, where they were snapping runner beans.

"My goodness, child. Come in. There's no need for knocking. What is it?" She came over to the doorway and smoothed Rosetta's hair back from her forehead. Rosetta had to stop herself from pressing her head against the woman's calloused hand. It felt so good to be touched.

After she had explained what had happened, Mrs. Fergusson shook her head. "Archie's looking for another man himself. Even with the extra hands he's hired on for harvesting, and our own Iain, he wants to get done quicker. He says the weather's been holding too good, makes him suspicious. There hasn't been one bad storm this month, and with all this hot, dry weather, it's bound to happen." She pumped a glass of water at the sink and handed it to Rosetta. "I'm sorry, dear. I'll ask Archie when he comes in tonight, and if he knows of anyone I'll get him to send him over. That's the best I can do."

~

Darkness was falling as Rosetta and Sigi hurried back across the fields. The air had a heavy, strange smell, and a small, humid breeze had come up out of nowhere.

"Did you get anyone?" Runa asked, as soon as Rosetta had filled Sigi's water dish and come inside.

"No. Mrs. Fergusson said she'd get Mr. Fergusson to look for someone though."

Runa looked out the doorway. "I don't like the feel of this. It's hail weather. The first year I was here, Albert lost the whole crop to hail. Everything." She turned back to Rosetta. "At least he's got most of it cut, but we could still lose a lot." She looked outside again. "Help me cover the garden, just in case."

They took armloads of old worn sheets outside and spread them over the rows of unpicked vegetables, and covered as many tomato plants as they could with pails and buckets. The breeze had turned into a wild, hot wind, whipping at the edges of the sheets, and Rosetta ran to get logs and stones, handing them to Runa so she could pin down the corners. When they were done, Runa straightened up her shoulders and rubbed the back of her neck. "At least if we get hail tomorrow we'll have saved most of the garden." She tilted her head back and looked at the sky. "I hope Albert gets home soon."

But he wasn't home by the time it was completely dark, and finally Rosetta went to bed, leaving Runa sitting downstairs with the glowing lamp.

~

"Get up, Rosetta, come on." As Mr. Thomas's voice called up the stairway, Rosetta rubbed at her eyes. It was still dark, but the air in her room was so humid she could hardly breath. Her nightdress was damp through. Throwing on her dress and wedging her sore feet into her boots, split up the sides now, she went down the stairs.

Runa was wrapping a scarf around her head to keep her hair out of her face, and Mr. Thomas was draining a cup.

"It's still night," Rosetta said. "What are we doing?"

"It's not night. Almost morning, but there's a storm coming," Mr. Thomas said. "I found a hand last night, but he can't come until tomorrow. Runa's gonna try and drive the second mower for me." He glanced at her, then back to Rosetta. "You get on out and make sure all the cattle's rounded up and back in the barn. Get everything inside; if any chickens are still out, scare them back into the coop and shut the door. Big hail can hurt animals bad if they don't get to shelter. When you're done that, bring us out water and something to eat. We don't have time to stop for anything." He looked out the window. "Only another three days, and I'd have it all in." He took a deep breath. "We'll get as much cut as we can. Once it's down, hail nor hard rain can't ruin the heads much."

The three of them hurried out into the wind and clouded sky. Rosetta heard a far-off rumble as the Thomases ran out to the field and she toward the barn. She got all the animals secured inside, even Sigi, and made some thick cheese sandwiches and filled a big jar with water. As she was hurrying through the cut wheat fields, the hot wind tore at her skirt. The sky was still eerily dark, and tiny bits of chaff and dirt kept blowing into her eyes. By the time she got to Mr. Thomas on the first mower, the whole front and back of her dress were wet with sweat. A sudden, huge clap of thunder almost made her drop the basket with the food and water.

Mr. Thomas jumped down from the mower and came over to Rosetta. He looked across the field to the other mower and waved at Runa. Rosetta saw the horses stop and the big blades slow. Runa picked her way across the field, half bent over in the wind. As she got closer, Rosetta saw that her face had a strange gray pallor.

Rosetta held a sandwich to the woman. Runa shook her head at the food, but took the water jar and drank thirstily. Rosetta and Mr. Thomas watched, seeing the way the water jar shook in her hands, spilling out half the water. When she had finished, she handed the jar back to Rosetta and lowered herself to the ground, resting her head on top of her bent knees.

"You best go on back to the house now, rest a spell," Mr. Thomas said, then put out his hand. Runa lifted her head and looked at his outstretched hand, then put her own into it. Mr. Thomas pulled her up, and without a word Runa started on her way to the house, her head lowered and one hand clutching her side.

"She managed it one other year," Mr. Thomas said, more to himself than to Rosetta. He looked at her. "You'll have to."

"The mower? Drive the mower?"

"I'll never get this field done in time, otherwise." He tilted his face to the clouds. "This might blow right over us, but it might open up any minute. Come on. I'll show you."

Rosetta followed him and climbed up into the seat. Mr. Thomas put the reins in her hands. "Hold tight, and don't let them feel you slacken. Thunder's spooking 'em a bit. If they try to break, they'll ruin the field. Ever drive horses?"

Rosetta shook her head.

"You just gotta be strong, let them know you're in charge. Think you can do it?"

"I can do it," she shouted over the wind. "I can do it."

~

At first, the demanding pull of the reins was intimidating, but after a few lengths of the field Rosetta started to enjoy the power she felt, pulling back against the leather straps, yanking hard to the left, or right, as she wanted the horses to turn. The mower churned along behind, the sharp blades rolling over the stalks with their tall, full heads, slicing them off. Rosetta put her face up into the wind, ignoring the stinging dust, ignoring the sweat running into her eyes, ignoring the cramping in her hands. She held tight to the reins, sometimes standing, and yelled "Gee! Gee!" to the powerful, hardworking horses. She never glanced over at Mr. Thomas on his mower, although he watched her from the distance, at first to make sure she was handling the horses. But even when he was assured that she could hold them, and make straight swathes, he still looked over from time to time, a grudging look of admiration just under the surface of his grime-streaked face.

~

The storm did blow over them. But it teased on for hours, the thunder keeping up its threatening growl and the black clouds bunching and coiling for hours. Finally, late in the afternoon, Rosetta and Mr. Thomas finished the field.

Rosetta's legs were shaking as she stepped down off the mower, and her hands seemed frozen into their curled position from holding so tight to the reins. Her upper arms and back ached from the unaccustomed stretching.

"Looks like she wants to clear," Mr. Thomas said, wiping his face with the back of his arm and taking off his hat. "I'll come back out while its still light and start on the next field. But we'll go up to the house and have something to eat now."

There was a big supper and a pitcher of cold tea set on the table. Rosetta looked into the bedroom, but saw that Runa was asleep, so she and Mr. Thomas ate silently. When they were done and Rosetta stood up to start the dishes, Mr. Thomas said, "Leave them for tonight. You get yourself off to bed early. Been a long day." He poured another glass of the cold tea, then cleared his throat. "Thank you," he said, his voice gruff, then quickly got up from the table, walking toward the bedroom.

Rosetta sat at the table for another minute, surprised. She threw a dish towel over the bread to keep it from drying out, then started to go upstairs. She glanced at the Thomases' bedroom and saw Runa sitting up, her back supported by her husband's arm. He was holding the glass to her lips and whispering something.

Rosetta felt a lump start in her throat. She went upstairs, holding back her tears. Everything hurt and throbbed painfully – but it wasn't that making her want to cry.

Chapter Fourteen

The next day at noon another man appeared with Mr. Thomas at the dinner table.

"This is Eli," Mr. Thomas said, as the short, heavyset young man sat down on one of the benches. "He'll be helping out now." Runa nodded at the young man and put another plate and fork on the table in front of him.

As Rosetta set a platter of cold pork in the middle of the table, Eli grinned at her. She gave him a curt dip of her head, then looked away. As soon as he'd entered the kitchen, she'd smelled the strong odor of tobacco and sweat and axle grease that exuded from his body and clothes. She wondered if he'd sleep out in the shanty, the original pioneer home of Mr. Thomas's parents, or if he lived nearby and would go home at night. She hoped so. Something about the way his eyes followed her around the kitchen as she sliced the bread, or got another spoonful of butter from the crock, or brought over the rich berry dessert filled her with an unpleasant sensation that she couldn't put a name to.

～

With Eli helping Mr. Thomas, the final threshing was finished in a few days. "He's a good worker, that fellow," Mr. Thomas said the day after Eli had left. Mr. Thomas had gone into town for the afternoon, and had just arrived home and was talking to Runa in the kitchen. "I hope to get him back for haying and seeding next spring. Maybe even stay on into the fall. That's it for old Ben."

"How is he?" Runa asked, covering the dough for the next morning's bread. Rosetta listened through the open door from the top step of the porch, brushing Sigi's thick fur with an old currycomb she'd found in the barn. "Have you heard?"

"I run into his daughter in town today. She told me doctor says it's his heart. He might have a few good years left, but not for workin'."

"Poor old fellow," Runa said, standing up to go to bed.

Rosetta gave the dog a pat. "Bedtime, Sigi," she said. The little dog turned and looked at her. "Yes, it is your bedtime. Go on now. Don't look at me with those sad eyes." Wagging his tail, Sigi turned from the step and went off to the back of the house, where a crumbling old doghouse stood. As Rosetta came inside, Albert stood up.

"Got these for you," he said, handing a wrapped package to Rosetta. "You can take 'em back if they don't fit. Runa told me what size you might be."

Rosetta looked at the package, then took it. She slowly slid the string off the lumpy rectangle and unfolded the edges of the paper. It was a new pair of sturdy leather boots. They were black, with laces up the front, not pretty at all. Underneath them was a large square of dark-blue cloth. Rosetta ran her hands over it.

"I'll help you make a new dress, as soon as we've finished the canning," Runa said. There was a small, pleased smile on her lips.

"Thank you, Mr. Thomas," Rosetta said. "Thank you, Runa." She drew a quick breath, realizing that she'd forgotten and had let Runa's name slip out in front of Mr. Thomas.

But Mr. Thomas seemed busy with his pipe, and didn't say anything, except for a quiet "welcome" just before Rosetta turned away to go up to bed.

~

Autumn descended on the farm almost as soon as Mr. Thomas planted his winter wheat, the first week of September. Over the next few weeks the days were still warm, but the bothersome insects had disappeared, except for the occasional sluggish buzzing of a bluebottle fly. The nights had lost their hazy warmth, with a full, soft white moon hanging in the fresh black sky for several nights in a row.

Then, one early morning toward the end of the month, as Rosetta went out to the barn to do the milking, she saw, in the gray dawn, that the stubble in the harvested fields seemed to float in a pale coat of white. But by the time she came out of the barn, the early sun was painting the sky a cornflower blue and had touched the fields. They were their usual color, as if the frost Rosetta had seen was her imagination.

In the next few days she saw that the maple had turned to rich crimson, and the sumach growing around the split rail fences burst into flame. The poplars' trembling leaves transformed to yellow and began to float off their branches and settle in soft piles around the slender trunks. Acorns rained down from the oaks, who still held tightly to their dark, scalloped leaves.

Rosetta thought of the four hard months. Two months to go. Two more months until she got her money and could be gone. She had accepted the fact that she wouldn't be able to send a letter off to Belleville, but at least when she got her two dollars she could take a train right there.

By October the garden was finally cleaned out, the vegetables and preserved fruit all put by, everything done but for one last job – the potatoes. Wearing her old boots in the muddy potato field and carrying a pail in each hand, Rosetta followed Mr. Thomas and his horse and single plow. After the potatoes were dug up, she would shake off the loose dirt and throw the potatoes into the pails. When the pails were filled, she'd take them to the side of the patch and dump them in a big pile. The ground was hard and cold, and her hands soon grew stiff and covered with mud.

Mr. Thomas had finished up and gone to get the wagon to load up the potatoes when Iain rode into the yard. Rosetta heard the hooves and watched to see who was coming, brushing her hair away from her face and leaving a big streak of mud down one cheek. She saw Iain tie the horse's lead to a branch and glance around the yard. When he saw her, he quickly turned away, toward the house, then stopped, as if thinking or talking himself into something, then walked in her direction. She bent down as if to pick up a potato, but wiped at her face with the hem of her skirt before straightening up.

"My ma sent you something," he called. He stood a good distance away, a bundle in his arms. Rosetta walked over the upturned furrows.

"Something for me?" She tried to see what it was.

He held it out, awkwardly. "It's one of her old dresses. She said to tell you she turned the seams and took it in some. She says she knows it will still be too big, but it's too tight for her now. And it will be years before it would fit Shelagh. And there's a shawl there, too. She says you or Runa can use it, whoever needs it."

Rosetta looked down at her hands. "I'm too muddy," she said. "Could you just put it there, on that stump? And please tell your mother thank you so much. I'm sure the dress will be fine." There are gold flecks in his eyes after all, she thought.

There was a moment's awkward silence.

"Well," Iain said and turned to go.

"Have you started school yet?" Rosetta asked, before he could get all the way around. "Your mother said you were going to go."

Iain studied the lump of dirt in front of him, touching a potato with one toe of his boot. "Archie hasn't needed me for a while now," he said, and Rosetta wondered why he'd call his father by his first name. "So I started a few weeks ago."

"A few weeks ago?" Rosetta cried, her voice alarmed. When Iain looked at her with a puzzled expression on his face, she said, "Well, I just don't want to miss too much. I'm not staying long, and I wanted to go as much as I could."

"You want to go to school?"

"Oh yes," Rosetta said. "Don't you?"

Iain stared at the dirt on her cheek until Rosetta put her hand up, wondering what he was looking at. "Well, I don't mind school, if the teacher's all right," he said, quickly looking around as if he was worried someone might hear him. "Especially over the winter, when there's not much else to do."

"But I won't be here for the winter. That's why I want to go now."

"You leaving?"

"Pretty soon."

"Oh," Iain said, and it wasn't the single word, but the quick look that passed over Iain's face for a split second that made Rosetta stoop to dig for a half-buried potato, her cheeks suddenly hot.

"Well, don't worry," Iain said. "You haven't missed much. The new teacher's still trying to remember our names."

Rosetta stood up, tossing the potato into the pail. "Is she nice? The new teacher?"

Iain shrugged. "Seems all right." He turned at the sound of the wagon. "You need help, Mr. Thomas?" he asked the man.

"Sure could use some," Mr. Thomas answered, holding out a second shovel, and Iain went to the pile of potatoes and started loading them into the open back of the wagon. The two men worked quickly. Rosetta brought over the last pail and stood watching them, arching her back. She had been bent over all morning.

Iain stopped to shrug out of his jacket and throw it over the dress and shawl on the stump. His shirt sleeves were rolled up to the middle of his upper arms, and Rosetta couldn't help but notice how his muscles moved easily under the smooth bronze of his skin with each heave of the shovel.

When Mr. Thomas left to take the load back to the root cellar, Iain put his jacket back on. Rosetta wiped off her hands as best as she could on her apron and picked up the dress and shawl. "I'll go back with you," she said, walking with him to his horse. They admired the horse, then they admired Sigi, who came to sniff at Iain, and finally, when they had even admired the size of a pumpkin left at the edge of the garden, Iain reluctantly got on his horse and left.

~

"Well, that's the last of it then. Everything done for winter," Mr. Thomas said, stirring his tea. "Even got that hog butchered, and a new house done for your little mutt. Right snug, too. Threw in some straw, and packed more around the outside. He'll be warmer than us. And just before rain, too. Felt it in the air all day. There was a halo around the sun this afternoon. Rain in twelve hours," he predicted.

Runa glanced at Rosetta across the table. They were sewing by the light of the lamp; Runa repairing the torn cuff on one of Mr. Thomas's shirts and Rosetta stitching a large rent in the side of her apron, where she'd caught it on a nail in the barn.

Rosetta looked back at Runa and raised her eyebrows and opened her mouth to ask if that meant she could go to school. As if Runa could read her mind, she shook her head no, ever so slightly, and Rosetta closed her mouth.

Mr. Thomas put tobacco in his pipe and tamped it down with his thumb. Then he lit a match and drew. Rosetta worked her needle in and out of the cotton, listening to the *putt putt putt* of the smoking pipe. She counted eighteen tiny stitches before Mr. Thomas moved. He stood up and set his pipe on a dish in the middle of the table. Rosetta kept her head bowed over the material in her hands, but the needle was still.

"Going to bed," he announced. Then, as he walked toward the bedroom door, he said over his shoulder, "Girl may as well get off to school come Monday."

As soon as the bedroom door had closed, Rosetta put down her needle and smiled at Runa. Runa smiled back and leaned toward the old teapot. She refilled her own and Rosetta's cups, then put her finger to her lips, got up and reached behind the tin tea canister on the shelf over the stove. She pulled out a paper package and, with hardly a rustle, fished out two large striped humbugs. She passed one to Rosetta and popped the other into her mouth.

Before she sat down again, she looked at the closed bedroom door, then went to the kitchen door and carefully, slowly, opened it a crack and slipped outside. In a minute she returned, with Sigi at her side. He immediately crossed the room and curled up under the table with a small, contented sigh. Rosetta reached down and rubbed his ears.

Then Rosetta and Runa, the little dog at their feet, sat in silence, listening to the pop and crackle of the fire in the stove and tasting the sweet bite of peppermint between sips of strong, cooling tea, each lost in their thoughts.

Chapter Fifteen

Rosetta used the sleeve of her coat to wipe the drops of rain from her face. It had been raining, an icy, steady rain, all weekend. On Sunday they closed up the parlor, fitting rags around the door to keep the cold air from seeping into the warm kitchen.

Rosetta had been up at five to start the fire in the stove. She'd made the tea and porridge, then gone out to the barn to do her chores. After breakfast she'd put a piece of bread and a slice of pork into the tin syrup pail Runa had given her, and now she swung the pail against her leg as she walked.

The thick yellow mud on the road sucked at her new boots, and after the mile and a half, passing the Fergusson farm, her thighs ached from the effort of pulling each foot up from the sticky mud. She plodded along, nervous about what she might find, but with growing excitement at finally going.

The schoolhouse came into view as she rounded a bend. It sat, a plain, square building, in a bare field bordered by a stand of jack pine, black in the rain. To one side were the two narrow privies, and on the other side of the school was a shed with a slanted roof. In it stood a wooden cart, and beside it, a horse, its back covered with a blanket. Its head hung down, and steam billowed out of its nose as it exhaled in the cool air.

There was no one else around, and Rosetta assumed she was early. The sodden gray sky held no hint of the time. She stood on the step, uncertain whether to go in. Just as she lifted her hand to knock on the door, a loud pounding sounded from inside. She put her hand down and listened. When the pounding came again, she pulled the rope handle and peeked in.

A woman was standing on a chair with her back to the door. She was hammering a nail into the wall behind a large, scratched wooden desk.

Rosetta stepped in and closed the door, watching the woman hammering. When the nail was finally in, the woman nimbly jumped off the chair. She turned around and gave a tiny start.

"Oh! You frightened me," she said. "I didn't hear anyone come in." Her smooth, round cheeks were pink, and her light-brown hair pulled back into a loose braided knot at the back of her head.

Rosetta clutched her lunch pail in front of her with both hands.

The woman looked at the pail. "I assume you're a new student?" she asked.

"Yes, miss," Rosetta said. Then she spoke a little louder. "My name is Rosetta Westley."

The woman smiled. She had small, even teeth. "I'm Miss Jasper," she said. "Hang your wet coat on one of the hooks, there." She pointed to a spot behind Rosetta. "In nice weather the students wait outside until I ring the bell, but as it's raining so hard, I expect they'll all be in shortly." She picked up a picture of Queen Victoria from her desk and climbed up on the chair again. After she hung it on the nail, she turned and called over her shoulder, "Is that straight?"

Rosetta looked at the picture of the stern Queen of England. Her Queen. It was the first time she'd seen her since leaving Manchester. The old monarch's usually expressionless eyes suddenly looked kinder. "Yes, miss," she said. "It's perfectly straight." She set her lunch pail down, took off her head shawl, and unbuttoned her coat.

"Good. It's been propped against the wall since I came in September, and every day I mean to hang it." As Miss Jasper put her chair back in place and busied herself with some papers on her desk, Rosetta looked around the room.

At the front was a slate board, with a chunk of chalk resting on the ledge below. Beside the board was a faded map. Tall windows lined both the east and west wall of the room, and a low, rectangular stove stood in the middle. Rows of battered double desks, with equally battered benches, ran on either side of the stove, with a short row in front and behind it. The desks were small in the first rows, and larger nearer the back. Oak framed slates sat on top of the smaller desks, with a piece of chalk tied to each. On the larger desks were steel pens.

There was a table at the back, holding a water bucket; a banged-up dipper hung over it from a nail in the wall. Beside the table was a bookshelf. On it was a pile of rather shabby notebooks, and underneath, two neat rows of worn books.

She breathed deeply. The familiar smell of chalk and paper filled her with warmth. As she squinted across the room, trying to read the titles of the books, the door opened. Two boys and a girl filed in, and before the door had a chance to close, it was pushed open again. This time it was Iain, with Shelagh and the two smaller Fergusson boys. Iain glanced at her, and an immediate flush reddened his high cheekbones. Seeing the color rise on his face made Rosetta glad. She smiled, and he gave a shy half-smile before turning to help the smaller of his two brothers reach the hook with his coat.

The door closed, then opened again and again as more children came in. Rosetta stepped away from the hooks, to one side, her coat still on. The students crowded around the coat hooks, some pushing, a few talking to each other in low voices. They all looked at her as they were hanging up their coats and setting their lunch pails on the floor under them.

"Hello," Rosetta said to Shelagh Fergusson, who grinned and said hello back. With a noisy scraping and rustling, the students all trooped to their seats. The younger ones went to the smaller rows of desks, the older ones to the biggest. Rosetta realized the rows must be grade levels. There were eight rows. She was still standing near the door with her coat on.

"Find any empty desk near the back for now, Rosetta," Miss Jasper called, "and we'll place you later." Rosetta hung up her coat and looked around the almost full room. Everyone's eyes seemed to be on her. She saw a spot beside one of the older girls. As she walked toward the seat beside the girl, the girl turned to face the front of the room, swinging her head around so fast that her braids swirled out around her. Rosetta hesitated, then sat in one of the empty seats, behind Iain and another tall boy with very protruding front teeth.

The morning started with the singing of "God Save Our Queen," and Miss Jasper reading from the Bible. As she read,

Rosetta relaxed and let her eyes roam hungrily over the books again.

"And before we begin our lessons," Miss Jasper said, closing the Bible, "I'd like to introduce a new pupil." She looked at Rosetta, and again, all heads turned and all eyes stared at Rosetta. Except for Iain. He looked straight ahead.

"This is Rosetta Westley," Miss Jasper said. "Welcome."

There was complete silence. Rosetta's mouth twitched in a tiny smile, and when she didn't see any returning smiles except from Shelagh Fergusson and Miss Jasper, she dropped her eyes to the toe of her boot, sticking out at the side of her desk. She studied the muddy leather while Miss Jasper said, "Well, let's all begin. Grades One to Three, take up your slates, please."

Miss Jasper asked the younger children to work on their printing, and passed out a few readers for the older students to share. She had each one of them, starting with the girl with the long braids, stand and read a passage or a poem.

Finally, everyone had read except Rosetta. Miss Jasper looked at her. "Would you read for us now, Rosetta?" Then she added, "I'm assuming you can read?"

Rosetta nodded, smiling. "Oh, yes, miss," she said, quickly standing, as she always had while speaking to her teachers in England. There were a few giggles.

"Iain," Miss Jasper said, "kindly pass Rosetta your text."

Iain half turned in his seat and handed Rosetta his book. "Thank you, Iain," Rosetta said, taking it. She tried to smile at him again, but he kept his face turned away. The boy with the prominent teeth nudged Iain. Iain ignored him.

"Read page sixty-two, please, Rosetta," Miss Jasper said. "The poem by William Wordsworth; 'I Wandered Lonely as a Cloud.'"

The book was tan, with Canadian National Series of Reading Books printed in swirly black letters. She ran her palm over the cover, then, without thinking, lifted the book to her nose, breathing in the smell of the ink and paper.

"Rosetta?" Miss Jasper's voice broke through the silence in the classroom. Rosetta quickly dropped the book from her face, opened it to the proper page, and began reading.

The words rolled off her lips, and Rosetta's mouth formed a smile as she read the familiar poem.

> "I wandered lonely as a cloud
> That floats on high o'er vales and hills,
> When all at once I saw a crowd,
> A host, of golden daffodils."

She read faster and faster.

> "Beside the lake, beneath the trees,
> Fluttering and dancing in the breeze."

Her voice grew louder, and her tongue was hardly able to keep up with her eyes, flying along the verses.

There was one snicker, then another, then a giggle. Rosetta didn't hear them, caught up in the joy of reading again, after five months. The giggles turned to laughter, and soon the room echoed with it. Rosetta stopped, and a line appeared between her eyebrows as she looked around the room to see what the laughter was about.

Miss Jasper called out sharply, "That's enough, stop it!"

She clapped her hands together, and the laughter turned back into snickers and whispers.

"But she sounds so funny, teacher," one of the small boys at the front said.

"Yeah. What's that she's talking?" the boy beside Iain asked, then answered his own question. "Turkey gobble?" He gave a hoot, and once more, laughter snuck through the room.

From the side, Rosetta saw Iain, his face still immobile, running his finger over the scarred edge of the desk. She felt heat rising from the collar of her dress, up her neck, to her cheeks and forehead, and she knew that this time it was her face that was crimson. She pressed the book against her chest.

"That's quite enough, James," Miss Jasper called, then, hitting the desk sharply with her pointer, shouted, "that's enough from all of you!" The laughter stopped, except for a few muffled squeaks and snorts.

"Would you finish up, please, Rosetta?" Miss Jasper said, her eyes slightly narrowed as she surveyed the room.

Rosetta looked back at the page, but the black letters swam dizzily around on the white background.

"Rosetta?" Miss Jasper's voice was softer now, seeming, to Rosetta, to come from far away. "Would you finish up the last stanza?"

Rosetta forced her eyes to clear and, staring straight ahead, slowly and carefully said the last two lines without looking at the book. She knew them by heart.

"And then my heart with pleasure fills,
And dances with the daffodils."

But now the words were heavy and wooden, and had lost their joy.

~

She didn't open her mouth again the rest of the morning. It was still raining at lunchtime, so Miss Jasper instructed the students to stay inside. Sitting alone at her desk, Rosetta ate her bread and pork. Even though she was very thirsty, eyeing the other children as they used the dipper, she didn't get up and have a drink. The girl with the long braids looked at her a number of times, and her look wasn't unfriendly, but Rosetta turned her face away every time. She had no intention of giving anyone a chance to make fun of her again. She especially didn't look at Iain, even when he came back to his seat early and sat there alone, ahead of her, flipping through the pages of his book again and again, while the rest of the class played games on the blackboard or talked.

It seemed as if the day would never end. When Miss Jasper finally announced that it had, Rosetta again waited until the other children had put on their coats and gathered up their lunch pails. She took an extra long time putting away her pen and notebook, and fussed with the lace of one of her boots.

When the last of them had shoved out the door, she got up and put on her coat.

"Rosetta?" Miss Jasper said. Rosetta looked at her. "The children will get used to you," she said. "Many of their parents or grandparents have accents from the Old Country. They're just teasing because you're new. My own first few days here weren't the best."

Rosetta nodded.

"You love reading?" Miss Jasper asked.

Rosetta nodded again.

Miss Jasper smiled. "I could tell by the way you read that poem of Wordsworth's. Where did you go to school before this?"

"There was a classroom at the Manchester Refuge, where I lived for the last four years. Before that I studied with Miss Arthur. She was my governess."

Miss Jasper's eyebrows rose a fraction of an inch. "A governess?"

"Yes. She came to our home and taught us there. Two of my friends came as well, and we learned together. As well as reading and mathematics, we studied history and geography, and music and botany. We were just starting on our first course of Latin when . . ." Rosetta stopped. "Well, there was no more money after my father died. And then my mother . . . then I had to go to the Home. The Manchester Refuge." She picked up her lunch pail and turned to the door. "Good day, miss," she said.

"Rosetta?" Miss Jasper said. Rosetta looked back at her.

"Would you like to take a book home? To read?"

Rosetta spoke softly. "Oh, yes please, miss."

"Come then, and choose one from the shelf," Miss Jasper said. Rosetta set her pail down and hurried to the shelf. "You may not find something you like," Miss Jasper continued. "Most of them are for the children who aren't quite as advanced in their reading as you."

But Rosetta didn't seem to hear her. She had dropped to her knees in front of the shelf and was running her finger along the titles printed on the spines. She stopped on one and pulled it out. "I'll take this one, if I may," she said.

"Certainly," Miss Jasper said. She looked at the girl on her knees in front of her, once more fingering the smooth front of the book, as she had the school text that morning. "*Gulliver's Travels.* Have you read it?"

"Yes. But I love it."

"Thank you, Miss Jasper," Rosetta continued, putting the book inside her coat to protect it from the drizzle that still fell outside.

She walked home in the chilled air, her breath making small clouds in front of her. The clay on the road seemed even deeper, pulling at her boots with rude sucking noises.

Rosetta hardly noticed the cold, or the condition of the road. She walked along, humming under her breath, thinking about the book she held tightly against her body with her arm at her side. She erased the first letter she had started writing in her head to Flora over the lunch break, the one about how awful the school seemed to be.

She thought about taking the extra lantern from the wood-shed upstairs, after dinner, after dishes, and chores, and, wrapped in her thin quilt, reading the adventures of Gulliver, reading it into the night.

Flora, how you would love to hear about Gulliver, Rosetta thought, imagining the little girl's laughter as Flora listened to the parts about the tiny Lilliputians. Remembering her sister's quiet, trusting giggles made the cold air a little less chilling.

"Soon, Flora," Rosetta said out loud, her breath coming out in a cloud. "Not long now. Maybe just another month or two. Just another month or two, that's all."

Chapter Sixteen

Miss Jasper was right; the children did get used to Rosetta. Rosetta learned to call Miss Jasper "teacher," like the rest of the students, and to speak slowly and carefully, flattening out her vowels. It only took a few days for her to make friends with Louise, the girl with the long braids, and another older girl, Gert. She joined them to eat her lunch, and the three of them walked square after square around the school-house at recess.

Rosetta loved the classroom now, with the warm glow of the kerosene lamps on the dark mornings and late afternoons, and the chanting of the younger children as they recited the alphabet and their addition and subtraction tables, and even the dusty smell of the old books. Miss Jasper kept everything tidy and orderly, and Rosetta felt more at home here than she ever did at the Thomas farm.

Some days she walked home with the Fergussons. The two little boys chased each other and ran circles around Iain and Rosetta and Shelagh, dashing ahead and then waiting for the others, sometimes wrestling, tumbling over and over in a flurry of arms and legs. Once, they found a tiny mouse, injured somehow, in a patch of yellow weedy grass by the side of the road, and yelled for Shelagh to come see it. She gently gathered it into a handkerchief she pulled from her pocket, cupping it in her hands.

"I'm going to run home, see if Ma can keep it alive," she called back to Iain and Rosetta, then raced off, her little brothers close on her heels.

"She is kind, like your mother," Rosetta said.

"Yeah. Both she and Ma like to look after little things, tend to them. Course, that was Ma's job."

"Her job?"

Iain stooped to pick up a glittering rock, and studied it as they walked along. "She was a midwife. Delivered lots of babies, before we moved out here from Toronto."

"Toronto? Where's that?"

Iain looked at her. "It's a real big city. Biggest in Ontario. We lived there when we first came from Scotland."

"You were born in Scotland? I thought only your mother was. Mr. Fergusson doesn't have an accent, nor do you."

"Archie isn't my pa. And I've lost most of my accent. I was only five when we came to Canada. But I remember how it felt to be new, get teased some."

"Mr. Fergusson isn't your father?"

Iain took aim at a tall oak and threw the stone at it. It hit with a *thwack*. "Nope." He was quiet for a moment, but Rosetta knew he was going to tell her more.

"My real pa had trouble with drink. He got killed, in an accident in the factory he worked at, only six months after we got to Toronto. Ma was already working, delivering babies in our area. One of Archie's daughters – he has three, all grown-up and moved away from here – had a baby, and Ma was looking

132

after her. Archie came in to see his daughter, and he and Ma met and hit it off right away. His first wife had died a long time since. Anyway, they got married, and Archie brought us to his home out here. Ma still delivers babies when she's needed."

They were almost at the Fergussons' turnoff. "I guess I did more than my share of talking," Iain said. "You never told me much about how you come to be here."

"I will," Rosetta said. "Next time."

~

Rosetta had been watching Shelagh in the school, listening to her as they walked home together. Shelagh was cheerful and bright, and seemed to love helping Miss Jasper with the smallest children and with little jobs around the classroom. Shelagh would be perfect, she thought to herself.

One night after supper, when Mr. Thomas had had his second cup of dried tansy tea and was smoking his pipe, Rosetta went and stood in front of his chair.

"Mr. Thomas, I was wondering about Shelagh Fergusson," she said. "What you and Mrs. Thomas would think of her." Runa looked up from her sewing, her mouth slightly open and her eyes wide.

Mr. Thomas took his pipe out of his mouth. "What about her?"

"Well, she seems clever and helpful. She's just nine, and although she's quite small, she's handy with lots of things." Rosetta threw a glance at Runa and smiled hopefully.

Mr. Thomas put his pipe back in his mouth, drew on it, and blew a cloud of smoke out around the stem. He took the pipe out again. "Why would you be telling me about the Fergusson girl?"

"It's close to my six months, Mr. Thomas. A few more weeks and then it will be time for me to collect my wages so that I can go. I thought that maybe you could arrange for Shelagh to come over, after school, and help –"

Mr. Thomas stood up, the chair skidding backwards on the wooden floor. "You're still that anxious to go, are you? Just up and leave, leave us flat? Leave her," he pointed to Runa, "with no help?"

"No! No. I don't want to do that. It's just . . . remember, I told you once, about my little sister, about how I know she's waiting for me, because they took her away after I promised I'd never leave her. And so I have to find her." She spoke as quickly as she could, so Mr. Thomas wouldn't have the time to get too angry again. Her fingers laced and unlaced on the front of her skirt. "And that's why I'm talking about Shelagh. Especially over the winter, when there's not too much outside work to do. And then, maybe by spring, when the heavy work starts, you could get someone else, maybe even another Home girl, or someone from –" she stopped again as Mr. Thomas raised his hand, palm out, toward her.

"Hold on up, just hold on up," he said. He pulled his chair forward and sat back down, putting his pipe in his mouth and looking at the ceiling. "So it's two dollars you're expecting, is it?"

Rosetta nodded, but Mr. Thomas looked over at Runa. "Get me the pencil," he demanded, "and the contract."

Runa got up and rummaged in the sideboard drawer, pulling out the wrinkled envelope and a yellow stub. She passed them to her husband. He turned over the envelope.

"We got a little figgering to do first, before we pay out any money," he said. He looked up at Rosetta. "I might not be so good at book learning, but I can figger. And there's a few damages here to be taken care of." He licked the end of the pencil. "I recall you broke one of them good teacups, from the set what used to be my mother's. She brung that all the way with her from down in New York State when she settled up here," he said, and wrote some numbers on the back of the envelope. "Them are good, expensive china." He looked at Rosetta. "And what about the broken glass from the lamp?"

"I didn't break that, Mr. Thomas," Rosetta said. "I just walked outside with it, to see if Sigi was all right, and it cracked, all on its own."

Mr. Thomas snorted. "Girl ain't smart enough to know you can't take a lamp from a heated room out into the cold." He wrote down another figure, under the first. "Runa," he said, looking up again, "didn't you tell me we'll need to buy another pair of stockings for the girl, because hers are almost wore clear through, and no amount of darning will patch them up any more?"

Runa nodded, lowering her eyes. Rosetta looked at her, then back at Mr. Thomas as he wrote the third figure. "And then there's the cost of the extra oil, for the lantern. Don't you think I know you keep a lamp going up there, until all hours? You must burn through a powerful lot of oil." He put down still another set of figures, and then Rosetta saw his lips moving as he slowly pressed the pencil onto each of the figures. Then he wrote the total and slid the envelope toward her.

"Look at that," he said. "Comes out to two dollars and twenty cents. So as I figure it, you best be careful, girl, or come the end of the next six months, you'll owe *us* money."

He set the pencil beside the letter. "Yup. You better be darn careful not to break anything more, or do any night-time reading." He put his pipe in his mouth and stared at the stove.

Rosetta didn't look at the envelope with its scribbled numbers. She stood very still, then said, "If you won't give me the two dollars that are my wages, so that I have money to leave this place, there's nothing I can do about it. But could you please give me even a bit of money, enough to buy a piece of paper and an envelope, and a stamp? A stamp is only two cents, Mr. Thomas. Surely you can let me have two cents."

"Who you want to write a letter to?"

"To the Marchmont Home, the Home in Belleville," Rosetta answered. Her hands gripped the sides of her dress.

"And what you need to write them about? Complaining? Well, you'll not get a single penny, nor two pennies, for that kind of whining letter. No, sir. Now get off to bed. There'll be no more talk about money from you. You got it darn good here, and you should be grateful. Now get off, like I said." He kept staring at the stove, sucking and sucking on his pipe, although Rosetta could see that it had gone out.

She looked at Runa, but the woman had her head down, one hand in a tight ball held in front of her mouth. Rosetta walked across the room and up the stairs into the cold blackness of her room. She left her stockings and petticoat on and pulled her nightdress over them and sat on the bed with the quilt around her shoulders. She pulled her knees up and wrapped her arms around them, rocking back and forth, shivering partly because of the cold of the attic room and partly because she couldn't think of what to do now.

In a moment she heard the low murmur of Runa's voice.

Usually they all went to bed at the same time, and she never heard any conversation between the Thomases.

Rosetta stopped rocking and listened. Runa's normally quiet voice rose a pitch. "I know you do. I saw you pay off our debt at Magrath's. Rosetta should be paid, Albert, and I should get my money, too."

"I'll see, I'll see," came Mr. Thomas's rumble. Then he said something else Rosetta couldn't hear.

"But it's mine," Runa cried. "You sold all the butter and cheese I worked on last summer. You took it to Thomson's Landing and you told me it all sold. That would be six dollars. So now I want the money. It's mine," she repeated, "to do whatever I want with. Buy what I want."

"And what is it you need to buy?" Mr. Thomas asked, his voice louder now. "A stamp, like that Home girl? You needin' to write to somebody, too?"

There was a moment of silence. "I want to buy some things for the house. And some new wool," Runa said. "I want to start knitting."

More silence. "No need to start that for a while. You know they don't always take with you. And besides," Mr. Thomas said, "them things you knit for the other ones will do fine."

Rosetta stared into the darkness, leaning forward so she could hear better.

"No, Albert." There was an even longer silence, and Rosetta heard sniffling, then the sound of Runa blowing her nose. "It's bad luck. It will bring a hex. I can't use those things. I have to knit new clothes for this baby."

Rosetta heard the hard thunk of Mr. Thomas's pipe hitting the table. "Well, you can't. You'll have to use the good things you already made, because the money's spent. This farm has a lot of expenses, woman, whether you know it or not. Getting the grain milled, and buying a new wheel for the wagon, and that Eli asking more wages than I ever paid Ben, and our winter supplies – that's pretty well cleaned me out. We got enough for a few emergencies over the winter, and that's it." His voice lowered, and this time Rosetta got up on her knees and moved to the end of the bed, her neck craning toward the stairwell. "And you need that girl up there, 'specially now, Runa. You know you do, if you want to keep this one, not lose it through working too hard again."

There was such a long silence that Rosetta thought they must have silently left the kitchen, gone to bed, and just when she was about to move back and get under the covers, Mr. Thomas spoke quietly. "And we have to think about money if we need the doctor, or you need medicine again. So there's nothing left over for foolish ideas like stamps. Or for clothes for a little one that don't know no difference. Now, come to bed."

Rosetta heard the soft *whoosh* of the lamp going out, and lay back down in the darkness. Another baby for Runa.

For the first time since she'd come to the Thomas farm in May, Rosetta fell asleep without thinking about Flora.

Instead, she thought about the two rough headstones under the little birch tree, and how Runa would never survive a third.

Chapter Seventeen

The next morning, Rosetta studied Runa's abdomen. It didn't look any different, still flat under the shapeless dress. Rosetta couldn't imagine a baby growing there. Runa's body hardly seemed to have strength enough to carry her around, let alone another body, no matter how tiny it was.

When Runa opened the sideboard to put away a spoon, Rosetta heard the rustle of paper, and thought about the contract again, about Mr. Thomas's words.

On the walk to school she hardly saw the scarlet cardinals as they hopped in the low berry bushes and cedars close to the road, or heard, from the taller hardwood trees farther back, the squawking of jays or the sudden hollow drilling of a wood-pecker. The wind blew hard from the north, behind her, snaking cold fingers up under her coat, and every so often it carried a rush of freezing wetness. It gave the air a bitter, despairing feel. After one such flurry, Rosetta stopped and turned around to face the wind, pulling the collar of her thin coat closer around her neck and looking up. The sky was solid gray, and although the end of October was still three days away, it felt as cold as any of the wintry days Rosetta remembered in England.

At least the road is easier to walk on now, Rosetta thought, and looked down at her greased boots as they stepped in the hardened, frozen wagon ruts. Runa had shown her how to grease them, every night, with goose fat, to stop some of the autumn rain and wet mud from creeping through the leather.

Since the first time Miss Jasper had asked Rosetta if she'd like to borrow a book from the school, Rosetta had been taking them back to the farm. After less than a month, she'd read all of them, and now Miss Jasper had started bringing Rosetta her own books, ones that she kept in her room at the Magraths'. Today Rosetta held a book of poetry by William Blake under her coat, pressed tight against her body with her arm, to protect it from the spits of cold rain.

The first thing that morning, Miss Jasper spoke to the class. "As is the custom, now that winter's coming on and we need the stove lit, I'll ask one of the oldest boys to take on the job of lighting it every morning before the teacher," she smiled, "and the other children arrive. It means getting here quite a bit earlier than usual, cleaning out the previous day's ashes, bringing in enough wood for the day, and stoking the stove properly. The pay is twenty-five cents a month, paid at the end of each month." She looked at a paper on her desk. "Mr. Leland left a note stating that Daniel Barker has done it for the last two years. But as he's no longer a student, I'll need someone else." She picked up a piece of chalk. "Anyone interested, please come and see me sometime today." She turned and started writing on the blackboard.

~

After everyone had eaten their lunch and gone outside, Rosetta shrugged on her coat and took the borrowed book to the teacher's desk.

"Thank you, Miss Jasper," Rosetta said, putting the book down. "All the poems were lovely. And some so sad."

Miss Jasper smiled. "'And by came an angel who had a bright key –'"

Rosetta finished the quote. "'And he opened the coffins and set them all free.' 'The Chimney Sweeper.' That was one of my favorites."

"I've shed more than a few tears with Blake," Miss Jasper said, and pulled open a cupboard door to take out her heavy brocade carpetbag. She looked at Rosetta, standing in front of her, her eyes shining and her hands clasped. The teacher saw that the nails were bitten and the tiny pieces of shredded skin around them red and raw.

"Do the Thomases have any books for you to read, Rosetta?"

"No," Rosetta answered, the light in her eyes ebbing. "Mr. Thomas thinks school and reading is a waste of time. He'd rather I was at the farm, working."

Miss Jasper nodded, looking from the girl's hands to her ill-fitting worn dress, the style too old for her, to the neatly darned elbows of her thin coat, and back to her fingers.

"Miss Jasper?"

"Yes?"

"About the job, lighting the stove. I could do it."

"Well. A boy has always done it, at least at the schools I've been, but . . . I suppose there's no reason you can't. Would you be able to get here that early? It means walking in the dark, and being here alone in the cold for the good part of an hour."

"Oh yes. I can do it as well as any boy," Rosetta quickly answered. She looked at Miss Jasper, holding her breath.

Miss Jasper picked up the book and put it in her carpetbag. "All right then. I've had to use the stove these last two days. You can start tomorrow."

Rosetta let out her breath, giving the woman a smile that opened her whole face. "Thank you, teacher," she said, and went out into the cold, wintery smelling air. She wandered around the noisy schoolyard, not even noticing Gert waving her over. Her mind was far away, composing a letter to Flora, one that she would actually be able to write and post, once she had the address from Belleville.

~

The hardest part was waking up at four so that she could get her chores done and leave for school an hour early. The temperature dipped lower and lower each night, and the cold air whistled through the chinks in the wooden walls of her bedroom. One morning there was a coating of ice crystals on the quilt, caused by her own breath. When Rosetta went out to the barn to do her chores, a fine dusting of snow in the yard crunched under her feet. She slept in her clothes after that, as the thin quilt wasn't warm enough. A few days after that first touch of snow, as Rosetta sat on the edge of her pallet, shivering while she laced up her boots by the light of a candle, she realized that the small, shining spots she could see in the corners of her room were tiny drifts of snow.

When she told Runa about the snow in her room, the woman told her to gather some dried cow pats from the barn, and showed her how to shove them into the cracks in the wood to keep some of the snow and cold out.

And that night, when Rosetta went up to her room, she found a thick woolen blanket on the end of her pallet. Rosetta picked it up and held her candle closer to it. The careful, tiny rows of knitting must have taken hours and hours to complete.

By the delicate pattern and the size of the blanket, Rosetta knew it had been made for a child's bed. She carefully spread the blanket over her quilt, and that night she slept warm and snug, and woke up feeling more rested than she had in a long time. And that morning, as she glanced out her bedroom window while she brushed her hair, the brush stopped in mid-air.

Overnight the world had turned white. Rosetta dropped her brush on the bed and sped downstairs into the dark kitchen. She quickly stoked the fire and set the kettle on to boil, then put on her coat and the mitts Runa had given her and quietly opened the door.

She stepped out into the strange snow-covered world, the new snow already a foot high and still falling steadily. She had never seen anything like it in England. She remembered a bit of snow some years, especially around Christmas, but it would be gone after a few hours, replaced by the usual wet cold. But this! She stood in the middle of the yard, looking up at the snow coming out of the darkness, feeling its soft touch on her face. She bent down and scooped up mittfuls of it, throwing it up around her. In a minute she heard a soft trampling sound, and saw Sigi bounding around the corner from his own little house trying to run through the snow that was chest high for him, tripping and stumbling, rolling, his tail wagging the whole time. He jumped at her skirt, black lips pulled back in a smile, and sneezed and snuffled to get the snow out of his nose.

"It's your first big snow, too, isn't it, Sigi?" Rosetta said, crouching to rub the dog's warm back. "Come on." And Rosetta and Sigi took off around the yard, running in circles, Sigi giving an occasional yip of joy, until Mr. Thomas opened the door, pulling up his suspenders and telling them to quiet down or they'd wake the missus, and for Rosetta to quit playing and get inside and put on the breakfast.

Chapter Eighteen

On December first, Miss Jasper gave Rosetta her payment for starting the stove all November.

Rosetta looked at the money laying in her hand, at the thinness of the two dimes and the thicker, larger nickel shining bright against the callouses on her palm. She took out her handkerchief and wrapped the coins in one corner, tying the cloth in a tight knot. She held the handkerchief inside her mitt the whole way back to the farm, and then ran up to her room and put it under her pallet.

Christmas preparations for the school pageant were underway. For three weeks the students paid little attention to their schoolwork. Much of their time was spent rehearsing and practicing lines and making decorations for the town hall. The school was too small to hold all the families of the students, so the hall, with its stage and faded but impressive velvet curtains, was to be used. Refreshments would be served, and the ladies auxiliary from a church in Peterborough had offered to provide special Christmas treats for the children.

The pageant was to take place on the Saturday night before Christmas. Rosetta immediately started planning. They would be going into Magrath Corners. That meant she might have a chance to buy paper and envelopes and stamps, and send the letter to the Marchmont Home. Maybe it would even get there by Christmas.

It was almost too much to hope for.

～

The night of the concert was cold and clear, with a white crescent riding high in the starless sky. There was no wind, and the now-packed snow on the road made the wheels of the wagon glide smoothly over the stony, rutted route. Rosetta rode in the back of the wagon, wrapped in an old bearskin, while Mr. and Mrs. Thomas rode up front.

"Albert?" Runa asked, as Mr. Thomas tied up the horse. "If there's time after the pageant is over, could I go over to the general store and put some raisins on our account?" Before he could answer, she added, "I want to make a special cake to take to the Fergussons' when we go over on Christmas day."

"I suppose," Mr. Thomas answered.

Rosetta kept her hand inside her pocket, clutching the handkerchief holding her own money.

"I'm going over to the feed store," Mr. Thomas said. "I'll come over to the hall when I'm done my business and meet you there." He turned to leave, then stopped. "And you may as well buy some hard candy. Christmas comes but once a year."

Rosetta watched Mr. Thomas walk away on the bustling street. It seemed that even he could be affected by the spirit of Christmas.

～

The Christmas pageant was a wonderful success, in spite of forgotten lines and off-key singing and one very small shepherd who wept with stage fright throughout the whole performance.

When it was over, everyone enjoyed hot chocolate and plates of cookies, and the youngest children, the ones not yet in school, received tiny net bags of candy. There was a gift, wrapped in brown paper and tied with string, for each student.

Rosetta unwrapped hers eagerly. It was a small book of poems by William Blake. She managed to catch Miss Jasper's eye in the crowd, and thanked her, with a smile, for choosing such a perfect gift.

Holding the present under her arm, Rosetta walked, with Runa, to Magrath's, thankful that Mr. Thomas had chosen to stay in the hall and talk with a group of men. Runa went straight to the dry-goods section and started fingering the bolts of cloth and running her fingers over the smooth sheen of ribbons.

"I'll look around on my own," Rosetta told her, and went to the shelf where the paper and envelopes lay in neat white stacks. She counted off five sheets of paper and envelopes. She didn't know if she'd get another chance to buy any.

Then, glancing to see that Runa had moved on to the huge jars of dried fruit, and was talking to a tall, rabbitty woman, she went over to the area Runa had just left. Looking over the skeins, she chose one of soft, fine white wool. She hid it as best as she could, under the paper and envelopes.

She paid for all her purchases, and before Mrs. Magrath could wrap them in brown paper, took out one sheet of paper and an envelope. Going to the post office wicket, she used the pencil tied there with a piece of string. She had composed the letter to the Marchmont Home in her head so many times that it only took her a few minutes to write it out.

Then she addressed the envelope, simply, Marchmont Home, Belleville, Ontario, and licked the gummy flap.

"Mr. Magrath?" she called. The man looked up from measuring out a paper cone of peppermints at the counter. "Could I buy a stamp and post this letter, please?"

"Soon as I'm done here," Mr. Magrath answered.

"How long will it take to get to Belleville?" she asked, as the storekeeper put the stamped letter into a canvas sack hanging behind the wicket.

"Not too many days," he said. "The mail gets taken down to Thomson's Landing once a week. The train there picks up the mail every weekday."

"Thank you," Rosetta said stiffly, remembering what the man had said about her the first time he'd seen her.

But this time he smiled. "You have a Merry Christmas now," he said, then hurried back to his customers.

"Merry Christmas," Rosetta called after him softly. The sight of the still-swinging canvas bag, holding the letter that would let her find Flora, was enough to make sure her Christmas was a wonderful one.

~

Christmas morning on the Thomas farm, with its early rising and outdoor chores, was much like any other, except for the delicious smell of the small goose Mr. Thomas had killed the day before. Runa and Rosetta had plucked it, and before dawn, Runa had put it in the oven, filled with bread stuffing. The special Christmas cake had been prepared a few days before.

Out in the barn, Rosetta suddenly burst into a loud rendition of "Hark, the Herald Angels Sing" as she milked one of the cows, her breath rising in clouds of steam with the song.

The cow swung her head in Rosetta's direction, her great jaws swiveling as she chewed her cud. "So, so, Bossie," Rosetta cooed, stopping her milking to run her hand over the cow's wide flank. "It's Christmas, and I've sent my letter." The cow stared at her, still chewing, then turned away, and Rosetta rested her forehead against its warm side, starting to milk again, singing the final verse more quietly.

They ate their Christmas meal shortly after one in the afternoon, later than usual, then changed their clothes and went over to visit the Fergussons. Rosetta wore the navy dress she and Runa had made in November. It was plain, with a simple rounded collar and a row of buttons up the back, but it fit Rosetta properly, and there had even been enough material to make a small ruffle along the bottom. Rosetta brushed her hair until it crackled, and left it hanging loose except for the side pieces, which she pulled to the back of her head and secured with a length of thread.

The stone house was alive with noise and laughter. Inside were decorations of pine and cedar, and the huge table had been covered with a sparkling-white bedsheet. Candles glowed up and down the table between the almost empty platters and bowls from the Fergussons' Christmas meal. "Just in time for dessert," Mrs. Fergusson said, giving Runa and Rosetta a warm hug. "Oh, now just look at that!" she cried, as Runa shyly uncovered the Christmas cake and handed it to her.

Extra chairs were found for them, and Rosetta sat beside Mr. Warren, a bachelor who farmed up the road past the Thomases'. One of Archie's grown daughters and her husband was there, too.

After they'd all filled up on the cake and shortbread cookies and pies of preserved fruit, Mr. Warren pulled a small flask of whiskey from his pocket and set it on the table. "For a Christmas toast," he said, "if you'll allow me."

Mrs. Fergusson made a loud sound in her throat and looked at her husband. "Well now, Ed," Mr. Fergusson said. "That's right kindly, but Ada doesn't approve of drink in the house."

Mr. Warren put the flask back in his pocket. "Sorry, ma'am."

Mrs. Fergusson passed him another slice of cake and a cup of coffee. "And now, the children's Christmas buns," she said, bringing out a tray covered with a cloth. The smaller children gathered around her. Iain stayed in his chair, while Rosetta took the dirty plates off the table and stacked them by the sink.

"Come on now, Iain, do you expect you're too old for one of your ma's buns? I couldn't keep you away, last year. We can't spoil our tradition." Iain shrugged, a sheepish smile on his lips, then got up and came over to his mother. Rosetta turned to watch, suddenly overcome with sadness, thinking of how wonderful it would be to have a tradition. To have things from the past that tied you all together. To have things in the future that you knew for sure. This was what a family was, being sure of what had happened, and being sure it would happen again. The only thing she and Flora had to count on was being together. And now . . .

"And you, my pretty lass," Mrs. Fergusson said, coming up to her and putting her arm around Rosetta's shoulders. "Don't be standing there with such a long face. 'Tis Christmas, and a new year coming on. Anything can happen in a new year. You mark what I say." She gave Rosetta a firm squeeze. "Get yourself over to the table. There's a Christmas bun for you, and all."

Each child was holding a small, shiny brown bun, studded with dried fruit, and there was one still sitting on the plate.

"Come on, Rosetta. This one's for you," Shelagh said, dancing around on her toes. "You have to break it open and look inside. Come on. We all have to do it at the same time."

Rosetta took the bun. It's fragrant, yeasty odor filled her nostrils.

"All right now. Everybody, on the count of three."

They all shouted out the numbers, even little Geordie, and then pulled their buns apart carefully. When Rosetta separated her bun into two, she saw something gleaming between the pieces of fruit. It was a dime, a new, shiny dime. She picked it out of the dough and looked up.

"It's our fun money," Iain said. "We always get a dime at Christmas, to spend how we like. We can't save it, but have to buy something we wouldn't think of asking for. We usually go into town to spend it before the end of the old year."

"What will you buy with yours?" Shelagh asked her.

Rosetta rubbed the glossy circle of the coin. "I'm not sure yet. Not yet."

~

After their dinner had settled, the children were all shooed outside to play. Rosetta stood uncertainly near the table, not knowing whether she was allowed to go, or should start on the dishes. Iain was still sitting at the table, but had the same uncomfortable look on his face as Rosetta.

"And do the pair of you think you're not children any

more?" Mrs. Fergusson said, her eyebrows two high arches in her forehead. "Well, maybe you are, and maybe you aren't, but get away with the both of you. Get outside and have a slide down the hill."

Rosetta and Iain looked at each other, then grabbed their coats and went outside into the frosty air.

The four younger children had organized a game of Fox and Geese, tramping a huge, dissected circle into the fresh snow at the side of the house. At first Rosetta held back, but when Samuel tagged her, she found herself running, running, running after the boy, laughing and panting as she tried to tag him. They played on and on, and Iain managed to catch Rosetta at least half a dozen times. At first he just tagged the back of her coat, or her arm, but the last time he grabbed her waist and whirled her about so that she was facing him, and for one instant they stood like that, in the falling snow, Iain's hands around Rosetta's waist, the fronts of their coats touching. Rosetta's heart, already racing from running, gave a strange, long dip that took her breath away. But Iain quickly dropped his hands, and the game went on.

After they were tired of playing, they went to a rise near the farm and slid down the long slope in a short wooden sled. The children impatiently waited their turn for a ride, sometimes just throwing themselves in the snow to roll down the snowy bank. Rosetta and Iain watched from the top.

"Your turn, Rosetta," Shelagh panted, handing her the rope that was strung through a hole in the front of the sled.

Rosetta gave a half-smile. "I've never gone sledding," she confessed.

The children stared at her. "Never?" they chorused.

"There's not much snow in England," she said.

"Are you scared, Rosetta?" seven-year old William asked. "Because if you are, I'll come with you."

"I'll go with her," Iain said. "Get in first, Rosetta."

Wrapping the skirt of her dress tightly around her legs, Rosetta sat down on the front of the sled, folding her legs, tailor-style, as she'd see the children do. She felt Iain crowd in behind her, his arms around her sides, holding the rope.

"Hang on," he said into her ear, and as they whizzed down the slope, Rosetta shut her eyes, not sure if her dizziness was from the speed of their descent or the feel of Iain's body pressing into hers.

They slid until the sky started darkening around them, and then trooped back to the house for hot chocolate and more Christmas dessert.

Rosetta didn't want to leave the warmth of the Fergusson house, but all too soon it was time for evening chores. Iain went out to the barn to get started.

"Thank you ever so much for a lovely Christmas," Rosetta said to Mr. and Mrs. Fergusson, as they all stood at the door.

"You're welcome, lass," Mrs. Fergusson said, giving Rosetta another hug.

As the Thomas wagon pulled away from the farm with Rosetta sitting on the back again, she saw Iain come out of the barn. He raised his hand and waved, and Rosetta waved back. They kept waving until the road turned sharply and the Fergusson farm was hidden from view.

~

The sweet taste of the hot chocolate and cake lingered on Rosetta's tongue even after she had changed and done the milking. When she came back in, Runa was slowly rocking by the stove, one hand resting lightly on her abdomen.

There had never been any mention of the baby. Rosetta had wanted to say something to Runa so many times, tell her that she knew, but then she would be admitting that she had eavesdropped on the conversation between Mr. and Mrs. Thomas.

Runa was still so thin that the only indication was a swell under her apron, so slight that Rosetta probably wouldn't even have noticed if she hadn't looked for it.

When Mr. Thomas came in through the shed door with an armful of wood, stamping the snow off his boots, Runa got up and put on the kettle. Then she rustled in the paper sack she'd put on the shelf after the pageant and pulled down her best glass bowl from the highest shelf of the dish dresser. She emptied a pile of brightly colored hard candies into the ruby glass. She made tea, and then passed the dish of candy to Albert and to Rosetta.

Then she went back into the bedroom and returned with her hands held behind her back.

"Merry Christmas, Albert," she said, holding out a pair of socks in her right hand. "And Merry Christmas, Rosetta." She pulled out her left hand and Rosetta saw a pair of mittens. Both the socks and the mittens were of thick gray and brown and white wool. Rosetta recognized it as the wool from the shawl Runa had brought with her from Iceland, the shawl she kept in her trunk with her special things.

"Oh, thank you," Rosetta said, smiling at Runa and putting on the mittens. They were wonderfully thick, and she knew they would keep her hands warm the rest of the winter, no matter how cold it got. But Rosetta felt a tug, knowing that Runa had unraveled her beautiful shawl to make the gifts.

Albert disappeared into the woodshed, then returned with a flat package, wrapped in brown paper. He gave it to Runa, and she smiled as she unwrapped the paper and saw the folded rectangle of cloth. "Linsey-woolsey," she said, fingering the mixture of linen and wool, woven in strips of dark green and blue. "It will make a beautiful dress, for good wear. Thank you, Albert." Mr. Thomas made a gruff sound in his throat. He picked up his new socks off the table. "Think I'll get me an early sleep," he said. "That big meal, and so much sitting, made me feel heavy-headed." He gave the socks a little shake. "I recognize this wool. There'll be no socks warmer than these."

He turned away before Runa could reply, and went into the bedroom, leaving the door partly open. After a few minutes, the dull buzzing of his snores drifted into the kitchen.

Hearing the snoring, Rosetta ran upstairs, still wearing her mittens. "Merry Christmas, Runa," she said when she returned, holding out the skein of delicate wool.

Runa looked at it, then at Rosetta. "How did you get this?" she asked, not taking it from Rosetta's mittened hand.

"I bought it. Miss Jasper has paid me for lighting the stove," Rosetta said, taking off her mittens. She lowered her voice, glancing at the bedroom door. "And I bought some paper and envelopes, too. I already sent my letter to the Marchmont Home." She pushed the wool toward Runa. "It's for you, Runa." She hesitated, glancing at Runa's apron. "To make something for the baby."

Runa gently cupped one hand over the small mound, as she

had earlier, her eyes not meeting Rosetta's. Then she reached out and took the wool.

"Thank you," she said, finally looking at Rosetta, and the girl saw tears glittering in her eyes. "I will make a fine little dress and bonnet." There was silence in the kitchen, and then Runa pulled at the wool of the skein so it formed a loop. Rosetta held out her hands, and Runa placed the loop around them. Then she began winding it into a ball. When she was done, she took a pair of very thin knitting needles out of her basket and started casting on the first row of stitches.

"You sent your letter? To find your sister?" she asked, her voice barely louder than the clanking of the needles.

"Yes. The night of the pageant," Rosetta answered.

Runa stopped knitting, and Rosetta could see the woman's mouth move as she counted the stitches on the needle. Then she shifted, ever so slightly, so that her back was facing the bedroom door, and started knitting again.

"Could I ask you a favor, Rosetta?"

"Yes," Rosetta said, lowering her voice to match Runa's.

"Could you help me send a letter, too?" She made a sound that was almost a sigh. "And lend me two cents for a stamp?" She didn't look up, but kept knitting, her fingers flying in a flurry of needles and wool.

"Yes," Rosetta answered again.

"I have been thinking, this last while, of what you said, before. And yes, I would like to write to my sister, to Gerdur, one more time."

Rosetta nodded, although she knew Runa was looking at her knitting.

"But I don't want Albert to know. After I write the letter,

could you take it, when you go back to school? Maybe you could ask your teacher, or one of your friends, to mail it at Magrath's?"

"Yes. Yes, I will."

Runa's needles finally stopped. "But I don't know when I'll be able to pay you back. Maybe in the summer, if I can get into town with some of my butter, or –"

"That's all right," Rosetta interrupted. She couldn't say to Runa that she didn't expect to be there in the summer. Once she had heard from Marchmont, and made a few more months' salary at the school, added to the dime from the Fergussons, she would have enough to get at least partway to Flora. Even if there wasn't enough for the train the whole way, by late February the weather would be growing nicer, and she could walk, or beg rides. No one would stop her this time. She fingered the mittens laying on the table in front of her and said, "Would you like me to read some poems from my new book? The one I got at the pageant?"

Runa nodded. "That would be nice." She turned up the lamp that sat in the middle of the table. Mr. Thomas's snores sounded from the bedroom.

Rosetta got her book and settled herself comfortably in the kitchen, glowing with warm yellow light. She started one of her favorite poems, "Nurse's Song." As she read the first few lines:

"When the voices of children are heard on the green
And laughing is heard on the hill,"

she heard a creak from the bedroom. Glancing toward the half-open door, she could see Mr. Thomas sitting on the edge of the bed. He was still in the shadows. She continued to read, her voice just louder than the dry wood snapping in the stove and the clinking of Runa's knitting needles.

"My heart is at rest within my breast
And everything else is still."

And as she read, she felt a stirring of guilt, because she realized she had been happy all day. It had been her first real happy day since she'd been separated from Flora. She thought about the look on Runa's face when she'd given her the wool. And she thought about Iain's hands on her waist, and the way they'd both waved until they could no longer see one another.

Chapter Nineteen

"Where do you think you're off to?"

Rosetta looked up from the oatmeal she was stirring. She was wearing her coat, ready to leave as soon as she'd prepared breakfast. "School, of course."

Mr. Thomas snorted as he sat down, placing his palms flat on the table, on either side of his shallow bowl.

"January twenty-seventh today?"

Rosetta nodded.

"And that would make you fifteen now, if I'm not wrong. I heard Runa wishing you birthday greetings yesterday."

Rosetta stood very still, clenching the handle of the wood spoon. The heat from the steaming porridge was making a damp spot on her wrist.

"So now that you're fifteen," Mr. Thomas continued, "I don't believe any more school is required. I had Mrs. Thomas read the contract over to me again, last night. It says we're responsible for seeing you get some schooling." He picked up his spoon, nodding at the pot.

Rosetta ladled a dollop of porridge into his bowl. Mr. Thomas's eyes never left her face, even as he dug a knob of butter out of the small crock on the table and dropped it into his bowl.

Rosetta watched it pool into yellow liquid on the hot oatmeal.

"Until you're fifteen, that is. Smart girl like you, you'd remember that," the man finished. "Bring me the salt."

The girl took the salt pot off the stove. She held it for a moment, then handed it to him.

"I know the contract did say that. But I would only go a little longer," she said, careful to keep her voice even. "Just another month. Miss Jasper is letting me write the Grade Nine examinations as soon as she can get them from the school trustees. She said they should be here in a few weeks. I need to have my Grade Nine standing." She watched Mr. Thomas spoon a liberal dose of salt into his bowl, then stir it around. "She told me I wouldn't have any trouble with the examinations. She says . . ." Rosetta stopped, watching the top of Mr. Thomas's head, the dark, thinning hair and the scalp shining through, as he shoveled the breakfast into his mouth. "Grade Nine is as much as needed to be a teacher, Mr. Thomas. Miss Jasper says there are lots of teaching jobs in the new towns opening up, especially to the west. She's going there, west, after this year. She says –"

Mr. Thomas threw his spoon, with a clatter, into the empty bowl. He leaned back in his chair so that the front legs lifted off the floor. "Ha. You? A teacher? That's a good one. I bet that teacher a yours is playing a joke on you. She's probably laughin', too, at how you believe anything she tells you."

Rosetta stared into Mr. Thomas's eyes. "She doesn't lie, Mr. Thomas. I believe her. I believe I could be a teacher."

Mr. Thomas stood up so suddenly that his chair screeched

across the wood floor, then fell over with a sharp crack. He took a step toward her, one hand curling into a fist.

"You'll stay here and work for us, for as long as we need you," he said, his voice barely a whisper. "Don't you ever look at me with those cow eyes o' yours and speak up to me, fancy as you please. Because I'm the boss in this house. You hear me? I'm the boss."

Rosetta was up against the stove. Even through her coat, dress, and petticoat she could feel the heat on the back of her legs and her behind. Mr. Thomas stared at her for another second, and his fist started to come up from his side. Rosetta forced her eyes not to blink, to keep drilling into his. She knew how Runa dropped her eyes whenever Mr. Thomas got angry about something, and she wouldn't drop hers. She wouldn't.

"Albert? What was that noise? It sounded like something fell." Runa's voice came, weakly, from the bedroom.

Mr. Thomas's hand dropped, and he grabbed his coat off the nail by the door. "It was nothing. Nothing, just a chair," he called toward the partly shut bedroom door. As he put one arm into his sleeve, he pointed his finger at Rosetta and shook it, but didn't say anything more.

The door slammed behind him, sending an icy swirl of air across the floor. Rosetta let her shoulders drop. She took off her coat, straightened the chair, and picked up the kettle, pouring the bubbling water over the dried mint leaves in the bottom of the pot she'd set on the table before Mr. Thomas had come in for breakfast.

"Tea's just brewing, Runa," she called. "I'll bring it in shortly." She finished pouring the water, hoping Runa wouldn't hear the clattering made by her shaking fingers as she tried to fit the lid into the scratched cast iron teapot.

She put a spoonful of maple syrup into the cup, stood straighter, and carried it into the bedroom.

"How are you this morning?" Rosetta asked. "Did you manage to sleep last night?" She set the cup and saucer on the top of the bureau and helped Runa to a sitting position.

"A little. I slept a little," Runa said. She turned her face toward the window, and in the dull-gray light Rosetta saw that her face was the color of damp putty.

Runa had three more months until the baby was due, but right after Christmas her body had suddenly ballooned out, and even her hands and feet were swollen. Rosetta knew she suffered from dizzy spells; she had seen Runa hanging on to the backs of chairs and touching the walls as she walked by them.

Rosetta smiled brightly, handing the cup and saucer to Runa. "Well, after you have your tea you should try to rest a bit more this morning."

"No," Runa said, one hand picking fretfully at a thread on the top of the quilt. "There's that mending to do. If you bring me the basket, I can work on it once the light's better."

"I'll do it," Rosetta said.

"You won't have time, will you?"

Rosetta turned and started through the bedroom door.

"Rosetta? Did he tell you you couldn't go to school today?"

Rosetta didn't answer, and Runa let out a small moan. "I knew it. It's all my fault. I should never have wished you a happy birthday in front of him. But I didn't think. Then, when he asked me to read the contract again last night, I knew what I'd done. I'm so sorry."

"It's not your fault," Rosetta said, then quietly closed the door behind her. She gathered Mr. Thomas's dirty dishes off the table. Her face felt like it was made of clay, almost set. She knew if she spoke or cried, it would crack.

She had to keep the clay fixed in place, so she could think clearly. If her face was still and hard, her mind could be the same way, and she would be able to think better.

She poured warm water over the dishes and put her hands into the dishpan, starting to scrub out a mug. If she didn't go to school, she couldn't make any more money for the train. All she needed was January's payment, and February's. And if she didn't go to school, she wouldn't write the examinations.

There seemed no point in staying. She should just leave now, show Mr. Thomas that he couldn't rule her life the way he ruled Runa's. She should just put on her coat, take the money she already had, and start out, heading back to Belleville. She still hadn't had a letter from Marchmont. She'd been able to check the week before, when Mr. Thomas sent her to Magrath Corners because he ran out of pipe tobacco.

I'll just go now, today. Yes, I will, Rosetta thought, and then stared down in shock at the broken-off handle of the mug in her hands under the water. She didn't know how she broke it. The bitter scratching of the blowing snow against the pane made her look toward the window.

But how could she leave, on foot, in the middle of winter?

"Rosetta? Rosetta, please come. Come and talk to me." She could hardly make out Runa's voice through the door.

And more than the weather, how could she leave Runa now? She thought of the woman, barely older than herself, lying still and pale in the dim bedroom. Alone, and sick. She thought of Flora. She had been sick so much of the time. Maybe she was sick right now. Still and pale, alone, in a bedroom, calling for her.

"I'm coming, Flora," she said. She closed her eyes, then opened them. "I mean Runa." Her voice grew louder. "I'm coming." And for the second time that morning, she squared her shoulders and went through the bedroom doorway.

~

The bitter cold snap lasted all week. Rosetta had to break the ice on the top of the washing water she kept in a jug in her room. In the dark barn, she'd milk the cows by the shadowy light of a lantern, the cows snorting in the cold air, blowing out blasts of fog from their large, wet nostrils.

Hurrying back inside from the still, glittering world, looking at the lifeless trees against the gray horizon, Rosetta wondered how people came to live in such an icy, bleak place.

But the week passed, and the temperature rose enough to make it bearable. On a bright, crisp Saturday, Mr. Thomas sat in the kitchen, oiling a plow blade. Rosetta peeled potatoes and put them to boil for lunch. She sliced yesterday's pork and fried a batch of johnnycakes.

Runa had managed to dress herself and come out of the bedroom, and Rosetta had helped her get seated in the rocker by the stove. But after half an hour she had gone back to bedroom, shuffling slowly, one hand under her protruding belly as if she needed to help support the extra weight.

A horse's whinny made Mr. Thomas and Rosetta stop their work. They looked at each other, then Mr. Thomas went and opened the door. He squinted in the harsh winter sunlight, then turned back to Rosetta.

"It's that teacher lady," he said, frowning at Rosetta as if it were her fault that Miss Jasper had ridden up in her buckboard.

Rosetta put down the big wooden spoon and went to stand beside Mr. Thomas. She saw Miss Jasper jump down from the wagon. She was carrying her carpetbag, as usual.

"Hello, Rosetta!" she called, waving. She hurried across the yard and up the steps, stamping her snowy feet just outside the door.

"Mr. Thomas, I believe," she said, holding out her gloved hand. "I'm Miss Jasper." She smiled at Rosetta, then at him. "Rosetta's teacher."

Mr. Thomas looked down at her hand, then stepped back. "I know who you are," he said.

"Well," Miss Jasper said, putting down her hand. "Well," she said again, her smile fading. "I came to see if Rosetta had taken ill. We all missed her at school. Especially on the cold mornings we had this week." She raised her eyebrows at Rosetta.

Rosetta glanced at Mr. Thomas, hoping he wouldn't ask what she meant. Mr. Thomas had no idea why she had left so early for school; as long as she had her chores done it didn't matter to him. And she had no intention of letting him know she had money, not after he'd taken it from her the first time.

Mr. Thomas sniffed and ran his hand through his hair so it stood straight up on top.

"I expect you better come in," he said.

Miss Jasper's smile returned. "Thank you," she said.

She stepped into the room, and Rosetta took her coat. "So you're all right, then?" she said to Rosetta. "Have you been poorly?"

Rosetta busied herself shaking Miss Jasper's coat. A few wet drops fell to the floor.

"She ain't been sick," Mr. Thomas said, sitting down again and picking up the oily rag. "No more need for her to go to school. She's past schoolin' age now. She's needed here, to help out the missus."

Miss Jasper was still standing by the door. "I see," she said quietly. Rosetta draped the woman's coat over the back of one of the chairs. She still hadn't faced Miss Jasper.

They all turned as the bedroom door opened. Runa stood there, holding the door jamb. "Good day, Miss Jasper," she said. "How nice of you to call on us. Please sit." She held her hand out in the direction of the rocking chairs.

Miss Jasper sat down, setting her carpetbag on the floor beside her. "Thank you, Mrs. Thomas. I was telling your husband that I came by to see if Rosetta was all right."

Runa lowered herself onto the seat of the chair across from Miss Jasper. She set her hands around the bulge in front of her. An awkward heaviness filled the air.

"Rosetta," Runa finally said, "you must make some tea for Miss Jasper. And I'm sure there are some biscuits left from breakfast."

As Rosetta bustled around, preparing the offering for Miss Jasper, the teacher pulled her carpetbag up on her lap.

"I brought Rosetta some books," she said, opening the bag. "I thought if she was ill, she would enjoy having something new to read. And the examinations will be arriving in a few weeks." She took the books out, put the carpetbag back on the floor, and set the books on her lap.

The heaviness returned to the room. Mr. Thomas went on

with his slow oiling, rubbing the rag in smooth, small circles on the already gleaming blade. Runa's hands moved in the same small circles on her abdomen, her eyes lowered, watching her own hands as if they were engaged in a fascinating activity.

Miss Jasper licked her lips and spoke again. "I understand your need for Rosetta's help, Mrs. Thomas," she said. "But if Rosetta can't come to school any more, perhaps I could come out, if the roads aren't too bad, for the next few Saturdays, and bring Rosetta her work. I suppose she's told you about wanting to complete her Grade Nine standards." She looked at Rosetta, but the girl was slicing biscuits and putting them on a plate. "There are just a few more areas she needs to cover. And then she could come to the school for a few days, and I'm sure she could do all the exams. It should only take a few days."

Mr. Thomas set the blade down and put the rag on top of it. "Look now, Miss Jasper. Rosetta is here to work, and that's it. We stuck by the rules of her contract, and let her go to school until she turned fifteen. And now she's finished with schooling, with all that. So we thank you for the visit, but we won't be needing any more of them."

He got up and put on his coat and hat and, taking the blade and rag, opened the door and went out. A blast of cold air billowed into the room as he slammed the door.

Rosetta brought the tea and plates and the biscuits to the table. Runa looked up at Rosetta as the girl placed a knife on the plate in front of her. "Rosetta? Open up the sideboard," she instructed, "and take out that jar of elderberry preserves." As Rosetta took out the jar, Runa continued. "Get down the fancy glass bowl, and use that." Rosetta did as she was told, and set the bowl of jam beside the biscuits. Then she sat down.

"I was planning to have the jam for Rosetta's birthday," Runa said, pushing the dish in Rosetta's direction, "but I wasn't feeling too well that day. It's the last jar," she said again, "so I wanted it for a special occasion. This seems a good day for it." She smiled at Miss Jasper and handed her the dish, and the woman took it and smiled back at her.

"I brought your pay with me, too, Rosetta. For January," Miss Jasper said.

Both women looked at Rosetta.

"Go on, Rosetta, take a biscuit," Runa said too cheerfully.

"Thank you," Rosetta whispered, and took one. She set it on her plate, opened it, and spread a thin layer of jam on it.

When Miss Jasper and Runa had covered their biscuits with the jam, and the tea was poured, Rosetta took a bite and chewed. The jam was sweet, and the powerful flavor of the berries reminded her of summer. Of warm weather.

It reminded her of England.

Of another time, when she had been another girl.

Chapter Twenty

February was a dreary, long month. It seemed to Rosetta that she lived in a world of candles and lamplight. Mr. Thomas was silent, grim, and restless. He'd repaired everything there was to fix around the house and barn and outbuildings and yard, and now even the ticking of the clock appeared to irritate him. An atmosphere of gloom hung over the house, as if suspended, like the gray winter clouds caught, for days on end, in the bare black branches of the tall trees at the side of the farm.

Rosetta brought Sigi into the barn with her when she went in to do the milking. After she was finished, she always spent a few minutes playing with the half-grown dog, and filling a battered old bowl with frothing warm milk for him morning and evening. She worried that the few scraps there were to bring him from supper weren't enough, but his body still felt firm and round under his thick winter coat. Runa told her he would have learned, by now, to catch the rabbits that populated the bush near the farm.

The dried peas and beans had been used up, as were most of the canned and pickled vegetables. The last of the oats had gone moldy, and only a pile of potatoes, a large sack of bitter turnips, and half a bucket of wildly sprouting onions were left in the root cellar. The butchered pork and beef, dried and frozen in the woodshed, seemed tough and tasteless. There was no more maple syrup for tea, or fruit preserves for the bread and biscuits. The endless thin soups and stews, spiced only by ground pepper, and the cornmeal mush all tasted the same, as sad and predictable as the weather.

The hardest part for Rosetta was thinking about a letter waiting for her in the post office in town. It had been two months since she'd written to the Marchmont Home. Mr. Thomas hadn't sent Rosetta into town, or even let her go to the Fergusson farm, saying Runa needed her all the time. But Runa seemed to need Rosetta less than she had in January. She was definitely a little stronger, even though her body, at least the front of her, was huge and cumbersome. A bit of color sometimes showed under the surface of her cheeks, and most mornings she got up and did a few simple chores, making breakfast or doing dishes.

"You seem better," Rosetta said to her one morning.

Runa smiled. "I know. It's a good sign. If I can hold on another month and a half . . . Ada says she can hear the baby's heart loud and clear now."

The only break in the monotony had been an occasional visit from Mrs. Fergusson and Shelagh. Each time they came, Rosetta peered out the window, hoping to see Iain, but he wasn't with them. On the last visit, Mrs. Fergusson had spent a long time in the bedroom with Runa, while Shelagh showed Rosetta a new knitting pattern.

When they had left, Runa sat down at the table. "Where's Albert?" she asked Rosetta.

"Out in the barn, I think," Rosetta said.

"I know how worried you are, about Flora," Runa said.

"And how much you want to leave. I know, too, how Albert is trying to bully you into staying. So I spoke to Ada about you going. I asked her about Shelagh. And she says that she can spare Shelagh, for a few hours after school, and weekends, until at least April, when the baby is due."

Rosetta watched the woman's face.

"After that," Runa continued, "we'll just have to see how things are. If the baby . . ." she let the sentence trail off. Her face hadn't changed. "I would like you to stay with me, but I know what it means to be separated from the sister you love. And I want you to go."

"But what will Mr. Thomas say? What will he do to you if you let me –"

Runa broke in, and now her face came alive, her mouth firm and her eyes a little brighter. "It's not your worry how Albert treats me. As soon as the weather turns warmer, it will be time for you to go. Go and find your sister. You have helped me to look for mine. I don't know if I'll ever hear from her, but you've given me the courage to try. Do you have enough money saved now?"

"I'm not sure. But I have some."

Runa nodded. "It's nearly spring. I will tell you when it is time, and then you will go."

Rosetta sat at the table with Runa, neither of them speaking, until Mr. Thomas came back inside, complaining about the winter weather for the fifth time that day.

~

March finally rolled in, and within a week the cold lifted. One morning Rosetta awoke to a tap, tap, tapping sound that she realized was the dripping of melting snow off the roof.

All of a sudden the air smelled different, and she saw small dark patches of bare ground in the south-facing yard. She was surprised to come downstairs one morning to find Mr. Thomas had already made himself a bowl of cornmeal and was shoving his arms into his coat.

"Going out sugaring before noon," he said. "Sap will be starting. If the weather holds and we get a real good run, I'll stay out two, maybe three days at the most before I come back for food. You can handle the chores on your own for a few days. I'll stop by the Fergussons' on my way out and tell their boy to come by and check up on things tomorrow, make sure everything is looked after proper."

Rosetta nodded. But as soon as he'd said good-bye to Runa and left with the horses, carrying some food supplies, she'd gone to Runa. "What's sugaring?"

Runa rubbed at her back with her hands. "The sap of the maple trees starts running at the first thaw. Albert puts a notch in the tree and a little spigot in it, and the sap runs into the buckets he hangs from the spigot. He and several other men have a camp, miles from here, where they boil the sap after they collect it. With the boiling, the sap turns into syrup."

Rosetta had never wondered about the pails of rich golden syrup. She was only sorry to see the last of it, at the end of January.

"This is the time," Runa said, a moist, anxious look in her soft eyes. She was still rubbing her back, and gave a little groan as she lowered herself onto the spool couch and put a small pillow behind her back.

"For me to go? Now?" Rosetta said.

"Yes. By the time Albert gets back, you'll have been gone

for a day or two, and there won't be anything he can do about it. And I won't let him, even if he tries this time." She looked down at her hands, now lying still in her lap. "I'll get Iain to do the chores tomorrow, and have him bring Shelagh over for a few hours later. Take one of the pillowcases to put your things in." She didn't look up as Rosetta slowly climbed the stairs.

~

"Do you want the pig, before I go?"

"Yes. That always helps this ache."

While Rosetta had been putting her things into the pillowcase, Runa had gone back to rest on the bed. Rosetta poured hot water from the kettle into the crock with a flat bottom and corked snout, and left it on the warm stove for a few minutes while she straightened up the kitchen. By the time she was finished, the crock pig was warm through. Using a clean square of flannel, she picked it up off the stove and wrapped it securely. "Here you are," she said to Runa, and slid the wrapped crock between the small of the woman's back and a pillow. She hovered in front of her for a few seconds. "I'll go out now and do the milking, even though it's still early, and make sure the animals have enough food until tomorrow. Then I'll come back in. Are you sure you're all right, Runa? You'll be all right, won't you? Should I stop at the Fergussons' on my way and tell them I'm going right now?" She thought about seeing Iain, and then about not seeing him, ever again.

"No. It's best if you just go. Iain will come around tomorrow morning, and I'll tell him you've left. Don't waste any more time. Go, go, before you burst." Her face showed the ghost of a smile.

"All right. I'll be right back." She went outside and gave the one sharp whistle that Sigi always came running to. Her eyes filled with tears as she bent over the little dog.

"You look after Runa," she said, holding his head between her hands. "You're a good dog, yes, a good dog. Stay out of Mr. Thomas's way." The dog licked her face. A low whine sounded in his throat.

"It's all right." Rosetta wiped her nose with the back of her hand. "I'm going away, but I won't forget you. And when I have my own dog, I'll call him Sigi, after you." She got up quickly, her chin trembling, and went to the barn and milked the cows and filled all the food and water troughs.

As she started back to the house, the dog followed her. "Go on, go away now," she said, sharper than she intended. Sigi gave her one quick wag of his tail and then raced off toward the bushes.

Good, she thought, closing the door behind her, not wanting him to follow her down the lane, look at her with his intelligent, loving eyes one more time. She picked up her pillowcase from beside the table and went into the bedroom, dreading what she had to do.

But Runa was turned away, her face to the wall, and her body so still that Rosetta thought she must have fallen asleep. "Runa?" she said in a low voice.

She didn't stir. Rosetta knelt by the bed for a moment, then reached out and touched the woman's back with soft fingers. She stroked the thin back once. "Good-bye, Runa," she whispered, and then was gone.

~

For the first little while, Rosetta's feet fairly flew over the road. She had to keep to the edge, where the snow was wet and sugary, to stay out of the deep pockets of thawing mud. She slowed down a little after the second hour, watching a great flock of geese overhead, the air filled with their nasal cries as they flew north.

When she finally reached town, she went straight to the general store. As usual, a few men were gathered around the stove, talking.

"Excuse me, but are any of you going over to Thomson's Landing?" she asked.

One of them nodded his head. "Not me, but I know the Doc's here in town. He'll be heading back that way come nightfall."

"Do you know where he is?"

"Last I heard he was just over at Mrs. Abbott's, at the end of town, checking on her boy. The one with the bad chest. But he'll be back here before he goes."

"Thank you," Rosetta said. She had already planned that if no one was going to Thomson's Landing that afternoon, she would wait until school was over and Miss Jasper had come back to her room. She knew the teacher would let her stay the night with her. And if she still couldn't get a ride tomorrow morning, she would set out on foot. Someone was bound to pass her on the road and pick her up.

While she waited for the doctor, she looked over at the post office. Mr. Magrath was behind the wicket, writing in a thick ledger. There was no reason not to try one last time.

"How can I help you?" the man asked when Rosetta came up to the wicket.

"Is there any mail for the Thomas farm?"

Mr. Magrath turned around and surveyed the wall of

narrow wooden slots, then reached toward one. "Well, I do believe there's something," he said, pulling out an envelope and handing it to Rosetta. "Here you go," he said, and started writing again, his pen busily scratching.

Rosetta's hands trembled so badly she could barely hold the envelope. All the way she'd told herself that maybe, just maybe, there would be a letter. And then she'd know where to go, instead of back to the Marchmont Home. And there was. It seemed almost too good to be true.

She read the writing on the front, then stared harder.

"Mrs. Albert Thomas," the spidery black letters said. Rosetta read it again. It was for Runa. A letter for Runa, not for her. She turned it over, and in the same fine writing was "Gimli, Manitoba." Her hand holding the envelope fell to her side.

"Excuse me, Mr. Magrath," she said. The scratching stopped, and the man looked up again.

"Yes? Do you have something to post?"

"No. But was there anything else for the Thomas farm? Any other letter? For Rosetta Westley?" She stood on her toes, trying to see in the slot he'd pulled the envelope from.

He looked again, bending and poking his fingers into the empty rectangle. "Sorry, that's it."

Rosetta picked up the bundle she'd dropped by her side and started to walk away from the wicket.

"Say, wait a minute," Mr. Magrath called after her. She turned around.

"I had my daughter here visiting from down at Port Hope last week, and she came in to help me out. She did some sorting, and I know she said there were a few . . . aha!" Mr.

Magrath had reached up to the top of the shelf and brought down five or six envelopes tied with string. He undid the knot. "Now, there were a few letters to people moved on and such, names she didn't recognize, that she didn't know what to do with." He looked at the top envelope, then back up to her. "It's Weatherly, you said?"

Rosetta shook her head, trying to read the upside-down writing on the envelope. "Westley, sir. Rosetta Westley."

Mr. Magrath put the envelope to one side and looked at the next. He seemed to take a very long time, reading the name on each envelope. When he got to the second last one, he picked it up. "Here we are. Miss Rosetta Westley. Magrath Corners." He handed it to her.

Rosetta took it. She pushed the letter for Runa into her pocket and, holding her bundle under her arm, read her name on the front of the envelope. She read it two more times, then pulled it open.

The sheet of paper had the letterhead of Marchmont Home on the top.

"Dear Miss Westley," Rosetta read. "Our records indicate that your sister, Flora Westley, was adopted by Mr. and Mrs. Harry Forsythe, of Cobourg.

"You may wish to contact them regarding your sister; their address is listed below. I trust this information will be helpful to you.

"I remain,

"Miss Beverly Lyle."

Just as she'd done with the envelope, Rosetta read and reread the letter. She ran her fingers over the address at the bottom of the page. Cobourg.

"Rosetta?"

With a jerk, Rosetta looked up. It was Mr. Warren. He held a can of kerosene in one hand and a wrapped package in the other. "Thought I recognized you," he said. "From Christmas, at the Fergussons'."

"Yes, hello, Mr. Warren," Rosetta said. She stuffed the letter back into the envelope and pushed it into her pocket beside Runa's.

"You on your own?" Mr. Warren asked, raising his ginger-colored, bushy eyebrows, looking at the stuffed pillowcase under her arm.

"Yes, I walked in," Rosetta said, wishing he'd leave her alone. She wanted to read the letter again.

"Well, I'm just off home, myself," he said. "Can I give you a ride?"

"Oh, no," Rosetta immediately said, "thank you, but no," and when Mr. Warren turned aside, she put her hand into her pocket, feeling the two envelopes. A letter for Runa. It was from Gerdur. She had a letter about Flora, and Runa had a letter from her sister. Rosetta thought about what would happen if Mr. Thomas got hold of the letter before Runa. If he'd ever give it to her. She could ask Mr. Warren to drop it off. But no, she decided, she wanted to give it to Runa herself. She wanted to know if Runa and Gerdur had found each other, after all this time.

She glanced outside. If she got a ride with Mr. Warren, it wouldn't take long to get back to the farm. It would be almost dark by the time she made it back to town again, and she'd miss her ride with the doctor, but she would stay with Miss

Jasper and somehow leave Magrath Corners early tomorrow morning, even if it were on foot. She would just have to wait until tomorrow if she were to help Runa one last time. She'd waited all these months; she could bear one more day.

"Mr. Warren," she called to the man's back. "I've changed my mind. I would appreciate a ride."

~

The wind had come up, and the earlier warmth of the day was missing. There was a definite chill in the air as Mr. Warren slapped the reins over his big Clydesdale's wide back.

"Wonder if our taste of spring is over?" he said, clucking at the horse to speed up.

"Where is Cobourg, Mr. Warren?" Rosetta asked.

"Cobourg? Not too far from here," the man answered. "A bit to the east, and south. Few days' trip."

"Is it expensive? The train from Thomson's Landing to Cobourg?"

"Oh, no need for the train. It's a more roundabout route by train. It doesn't run direct from Thomson's Landing to Cobourg. It's shorter, easier, by wagon. Only a few days by wagon, if the roads aren't too bad."

"By wagon? Only a few days?" Rosetta's voice rose shrilly on the last word.

Mr. Warren looked at her. "Yes. Not far at all."

Rosetta beamed at him. "Thank you, Mr. Warren."

The man grinned back at her. "Don't thank me," he said. "I didn't put it there. You know someone in Cobourg?"

Rosetta nodded. "My sister. My little sister is in Cobourg," she said. "And I'm going to her. Tomorrow."

Mr. Warren slapped the reins again. "That's real nice," he said. "Nice to have some kin nearby, 'specially if you're far from home."

"Yes," Rosetta said, "yes."

~

By the time they reached the Thomas farm, heavy cloud had rolled in and small, hard dots of snow swirled around the wagon. Rosetta looked at the house. There was no light shining from the window.

"Looks like no one's at home," Mr. Warren said, as Sigi came running toward the wagon, no welcoming bark, his tail straight out behind him.

Rosetta scrambled down. "Mr. Thomas is out sugaring. But Mrs. Thomas is at home. Thank you for bringing me back, Mr. Warren," she said, stooping to touch Sigi's head. The dog looked up at her, his muzzle wrinkling.

"You sure you'll be all right?" Mr. Warren asked, frowning at the still, dark house, then raising his eyes. "Looks like the stove's gone out, too."

Rosetta followed his gaze to the chimney. The stove hadn't been out since early October. "I'll be all right," she called over her shoulder, already halfway to the house. She pulled the collar of her coat up higher, trying to ignore the cool finger of doubt reaching out to touch her, just at the back of her neck.

Chapter Twenty-One

Rosetta stepped inside and shut the door behind her. She stood, listening, feeling the chill in the room. She had never seen the house like this, with no light, no sound, no smell. Even through her dress and coat sleeves, she could feel the hair on her arms prickling.

Out of the stillness came an unexpected, twisted cry, almost like the muffled mewing of a kitten. Rosetta's breath caught in her throat.

"Runa?" she called, barely above a whisper. She started toward the bedroom. "Runa? Is that you?"

"Rosetta. Rosetta, you're back?" Runa's voice had a strange dullness that frightened Rosetta even more than the mewing sound. She dropped her bundle and ran to the doorway, but didn't go in. She put her hand on the doorjamb, gripping it tightly.

"What is it, Runa?"

"Go get Mrs. Fergusson," Runa said, still in that frightening, dead voice.

"Is it the baby, Runa? Is it?" Rosetta couldn't see the woman's face in the late-afternoon shadows, just the hump under the quilt. "But it's too soon. It's only the beginning of March. That's much too soon, isn't it? You said spring, springtime you said, you told me late April is a good time for . . ." She watched in horror as Runa's body suddenly wrenched and then rose under the quilt, the bulge of her abdomen contorted and stiff. Just when Rosetta thought she couldn't stand it any longer, couldn't stand the thin whistling that came from between the woman's teeth, the unnatural arch of her body, thought she must run and shake Runa, shake her out of the spasm, Runa's body let go, dropping down as if it were made of heavy stone.

Rosetta started into the bedroom. But Runa stopped her, her hand slowly lifting a few inches from the quilt. "Go. Go quick," she whispered.

Rosetta wrapped the shawl that had slipped down around her shoulders over her head again. She noticed that her own hands were shaking. "I'll run. I'll run all the way, and be right back with Mrs. Fergusson," she said, turning. "Mrs. Fergusson will know what to do." Then she looked back, over her shoulder, at the still form on the bed. Even from the distance she could see the damp stains on the pillow under the thin white fan of Runa's hair. "Should I start the stove? Do you need anything, Runa? Can I bring you something, before I go?"

Runa's head moved weakly on the limp pillow. "Never mind about the stove. A spoon. Bring me the big wooden spoon."

Rosetta ran to the stove. She grabbed the spoon out of the soup pot and wiped it on the wet rag by the water pail. Holding it in front of her like a sword, she raced back to Runa.

"What shall I do with it? The spoon, what shall —"

Runa grabbed the spoon out of Rosetta's hand. "Tell Mrs. Fergusson they're coming close and hard," she said. Her lips started to tremble. "Tell her . . ." she turned her face away from Rosetta. "Go now," she whispered.

Rosetta backed away from the bed, pulling on her mittens. "And Rosetta?"

Rosetta stopped, one mitten on. Runa had turned her face back toward Rosetta. There were tears on her pinched cheeks, the furrows on her forehead deep.

"Please pray. Pray for this baby not to die."

Rosetta nodded once, and when she saw Runa put the handle of the spoon to her mouth, clamping her teeth on it, she turned and ran through the kitchen, kicking the pillowcase out of the way, and on out the door into the falling purple twilight.

"Stay," she ordered Sigi, as he started bounding along beside her, his tail wagging playfully. "Stay, I said," she shouted, and the dog stopped abruptly at the unfamiliar tone. He stood, watching her until she was out of sight. Then he went up the steps and sat down in front of the door, staring at the empty road.

~

Rosetta ran down the snowy ruts left by the wagon wheels for as long as she could. Her lungs were throbbing with liquid fire, and the stitch in her side was a cruel knot. It was shorter to go through the fields, but she was afraid the thaw would have turned the ground into an impassable mess of mud.

She walked a few paces, pushing in on her side, then started running again. By the time she reached the Fergussons' farm, it was dusk. Lights from the house cast long rectangles of yellow on the blue shadows of the snow in the front yard. A few feet from the house something silently threw itself against her back, knocking her to the ground.

"Get off, Bonnie," she panted, pushing away the dog's slobbery, grinning mouth. "Off!" The big dog danced around her, excited at her visit, smelling Sigi on Rosetta's clothes.

Rosetta flung herself against the door, banging with her fist. "Mrs. Fergusson!" she shouted. "Please! It's Rosetta." The door opened almost immediately, and Mrs. Fergusson's round, startled face peered out at her.

"Goodness sakes! What is it, child? Come in, come in." She pulled at Rosetta's snow-covered arm, drawing her into the warmth and light of the kitchen. "You look all worn out."

"It's Runa. It's Mrs. Thomas," Rosetta panted. "The baby, Mrs. Fergusson. It's coming now. Too early, and Runa is in a bad state." Her words came out shaky and squeaky. "I ran all the way, because Mr. Thomas took the horses when he went sugaring; I ran all the way, but it seemed to take so long, and she's all alone, all alone, and it's awful, Mrs. Fergusson, it's –"

"Shush, now," Mrs. Fergusson said, already pulling on her brown wool coat. "You catch your breath. Archie," she said to her husband sitting at the scrubbed wooden table with the staring children, a forkful of potatoes covered with yellow gravy halfway between the plate and his mouth, "go out and get the trap ready. With Moses. He's fastest."

"I'll hitch him up," Iain said, "and drive you there." He stuck his cap on his head and had one arm in his jacket sleeve as he went out the door.

"Why didn't you come over and get me at the first sign?"

Rosetta was still trying to take deep breaths. "I left . . . I went into town. I left Runa alone. I know I shouldn't have, but I, but . . ." She stopped, thinking, as she had all the way to the Fergusson farm, that if she hadn't gone she would have been

184

with Runa when the pains started, and she could have come for Mrs. Fergusson right away, and maybe somehow the woman would have known how to stop the baby from coming. Or if she had stopped at the Fergussons' and told them Runa was alone, as her instincts told her to, Shelagh or Mrs. Fergusson herself would have been with Runa.

"Well," Mrs. Fergusson said, "I can see how cold and tired you are. I should tell you to stay here, get some warm food in you," she said, "but with the way Runa's troubles take her, I might need another pair of hands. Here," she said, taking a high, soft bun from a pile of them in a bowl on the table. "Eat this on the way." She gave Rosetta a small smile as she put the warm bun into the girl's snowy mitt. "You'll soon be married and doing this yourself. Now you'll learn what it's all about."

She gave a few instructions about the children to Mr. Fergusson, then took the carpetbag that sat on the floor under her coat.

Rosetta followed Mrs. Fergusson's broad back out into the night. Marry? Have her own babies? She thought, as she had many times since Christmas, about Iain's slow smile, the shine of his hair, his strong hands on her waist, catching her in the snowy circle, and the warmth of his breath on her cheek as they slid down the hill together.

But she couldn't let herself think about it, not about marrying or babies. Not about anything else, until she found Flora.

~

"Come now, lass, keep the fire going, strong and hot," Mrs. Fergusson urged Rosetta, as she came out of the bedroom. "And give your hands a good wash before you come in to help."

As Mrs. Fergusson had hurried into the bedroom with her

coat still on, Rosetta worked at the stove, starting a new fire and giving the growing flames a violent jab with the poker. She heard the soothing murmur of the woman's thick brogue over Runa's rasping voice.

Now she handed Mrs. Fergusson the kettle, and the woman bustled over to the sink. She filled the washbowl and, rolling up her sleeves, plunged her hands into it. "We'll want the place especially warm, for the baby." She grabbed a sliver of soap and washed and washed her hands, then dried them on a clean piece of flannel she pulled out of her carpetbag. She took the bag and went into the bedroom.

Rosetta scrubbed at her own hands and nails. Then she went to the bedroom and stood in the doorway, twisting her fingers together.

Mrs. Fergusson was at the foot of the bed, pulling the quilt back up over Runa's raised knees. "Good," she said. "Baby's the right way this time, Runa." She glanced over her shoulder. "You go and talk to her, Rosetta."

Rosetta went to the edge of the bed. Runa had her eyes closed and the spoon clamped between her teeth. Her breath came in harsh grunts around the wooden handle. As Rosetta watched, Runa's eyes flew open, and a desperate moan rose from her throat. The spoon dropped from her mouth, and she began chanting something in Icelandic, her eyes fixed on a spot over Rosetta's head.

Rosetta looked at Mrs. Fergusson. "What should I do? I don't know what she's saying."

Mrs. Fergusson shrugged, digging in her bag. "She's likely telling herself some story, to take her mind off the pain. It's good. You talk to her, help her through it."

186

Rosetta nodded, kneeling on the floor beside the bed. "Runa? Runa, look at me! Is it another of your poems, or one of your Icelandic sagas? Tell it to me. Tell me what you're saying."

Runa's eyes left the wall behind Rosetta, and she focused on the girl's face, shaking her head.

"Please. It will help. Tell me."

Runa tried to lick her lips. "The Sayings of the High One," she whispered. "There are eighteen verses. Eighteen."

"Good, good lass," Rosetta heard Mrs. Fergusson murmur. "That's the way."

"Which one were you saying, just then?" Rosetta asked, picking up one of Runa's hands and rubbing it between her own.

"The eighth. I was up to the eighth."

Rosetta rubbed Runa's hand harder as the woman's breath caught in her throat and her face contorted. Through it she spoke in Icelandic again, louder this time.

"Was that the ninth?" Rosetta asked. "Tell me the ninth saying."

Runa relaxed back a bit and closed her eyes.

"I know a ninth: If I ever need
to save my ship in a storm,
it will quiet the wind and calm the waves
soothing the sea."

"Quiet the wind and calm the waves," Rosetta repeated. "Soothing the sea. I like that. Think of it, Runa, the calm sea, the waves, just lapping –"

Runa suddenly struggled to a half-sitting position, whimpering. Rosetta dropped her hands and stood up.

"All right, all right, get ready," Mrs. Fergusson said, although Rosetta didn't know whether she was talking to her, to Runa, or to herself. The woman threw back the quilt and leaned between Runa's bony knees. "Go ahead, dear, go on now," she said, glancing up at Runa, then, seeing Rosetta standing there, she ordered, "Grab her hands, and let her pull."

Rosetta took hold of Runa's hands, and the woman gripped them firmly. Leaning back, she pulled so hard that Rosetta thought her shoulders would be yanked out of their sockets. She was shocked at Runa's strength.

As she pulled, Runa kept her eyes squeezed shut, and the moan stopped. It was replaced by a kind of low, fierce growling in her throat. Four times Runa pulled on Rosetta's hands, and each time Rosetta thought Runa couldn't do it any more, couldn't stand the pain. Her thin face was damp and white as paper, except for two bright spots high on her cheeks.

"That's it, lovie, that's it, you're doing fine," Mrs. Fergusson said during the fifth push. "Just a little longer, just a little –" She stopped abruptly, was busy with her hands for a moment, and then spoke again, the soothing tone of her voice changed. "Stop," she demanded. "Stop pushing, Runa. Rosetta, come!"

Rosetta drew her hands away from Runa and went to stand beside Mrs. Fergusson. Leaning over, she peered at Mrs. Fergusson's hands and saw a scowling face, no bigger than an apple. Twisted around the little bit of neck that showed was something that resembled a thick, grayish rope.

"Support the head, Rosetta, while I unwrap the cord," Mrs. Fergusson said. She deftly pushed and pulled as Rosetta replaced the woman's hands and cradled the tiny head, covered in fine, wet down. Then Mrs. Fergusson took a piece of flannel out of a wrapping of more flannel and quickly and expertly wiped the nose and mouth. She pinched the still cheeks and carefully inserted her smallest finger into the baby's mouth and scooped around.

"All right, all right, we're all right now," Mrs. Fergusson whispered, taking out her finger, then, louder, "one last push, Runa, and you'll have your baby." She looked at Rosetta. "You hold on now, Rosetta, and help me catch the baby." Before Rosetta had a chance to think, she felt the head slide forward, and then, in one smooth rush, the rest of the baby flowed out of Runa, into her own hands and the hands Mrs. Fergusson had placed just in front of Rosetta's.

She stared down at the perfect little body. Then she looked at Mrs. Fergusson. The woman pulled the baby upright and stroked and tapped the bottom of its feet.

"It's a girl," Rosetta whispered. Then, louder, "It's a girl, Runa. A baby girl."

She looked up at Runa. Runa was propping herself up on her elbows, staring at the top of Mrs. Fergusson's head, bent over the baby.

"Is she all right, Ada? Is she alive? She's not crying. Is she breathing? Ada?"

Runa's voice was loud, louder than Rosetta had ever heard her speak. She was surprised that Runa still had so much strength, could still call out so firmly.

"Ada?" Runa repeated. Then her voice sank, back to the quiet, uncertain tone Rosetta was more accustomed to. "Ada?"

Mrs. Fergusson finally looked up. "She's alive, Runa. She's very wee, but she's taken a few breaths. She's just too weak to cry."

Runa lay back. "She's alive," she repeated.

Mrs. Fergusson looked at Rosetta. She had the baby lying on a piece of clean flannel in her lap and was massaging its unmoving arms and legs. "Go and fill the washbasin with warm, clean water and bring it in," she said.

Rosetta nodded and did as she was told. "Thank you," Mrs. Fergusson said. "Now you go on out and wait in the kitchen. Make a bite to eat, for later. We'll all need our strength."

~

Mrs. Fergusson came out of the bedroom half an hour later. Rosetta turned from the stove. "Is she, is the baby all right, Mrs. Fergusson? Is she going to be all right?"

Mrs. Fergusson's head gave a tiny shake. "We'll know more by morning's light, dearie. If this little thing survives the night, then . . ." the woman paused, a concerned look in her eyes. "Well, best to look at things in the morning." She pointed her chin toward the pot on the stove. "Is that soup you've got there? I want Runa to eat something."

"Yes," Rosetta said. "It's from last night, only turnip and onion."

"That's fine," Mrs. Fergusson said. "Now, I'll stay on awhile. You have some of the soup, and then get some sleep. I have to be home before sun-up, for my own little ones, and then you'll take over. So best sleep while you can." She poured a ladle of soup into a bowl. "When will Mr. Thomas be home?"

"I don't know. He just went out sugaring today. He said he didn't know how long he'd stay, depending on the weather. He might not be home for another day. Maybe even two." She shook her head and pushed away the soup Mrs. Fergusson set in front of her. "I'm not hungry."

When Mrs. Fergusson went back to the bedroom, Rosetta added wood to the stove, then went upstairs and took the quilt from her bed. She brought it down and wrapped herself in it and sat in the rocking chair. Mrs. Fergusson was going back into the bedroom with more warm water. "You intend to stay down here?"

Rosetta nodded.

"All right then, make sure the stove doesn't go out." She looked at the girl in the lamplight, studying the paleness of her face and the dark shadows under her eyes.

Rosetta started rocking, slowly, her eyes glued on the bedroom door.

~

Each time the bedroom door opened throughout the long night, Rosetta sat up sleepily, her lips opening to ask the awful question. But each time, as Mrs. Fergusson made tea or took more warm water and clean flannels, she simply smiled a small, tight smile, and Rosetta knew there was no news, good or bad.

And all night, as she put wood into the stove and kept on turning up the wick on the oil lamp, she listened for the sound she wanted to hear.

But no baby's cries came from the bedroom, and the night passed, black and silent.

Chapter Twenty-Two

In the grayest hour, just before the sun struggled to make a shrouded appearance in the heavy morning sky, Mrs. Fergusson came out of the bedroom once more. This time she was wrapping her shawl over her head and shoulders. She held her finger to her lips as Rosetta jumped up, the quilt falling to the floor.

"Well, the bairn is still alive," Mrs. Fergusson said, then, seeing the smile breaking across Rosetta's face, shook her head. "It's still early to know if . . ." She stopped, then continued. "But the wee thing's color is a bit better, and Runa's trying to feed her now." She pinned the shawl securely in place. "Iain's here to fetch me, so it will fall on you to look after Runa. I'll come back tonight, for a quick look, and I'll send Iain into Magrath Corners to send word for the doctor."

Rosetta blew out the lamp. The room was still dark, but she knew that in a few minutes enough daylight would come through the windows to chase it away.

Mrs. Fergusson picked up her bag and opened the door. Rosetta caught sight of the Fergussons' wagon. A figure huddled on the seat, the reins loose in his mittened hands. The horse tossed its head, white frost coating his long muzzle.

"I'll get Iain to come back, after he takes me home, and do the milking and chores for you."

"I can do them."

Mrs. Fergusson studied Rosetta's face. "You let him. You've got enough to do with taking care of Runa."

Rosetta nodded, not quite able to hide the relief on her face.

"All right then. Try and get Runa to take some food. She'll need her strength for whatever is to come." She looked into Rosetta's face, shadowy in the dim room. "And so will you, dear. So will you," she said, then was gone.

~

Mr. Thomas arrived home at nine o'clock that morning. He came into the house, shaking the snow out of his clothes, and sat down at the table.

"Got everything done out in the barn?" he asked. Rosetta knew he would have checked when he put the horses away, but she answered anyway.

"It's done. But yesterday –"

The man cut her off. "Sap runnin' like water at first, but the cold slowed it down. Thought I may as well come back until this afternoon, when it warms up. Now I need some hot food, and a few hours' sleep before I go back out."

Rosetta could hardly stand it. "Mr. Thomas, Mrs. Thomas had –"

Again, Mr. Thomas interrupted. "I'll have my mush now. Had a cup of tea in camp, but I'm near froze. Make a fresh pot, and get my breakfast."

Rosetta ignored his requests and came and stood in front of him. "Mr. Thomas, Mrs. Thomas had the baby yesterday."

Her voice rang in a singsong; she spoke as quickly as possible so she couldn't be interrupted again. "A little girl, but she's very poorly. Mrs. Thomas is all right; she's sleeping."

Mr. Thomas stood up, blinking. "Yesterday? She birthed yesterday? Why'd she go and do that? Not time." He stood up, and although his voice and words were surly, his eyes darted from side to side. He rubbed his hand over his whiskered chin and strode toward the bedroom door.

Rosetta stepped in front of him. "She's sleeping," she said again. "She hasn't slept much, and I think it's good for her to sleep right now. Mrs. Fergusson said she needs to rest."

But Mr. Thomas didn't pay any attention to her. He opened the door and went in. Rosetta followed him. He went to the bed and looked down. Runa opened her eyes.

"Well," Mr. Thomas said.

"A girl, Albert," Runa said. She smiled.

Mr. Thomas looked down at the bundle in Runa's arms. "Doesn't look much like the others." Rosetta could see Runa in the miniature face and finely arched brows, and in the coating of white-blonde hair, fluffy and even lighter after it had dried. The baby's skin had the translucent bluish tinge of skimmed milk.

Runa's smile faded. "No," she said. The baby made a squeak, and Runa sat up, wincing, but her smile returning. She gazed at the baby, and caressed the soft blanket wrapped around the tiny form.

"Don't set your hopes too high on this one neither," Mr. Thomas said. "Her being a girl and all, and lookin' so puny." He stood for a moment, looking down at his wife and baby, and then turned and started out of the room.

Runa tore her gaze away from the baby, and Rosetta watched the woman's eyes follow her husband as he left the room.

"I want to call her Soffia," Runa said. "It was my mother's name."

Mr. Thomas stopped, but didn't turn around. "Too fancy. Never heard of no girl 'round here called Soffia."

Runa's lips pressed together. "I will call her Soffia."

Rosetta stood perfectly still.

After a long moment, Mr. Thomas shrugged and went through the doorway. "Do what you want," he said. His voice sounded strange. Rosetta thought that maybe he didn't care what Runa called the baby because he didn't think she would live anyway. She looked at Runa, still sitting there, staring at her husband's disappearing back.

And now there was something in her pale eyes, a cold glitter, that Rosetta had never seen before. It made Runa look a whole lot different.

When Rosetta went back into the kitchen, Mr. Thomas wasn't there. She looked out the front door, but there was no sign of him. Then she looked out the window over the sink and saw him, a lone figure, walking out to the barn. She saw that he had forgotten to wear his hat. He always wore his hat outside. But as she watched, he passed the barn and kept going. Rosetta realized that he was going to the old tree. When she saw him stop there and stand, his bare head lowered, she turned away, feeling as if she was spying on something she wasn't supposed to see.

~

Runa and the baby slept most of the day. Mrs. Fergusson came in the late afternoon and stayed in the bedroom for half an hour. When she came out, she spoke to Mr. Thomas.

"Now, Albert, you make sure you let Runa rest a spell. Don't make her get up; she's weak. Remember what —"

"I know, I know," Mr. Thomas interrupted. "But I didn't have no help in the house that last time, and it was harvest time. Someone had to make the meals."

Mrs. Fergusson looked at Rosetta. "Well, you have Rosetta now, so there's no reason Runa can't stay right abed for at least four or five days. Doctor's up at Millbrook; there's an outbreak of scarlet fever there. He won't be back until the weekend at least. Mind, there's not much he can do anyway. It's not in our hands whether that little one lives or dies. The fact that she's still alive shows she's stronger than she looks."

Mr. Thomas just nodded glumly, and after Mrs. Fergusson left, Rosetta gave him his supper. When he went out to the barn to do the chores, she carried the lamp and a plate of food to Runa.

Runa was awake, holding Soffia, staring down into her face.

"How is she?" Rosetta whispered, setting the lamp on the dresser.

Runa nodded. "I just fed her, and she seemed to take a little more than last time." She smiled at Rosetta. "You don't have to whisper. Babies don't wake up that easily." The smile left her face. "Why did you come back, Rosetta? What made you come back, after you'd left?"

Rosetta put the food on the dresser beside the lamp. "I've been waiting to show you. There hasn't been a chance before now. Wait."

She ran back to the kitchen and fished in the pocket of her coat, pulling out the letter for Runa. She glanced out the window and saw Mr. Thomas swinging the ax near the woodpile, then hurried back to the bedroom.

"Look! A letter, for you." She fanned the air with the envelope.

Runa's mouth opened. She held out her hand, took the envelope and studied the writing on the front. "Yes. I could never forget her handwriting." She stared at it for a long time.

"Well? Aren't you going to open it?" Rosetta asked. "Here, I'll take Soffia." She gently took the sleeping baby from the crook of Runa's arm and laid her in the cradle Mr. Thomas had brought down from the upstairs room.

Runa picked at the sealed flap of the envelope. She slowly withdrew the single folded sheet of paper, and as she began to open it, a few worn bills fell to the quilt. Runa looked at them, then up at Rosetta.

"Read it, Runa, read it," Rosetta urged.

Runa nodded, and her eyes started to move back and forth over the page, covered with tiny, cramped words.

Rosetta listened to the rhythmic chopping of the ax. Finally, Runa set the letter on the quilt, beside the money.

"She never got any of my letters, Rosetta. All the ones I wrote those first few years. When she got to Gimli, Papa wouldn't give her any freedom. She had her baby, and she had to do what Papa said, so he'd let her stay. She had nowhere else to go. And he never gave her any letters. She never even knew I wrote, Rosetta." She stopped, then shook her head and went on. "Papa died over two years ago. Gerdur married last year, and she has a nice husband and is expecting a baby in the summer. Her son, her first child, is a big, healthy boy." She ran her fingers over the paper. "She says so many things,

Rosetta. About how young we were. About how people change."

Runa picked up the bills. "Her husband gave her these to send to me." She folded the money in half and set it down on the quilt again. "Gerdur wants me to come there, to Gimli. The money is for the train ticket. She wants me to come right away, and have the baby there." She looked at the cradle.

Rosetta put her hand on its polished hood, rocking it ever so gently. The chopping stopped.

"Will you go?" she asked.

Runa looked up at her. "I don't know, Rosetta." She looked back to the cradle. "I'm afraid to go, but I'm afraid to stay. There's been only bad luck for me here with my babies. But Albert . . ."

Rosetta nodded.

"I have to think about it," Runa said. "So much depends on Soffia." She fingered the bills. "You take some of this." The sound of feet crunching through the snow came close to the house.

Rosetta shook her head. "No. You'll need it."

"Can you keep it for me?" Runa asked, scooping up the bills and letter and shoving them into the envelope. "Put it with your things. He might find it here. And Rosetta?"

The woodshed door crashed open.

"I know I told you to go. But now I'm asking you to stay, for just a little longer, a few weeks. Will you? Please? Until I decide what to do? Until Soffia . . . until we know that she . . ." She grabbed Rosetta's hands. "I'm more afraid, now, now that I have her." She looked at the cradle. "I'm braver when you're here. Please don't leave. Please."

Chapter Twenty-Three

Winter eased in and out, seeming to lose its strength each time it tried to return, and as it grew weaker, Soffia grew stronger. Day by day she nursed a little more, and her arms and legs started to lose their stick-like appearance. Her eyes began to focus, and her cheeks were no longer flat.

And soon there were only a few mounds of rotted snow on the north side of the barn, and the rest of the farmyard was oozing mud, drying in the persistent wind that blew in from the west.

Rosetta was busy around the clock. Although the baby's health was improving, Runa's wasn't. She seemed weak, uninterested in eating, and Rosetta had a hard time to even convince her to change her nightdress or brush her hair. The only thing she showed interest in was Soffia. She kept her in her arms at all times, not even wanting Mrs. Fergusson to take her for a few minutes to look her over. Mrs. Fergusson had shown Rosetta how to bathe the baby, and how to rub her back and walk with her when she drew up her tiny knees and cried after some of her feedings. Runa watched from the bed, wearing a distressed look the whole time.

Rosetta had scrubbed down a crate and lined it with an old piece of a quilt, washed soft and smooth. She put it on the kitchen table, and whenever she could, she convinced Runa to let her take the baby so the woman could have a few hours of sleep. Then she'd put Soffia in the crate so she could keep an eye on her while she worked, and so that the baby's small squeaks and occasional cries didn't waken Runa. When she noticed the baby staying awake for longer and longer periods, Rosetta propped her up with a little pillow. She was sure the baby followed her movements around the kitchen with her round eyes. They were still a dark, murky blue, but Rosetta thought she could already detect them lightening.

"You need to get up, and get out, Runa, love," Mrs. Fergusson said after one visit. "It does you no good, lying abed all this time. Your wee girl there is a little fighter, she is, and you mustn't spend all the hours God gave you worrying that she won't live. Now, I want Albert to bring you over for Sunday dinner. Get up and dressed, and get Rosetta to do something nice with your hair, and come over in the carriage. It will be good for the baby, too, to have some fresh air. The bite is gone from the air now. It won't harm her to take her outside." She looked over at Albert. "You hear me now, Albert Thomas. Bring your little family over to our place this Sunday. I won't settle for any excuses."

~

When Sunday came, the sun shone with its first genuine warmth. Mr. Thomas hitched the horse to the wagon.

"Reckon it's a good day for a visit after all," he announced, coming into the kitchen and leaving the door open to let in the soft, fragrant air. "And like Ada said, sitting around ain't doing you no good." Runa was out of bed, in a chair near the table, holding Soffia tightly against her. Rosetta had helped her into her second-best dress, and had made a looser knot with her hair and tied a light blue ribbon around it.

Runa picked at the cuff of her sleeve. "I'm not sure I'm feeling well enough to go, Albert. Maybe a few more weeks."

"Nonsense. You're just feeling sorry for yourself. You look fine today." He hesitated. "Real pretty. Now, I'll be waiting. Come outside when you're ready."

As he started to go toward the door, Rosetta said, "I'll change Soffia one more time before I put on my navy dress."

"No need for you to go," Mr. Thomas said. "You stay here and open up the parlor. Needs doing now spring is here. And have supper ready."

Rosetta silently took the baby from Runa's arms and carried her into the bedroom and undressed her. As she changed Soffia's diaper, Rosetta noticed, for the first time, that the tiny legs had enough fat on them to show the beginnings of dimples on her knees. The baby waved and kicked her bare legs in the air. When Soffia was in fresh clothes and bundled in a warm blanket, Rosetta kissed the baby's satiny cheek and handed her to Runa.

"I'm sorry you can't come with us," Runa said. Her hands shook slightly as she tied her bonnet ribbons beneath her chin.

"It's all right," Rosetta said, trying not to think about Iain while she listened to Runa's instructions on opening the parlor.

~

After the wagon had rolled out of the yard, Rosetta looked into the darkened parlor and sighed, then got to work. First, she opened all the curtains and pulled up the blinds. She carried the rag carpet to the clothesline, where she thwacked and thumped it with a wire beater, trying to stand back as the dust billowed out. Leaving it there to air, she went back inside and dusted all the parlor furniture and washed the wooden floor. Then she brought the rug in, laid it down, and sprinkled it with pepper to discourage insects.

She worked hard and fast so she would still have a few hours to call her own before the Thomases returned. She kept thinking about Runa. What was wrong with her? Soffia was growing and thriving. If only Runa would start acting like her old self and tell Rosetta she didn't need her any more.

Rosetta had written to Flora the day after Soffia was born. She told her that she was coming to her, right away, that she knew where she was, only a few days' away. "There's a new baby girl here, Flora," she wrote. "And as soon as the mother is better, I'll be coming to you. The baby's name is Soffia, and she's lovely. When I hold her, I think about you when you were a baby. Can you remember when I used to hold you and sing to you? Do you remember all that, Flora?"

But she hadn't been able to mail the letter yet. It sat under her pallet with her money and the books Miss Jasper had left that long-ago Saturday.

When she was done, she walked around the yard, giving the whistle that brought Sigi racing to her from wherever he was. She stroked the dog. "Come on, Sigi," she said. "Let's go." She ran down the lane to the road, then back up, the dog running beside her, his ears straight back and his tongue lolling out of one side of his mouth. As Rosetta ran, jumping over the wettest patches of yellow mud, she unpinned her hair and dropped the pins in her apron pocket. Now her heavy, waist-length hair flew out behind her. In the middle of the yard Rosetta closed her eyes, put her head back and, with her arms straight out at her sides, started spinning. She spun and spun, with Sigi barking and running in his own frenzied circles around her. Then she would stop and open her eyes and laugh out loud as the house and barn and fields beyond dipped and swayed.

She kept up her game until she was breathless and strands of hair stuck to her cheeks and neck. She undid the top button of her dress, then, as she combed through her hair with her fingers, decided to take a bath.

As she hauled pail after pail of water from the pump to the stove, heating enough to fill the copper bathing tub much deeper than usual, she hummed. How wonderful it would be to take a real bath, a long, quiet, private one, not like the usual hurried ones in the corner of the kitchen, behind the blanket temporarily strung between two nails, with barely enough water to cover the bottom of the tub.

She planned to bathe, dry her hair in the sun, then go out to the loft to look for any new kittens or the beginnings of swallows' nests, then wander into the wooded area and see if the trilliums were up.

Just before she undressed, she opened the door for Sigi. "No one's here. You can stay inside with me for a while." The dog scampered in, sniffing excitedly in each corner of the room. "Down," Rosetta said, as she laid her clothes neatly over the back of a chair and climbed into the tub. The dog curled into a lazy circle beside the tub, his chin on his paws, his golden eyes dreamy and relaxed.

Rosetta sang out loud as she washed herself with the

biggest piece of soft soap she could find in the cup. Then she slid under the water and scrubbed her hair with it. Sitting up again, she rinsed it with clear water from the pail she'd put beside the tub, pouring dipper after dipper over her head until her hair squeaked between her fingers.

Getting out of the tub, she dried herself with a large, clean flannel. As she was briskly rubbing at her hair, Sigi jumped up and stared at the door, his legs stiff, the hair along the back of his neck bristly.

"What is it, Sigi?" As a low rumble started in the dog's throat, she grabbed her petticoat and yanked it over her head. She picked up her dress, but before she could put it on, the door banged open. Rosetta gasped and held her dress up in front of her.

Sigi raced forward and grabbed at the pant leg of the man in the doorway. The dog shook the pant leg, growling and snarling.

"Stop! Stop it, Sigi," Rosetta called. "It's only Eli."

Sigi stopped, but kept the material in his mouth, half looking back at Rosetta.

"I said stop, Sigi," Rosetta repeated.

The dog let go of the cloth and took a step back, but the rumbling, like a trapped bumblebee, still came from his throat.

Eli stood there, turning his cap in his hands. His lips opened in a grin, showing a row of stained teeth.

"Beg pardon, Rosetta," he said. "I come to speak to Mr. Thomas, about when he wants me to start taking off the hay." He took a step into the kitchen, then moved back again as Sigi's growling rose a tone.

Rosetta gripped the cotton of her dress tightly against her. "He's not here," she said, and then glanced at the closed bedroom door. "Mrs. Thomas is resting," she said, the lie coming out of nowhere.

Eli looked at the door, then back to Rosetta. His eyes traveled down her body, resting on her bare ankles and feet. "Well, I best not disturb you at your Sunday scrub," he said, still staring at her feet. "Tell Mr. Thomas I'm free whenever he wants me."

"I'll tell him," Rosetta answered, holding her chin high, aware of her wet hair dripping down the back of her petticoat.

"Good day to you, then," Eli said, still grinning. But just as he put his hand on the doorknob, he looked back at her. "Glad we'll be able to get to know one another better," he said. "You and me, I think we'll get along real well." Then he left, the door standing wide open behind him.

Rosetta waited until she heard his footsteps thud down the wooden porch steps, then ran to the door and closed it, leaning against it for a moment. She peeked out the window and saw Eli on his horse, plodding down the lane.

She dropped to her knees and put her arms around the little dog's neck. "Good boy," she whispered. "Good, good dog, Sigi." The dog looked at her and wagged his tail slowly.

After Rosetta finished dressing, she went outside and sat on the top step, turning her face upward and closing her eyes. She raked her fingers through the strands of shining chestnut hair, holding them out to let the sun through to dry them.

But every few minutes she opened her eyes and peered down the lane. Now she didn't feel like going out to the loft, or looking for trilliums, or playing with Sigi any more.

The image of Eli's dull eyes, with their puffy pink lids, roaming down her body wouldn't leave her mind.

~

The Thomases came back shortly after Rosetta had laid out a cold supper and was darning a pair of Runa's stockings. Runa went into the bedroom, and while she was there, Mr. Thomas came in and washed up, then sat down at the table. When Runa joined them, the baby still in her arms, she had changed back into her everyday dress. She looked at Rosetta, sitting with the stocking in her lap. "Won't you be eating?"

"No, I had something earlier," Rosetta answered. "Mr. Thomas, Eli came by. He said to tell you to let him know when you're ready for him."

Mr. Thomas gave a nod and dug into the food. "Hope he can start right away. We'll get at that first haying in another week, if it don't rain too much. Animals all looked after?" he asked.

"Yes," Rosetta answered, going back to her darning.

"I best check after I eat anyways," he said. As soon as he'd wiped his plate with the last crust of his bread, he got up and went out.

Runa had hardly eaten a bite. "Rosetta," she said. "I have to tell you something."

Rosetta put down the stocking with the darning egg in the toe.

"What I want to tell you is that I've made up my mind. I want to go and see Gerdur for a while." Rosetta saw that there was actually some color in Runa's face.

"You're really going? All the way to Gimli? To Manitoba?"

Runa nodded. "I talked for a long time with Ada. I don't know why I feel so sad, even with Soffia here. She told me it happens sometimes. That maybe I need a change. To be somewhere else. I told her about the letter from Gerdur, and she said it was important for me to go. If I want to get better."

Runa clasped her hands in her lap. "I think she's right. It is this place that scares me right now, with Soffia, because of what happened to my little boys. I know that she's already lived longer than either of them, but still . . . once she's a little older, even a few months, I'll stop worrying, but for now, oh, I can't sleep, or eat, without thinking that she's stopped breathing.

"But I'm frightened. When Albert finds out . . . I can't tell him." She looked down at Soffia, running the back of her forefinger up and down the sleeping baby's cheek.

Rosetta snipped the darning thread with her teeth and sat quietly with her.

"But the hardest thing," Runa said, "will be to have to say good-bye to you again."

Rosetta watched Runa's mouth.

"It's because of you that Soffia was born safely, and because of you that I wrote to Gerdur again. So now, before I go, I will tell Albert that you are going to write your examinations. I have asked Ada to take Shelagh out of school and send her over for two days this week. I owe at least this to you."

"When will you go?" Rosetta asked.

"By the first of May. By then, I know that Soffia will be ready to travel," Runa said. "If you help me. Just this one more time. I will only tell Albert on the day I'm going, when Iain comes to take me and Soffia to Magrath Corners. Mrs. Fergusson is arranging a paid carriage for me to Thomson's Landing, and I'll take the train from there to Winnipeg.

Gerdur told me, in her letter, that by the end of April there are barges and tugboats that run regularly from Winnipeg to Gimli.

"And Rosetta, once I am gone, then you must go, too." When she finished all of this, she suddenly got up and laid Soffia in the crate beside the table. She came to Rosetta, leaned down and hugged her tightly. It was the first time they had touched, really touched each other, except for one handshake and Rosetta helping Runa when she had Soffia.

Rosetta sat still, too surprised to move, and then put her arms around Runa's thin back.

She didn't know why the hug made her feel so sad, only that it felt more like a good-bye than anything else.

Chapter Twenty-Four

Rosetta wiped her forehead on the sleeve of her dress. It was hot, hot for the first day of May. She looked toward the far field and saw the billows of dirt clotted over Eli as he followed the horse-drawn seeder drill. He'd been working at the farm for the last two weeks. Like Ben had the year before, he slept out in the old shanty.

Rosetta hated him, hated the way his eyes followed her everywhere, whether he was sitting on a stump outside the shanty after work at night, smoking one of his rolled cigarettes, or in the kitchen for meals. He always appeared, out of nowhere, it seemed, as Rosetta was coming out of the barn in the morning or worked at putting in the garden after supper. She would come around a corner, or look up from what she was working on, and he would be there, his eyes burning holes into her, his thin lips pulled back in a leering smile.

She knew Runa was almost ready to go, and that meant she would be going, too. It had been a busy few weeks. Runa had kept her promise, and one early morning little Shelagh appeared at the door during breakfast.

"Go to the school, today, Rosetta," Runa said. "Go and do your examinations. And good luck." Rosetta had put down the frying pan and stared at the back of Mr. Thomas's head as he ate his breakfast. It didn't move, except for the steady up and down of his ears as he chewed. Rosetta didn't wait to do anything but wash her hands, and then was gone.

The school was empty except for the smallest children. All the older ones were at home, helping with the seeding or gardening. Miss Jasper smiled at her warmly and set a thick stack of papers in front of her.

It took Rosetta two days to work through the provincial exams, but she completed the last one just before three o'clock on the second day.

"Wonderful," Miss Jasper said. "I'll forward these on to the school board to be marked. They'll send me the results as soon as they're done. I know you'll have passed them all with flying colors. They'll keep the records there, in Peterborough, and all you have to do, if you need your recommendation to teach, is write them, and they'll send on your verification. That's it. You've done it, Rosetta."

"Thank you, Miss Jasper." She drew an envelope and a few pennies out of her pocket. "Could you mail this for me when you go home tonight?"

Miss Jasper took the envelope and looked at the name on it. Her face broke into a smile. "Is this your sister? You've found her then?"

Rosetta grinned back. "Yes. And I'm going to her, in Cobourg. Any day."

"I'm glad for you," Miss Jasper said. "Good luck. Perhaps some day we'll run across each other, both teachers in a school."

"Perhaps," Rosetta said, still smiling.

She had walked home slowly, thinking about Flora's birthday. It was May sixteenth, and she intended to be with her for it. Flora's sixth birthday had been at sea, on the *Corsican*. There had been nothing to celebrate with, but at least they had been together.

After she'd finished her work for the day, Rosetta looked through the rag basket. As well as a wool sock that had the whole toe gone, there was a threadbare muslin petticoat of Runa's and a piece of a large checked handkerchief. Rosetta started to cut and sew.

Over the next few days she worked on the muslin in time snatched between chores, finishing it off in the near dark in her room. When she had it done, she smiled, pleased. It was just a small white doll, a little bigger than her hand. From the handkerchief, Rosetta had even made a tiny dress to go over the muslin-stuffed torso and arms and legs.

The doll was nothing like the beautiful, porcelain-headed ones with painted features and fancy dresses that Rosetta remembered from her own early childhood. But the stitches were tiny and neat, and the line of the red thread mouth and the blue x's of the eyes were cheerful and friendly.

Her eyes had burned after working over the doll in the fading light, and her shoulders were stiff from hunching forward on her bed. But the doll was perfect. It was a birthday gift for Flora, and Rosetta would be with her to give it to her. In a sudden rush of excitement, Rosetta had kissed the little doll's face. Then she put it into her trunk and closed the lid, imagining the look on Flora's face as she gave her the doll.

~

Rosetta went into Runa's bedroom. Runa was sitting in the rocking chair in the corner, nursing Soffia. "Will you be going soon? It's the first week of May, Runa."

Runa shrugged dully. "Yes. I know I should."

"It's Albert, isn't it? You're afraid to tell him."

"Yes. He won't let me leave. I know it."

Rosetta took a deep breath. "Then you should just go."

Runa caressed the baby's feathery hair. "How can I do that? He'd think I was running away, leaving him, just like Gerdur did. But I'm not. I would come back to him." She rested her hand on the baby's head. "But I'm tired, and scared. What should I do, Rosetta?"

Watching her and the way her limp hands touched the baby, Rosetta knew Runa might not go at all. And then how would she leave? Already Shelagh was needed more and more by her mother for the summer work. It was only going to get harder.

"I'm going over to talk to Mrs. Fergusson today," Rosetta said. "I'm going to tell her that you're ready to go, and we'll decide on the day."

Runa looked up, her face stricken. "But I'm not ready."

Rosetta sat down beside her. "You might never be, Runa. But it will be good for you. You'll come back with Soffia big and healthy, and feel better about everything. And I'll get Mrs. Fergusson to help me tell Mr. Thomas, so he'll understand."

Runa shook her head. "I don't know," she said listlessly.

"I do," Rosetta said.

~

A few days later Mr. Thomas and Eli went out to plant the back field. They took the lunch Rosetta had made them, wrapped in a dish towel, and two jars of water.

"If we don't stop, me and Eli can get it all done before dark," he said to Rosetta. "Make sure you work on the garden today."

"Yes," Rosetta said, bending over the table as she kneaded the bread dough on a floury circle. As soon as the door closed behind him, she hurried into the bedroom.

"All right. It's time. They're gone for the whole day. Get your bag packed, and I'll get the baby ready." When Runa started to shake her head, Rosetta took her by the hands. "Come on. Mrs. Fergusson has arranged everything. Don't worry." She took the carpetbag from under the bed.

"Can you give me a piece of paper, and the pencil?" Runa asked.

Rosetta nodded, then took the baby out to the kitchen, leaving Runa sitting on the edge of the bed. The baby cried sleepily, fussing at being awakened, but Rosetta bathed and dressed her and put her into the padded crate. Then she ran upstairs to get the letter and money from Gerdur that was still under her pallet, and also took one of the two sheets of paper she had left. She hurried downstairs with it, grabbing the little pencil out of the sideboard on her way through the kitchen, and took it all into the bedroom.

At least she's up and has brushed her hair, Rosetta thought. "Here's the paper and the money for your ticket. Put it in your bag. I'll pack you some food," she said, taking Runa's new linsey-woolsey dress down off the peg and laying it out on the bed. "Put this on."

Rosetta went out to the kitchen to cut bread and cheese, and shortly Runa came out of the bedroom, half dragging the bulging carpetbag with both hands. She had the piece of paper between her teeth.

As she dropped the carpetbag to the floor with a thud, she gave Rosetta the paper, her eyes darting around the room. "This is for Albert. Have I forgotten anything?"

"No," Rosetta said, opening the carpetbag and putting Soffia's clothes and diapers on top. "I'll take your bag and the food out to the barn. You just carry Soffia."

Runa held Soffia while Rosetta struggled to get Josie harnessed to the wagon, then both women climbed up. As they started toward the road, Sigi chasing the cart out of the yard and then going back to his shade by the porch, Runa turned in the seat and looked back at the old tree until it was out of sight.

~

Rosetta wiped Josie down and gave her fresh water.

In the house, she saw that the dough she had been kneading for bread had risen and fallen and was useless. She threw it into the slop pail for the pigs and started some more and fried some pieces of chicken, rehearsing what she would say to Mr. Thomas when he came home. She put the folded piece of paper on the shelf in front of the pine clock. Then she spent what was left of the afternoon pushing the small hand plow through the clods of earth in the big garden behind the house.

Just before five o'clock, she set the table with three places, and then went back out to work in the garden.

She looked up as Mr. Thomas came into the yard and splashed water over his head and arms at the pump.

"Supper ready?" he called to Rosetta.

"Yes," she called back and, wiping her hands on her apron, slowly walked to the house. When she came in, Mr. Thomas was standing in the middle of the kitchen. The parlor and bedroom doors were wide open.

"Where's Runa?" he demanded.

Rosetta looked down. "There's a note, by the clock."

Mr. Thomas strode over to the shelf and snatched at the paper. He opened it, then flung it at Rosetta. It fluttered to the floor like a small, weary bird and rested there, between them.

Mr. Thomas kicked it toward her with his toe. "Pick it up and tell me what it says."

Rosetta bent and picked up the paper.

"Dear Albert," she read, "I have gone to visit Gerdur. I know you will be very unhappy, but I think it will be good for me, and for Soffia. I will be back, I promise, and I will write, soon. Please try and understand. I'm sorry."

Rosetta looked up. "It's signed, Runa."

She gasped as Mr. Thomas grabbed her wrist and pulled her toward him. "You did this, didn't you?"

Rosetta looked away from the fury in his eyes.

"She's my wife, girl. She can't just go off like that. She had no money." His voice rose, until he was shouting. "She would never of gone if it weren't for you, aren't I right?" He squeezed Rosetta's wrist harder, shaking it, and Rosetta had to bite her lips not to whimper.

"Mr. Thomas,," she said, loudly. "This is between you and Mrs. Thomas. The letter said she'd write."

Mr. Thomas stared at her.

"Let me go," Rosetta said, not as loud, but firmly.

Mr. Thomas stared for another minute, then let go of her wrist. Rosetta rubbed it with her other hand.

"But you know all about it, don't you? Don't you, girl?" There were flecks of saliva at the corners of his mouth.

Rosetta motioned at the table. "I made supper." She knew food wouldn't distract him, but she couldn't think of anything else to say. "And Mrs. Fergusson is coming over to talk to you."

The man's face was still contorted with shock and anger. "They were in on it, too? They're supposed to be our friends." He looked at the table, then ran his hands through his hair, still wet from the pump, making it stand up in straight spikes. He looked back at Rosetta, opened his mouth as if he was going to say something, but closed it again.

Eli came into the kitchen, but stepped aside as Mr. Thomas pushed passed him and headed to the barn. Rosetta went outside and sat on the step, brushing Sigi until Eli had finished eating and silently went out to the shanty. He leaned against the rough logs of the little old house, smoking and watching Rosetta.

She went inside and took the two clean dishes off the table and set them back on the shelves and put away the leftover food. Then she sat down at the table, and waited.

Chapter Twenty-Five

It was growing dark by the time Mrs. Fergusson came over. "I'm sorry I was so long, dear. Geordie is down with a bad stomach, and all he wanted was his ma. I had to wait until he fell asleep. How did Albert take it?"

"About how we expected. Mad. He's gone off somewhere."

"Well, he's bound to be back to sleep. And I'll wait right here with you, until he comes. I won't leave you until I know you'll be all right."

Rosetta lit the lamp on the table. "Mr. Thomas gets terribly angry, but I'm not really afraid of him." She turned up the wick a bit. "It's that Eli," she said, studying the flame.

"I don't know much about him. He's not from around here, but he doesn't look a pleasant sort." She stood up and looked out the doorway. "I hear a horse coming."

In a few minutes Mr. Thomas strode into the kitchen, his hat and clothes covered with a layer of grime from the clouds of dust a galloping horse would have made on the soft road.

"What do you have to tell me, Ada?" he said, his eyes glittering. "You not actin' very neighborly."

"You just sit yourself down here, Albert, and listen to me. That wife of yours was in a bad way, with no sign of getting better any time soon. Having a baby will take a woman like that. I know, I've seen it before, and more than once. And with your Runa, there was even more to make her so blue. All the worry about misfortune repeating itself, with Soffia coming early and being such a wee thing to start off, and still not exactly thriving. And so yes, I thought it was best that she go and visit her sister, have something else on her mind. I don't approve of the way she did it, going off without talking to you about it first, but that was her only way of dealing with it."

"You give her money to go?"

Mrs. Fergusson looked at Rosetta. "That's not important. That sister of hers will most likely tell her she's got the most beautiful baby in the world, tell her everything will be all right, and make her believe it. Apart from a mother, there's nothing like a sister when a woman needs comfort."

Mr. Thomas made a noise in his throat, but Mrs. Fergusson tapped the table.

"I'm not done yet. And speaking of sisters, this girl here is off to hers now. She's helped you out here for a whole year now, with not much to show for it, and done a good job, as far as I can see."

Rosetta traced a crack in the tabletop with her fingernail. "And besides, it's not right, a young girl alone here with two men. Runa knows Rosetta has to go, and they've said their farewells."

"And what about when she comes back? Will she be able to manage again, without the girl?"

"For now, old Ben's daughter is going to come over for a few days a week. We already talked to her in town. You know she's a widow, with her own children almost grown, and now that her old father can't work any more she's looking for anything going. Says she'll be willing to cook and do laundry and tend the garden while Runa's gone, in exchange for what you have to give her. Eggs, milk, garden produce, a chicken now and then. And when Runa comes back, she'll most likely keep coming out to help as needed."

Albert looked away.

"Well, that's all of it. Rosetta will go tomorrow, as soon as she's got her things together," Mrs. Fergusson said and stood up. "You won't be giving her any trouble, will you now, Albert? Because if I think you will, I'll take her on home with me right now."

Mr. Thomas shook his head.

"Good. Then I'll say good night and be away home. Rosetta, I'll send Iain for you in the late afternoon, after he's finished helping his pa, and you come on over and stay for supper and the night, and then we'll find a ride for you up to Cobourg."

Rosetta stood up and faced the woman. "Thank you, Mrs. Fergusson, for everything."

There was a muffled sound from Albert. Mrs. Fergusson glanced at him, then patted Rosetta's arm.

"We'll see you tomorrow, then, dear."

"Yes. Tomorrow," Rosetta said.

~

Rosetta couldn't fall asleep. She was too excited about the thought of being in Cobourg in only a few days. She had gone up to bed as soon as Mrs. Fergusson left, not wanting to be around Mr. Thomas. She heard him go outside, then heard him come in again. His footsteps were heavy, stomping around the house, and she heard him pumping water in the kitchen, the clatter as he dropped something heavy, and then a loud string of curses. He went in and out again. Finally, he called her, not seeming to realize it was close to the middle of the night, or not caring.

"Rosetta! Get down here."

Rosetta wrapped her quilt around her and came down the stairs, peeking around the opening. The kitchen was a mess, food spread on the table, the kettle laying on its side on the floor. A tall bottle half filled with amber liquid stood in the middle of the table. Mr. Thomas looked wild, his hair every which way, his shirt only partly buttoned, and the pupils of his eyes huge and black.

"I'm going," he said. "And when I get back, you better be gone, too. Go! Just like she did. And don't you ever let me see your face again." Fine drops of saliva flew from his mouth. His words were heavy and some ran together. "Got no use for women. All they do is leave. So you hurry up and get outta here, too. You be gone when I get home."

He grabbed the bottle and stumbled out. Rosetta heard him cursing as he walked away from the house, and by the time she had gone back up to her room, the thundering of a horse's hooves echoed outside her open window.

Chapter Twenty-Six

Rosetta slept longer than she ever had on the farm, the sun already quite high by the time she opened her eyes. The house was quiet, not a sound anywhere. She quickly got up and dressed, and went to the kitchen. She stood in the middle of the room, where she could see into the bedroom. The cover of the bed was still pulled neat and straight, as she had made it when Runa left the day before.

It took her a while to tidy up the mess Mr. Thomas had created. She heated water and put all the dishes into the dishpan and swished the warm water around, staring ahead of her, out the window. She could see Eli, just visible as he bent over in the field behind the barn, repairing a fence. Clouds of dry yellow dust swirled in lonely circles around the barn.

This is the last time I'll look out this window, Rosetta thought, and just then Eli stopped, straightened, and looked at the house. Rosetta took her hands out of the dishpan and backed away from the window, even though she knew Eli couldn't see her through the window from this distance. Her wet hands dripped dirty dishwater into a tiny pool at her feet.

~

Standing beside the stove, Rosetta ate a few spoonfuls of the thick soup she had just finished making. She had to wait until

Iain came for her, and she'd rather keep busy inside the house then go out and risk having to run into Eli. She would try to avoid him all day, and as long as there was food ready when he came in at noon, he'd have no excuse to call her or come looking for her. She put a bowl of it on the table, covering it with another bowl to keep it hot. She put out a platter of ham, and sawed thick slices of yesterday's bread, and set it, alongside the crock of butter, on the table. She covered everything with a cloth, set a pitcher of cold tea beside it, then looked out the kitchen window. She could still see Eli in the field, but knew he'd be in for his dinner at exactly twelve noon, like always.

She had already taken the old pillowcase and put all her things into it, everything except the letter with Flora's address in Cobourg and the little doll. These she put into the big pocket of her dress, beside her little book of poetry. The pillowcase waited on her bed.

She undid her apron and hung it on its hook, then slipped out the door and walked away from the house. She caught a movement out of the side of her eye, and looked down to see Sigi bouncing along beside her, his ears blowing straight back and his tongue hanging out in the usual grin of pleasure.

Rosetta hurried to her favorite spot in the woods. She sat down on the hard dirt between two tall trees. Sigi stood in front of her, his tail a furious blur, eyes sparkling. "I'm leaving, Sigi. This time for sure," she said. "Runa won't be back for a while, but you'll be all right." She put her nose on Sigi's silky head, breathing in the dog's outdoor scent, and then stroked his smooth sides. "You'll be all right," she said again. She knew he would be able to catch rabbits and squirrels if Mr. Thomas didn't bother to feed him, and she had seen him drinking from the trough by the barn fence when his water dish was empty. And probably Ben's daughter would put scraps out for him if she saw him around the yard. "But there'll be no one to give you leftover johnnycake and syrup, like I do, will there? You'll miss your treat." The dog licked her face.

Rosetta wriggled around until her back was comfortable against a tree trunk, then reached into her pocket and took out the poetry book. She opened it and tried to read, but the sharp edges of the sun through the fluttering leaves above her made slashes of light and shadow on the pages. Rosetta put the book back in her pocket and just sat, listening.

In the still heat of the bright day the minutes passed slowly. A fly buzzed around her face, and she brushed it away without even noticing. Then she heard the kitchen door opening, followed by the hollow slam as it closed, the sound creeping across the distance to where she sat. She pulled her knees up in front of her, putting her arms around them and resting her cheek on top of them. Eli would be eating his dinner. As soon as he was finished, she would go back in and get her things and walk over to the Fergussons, save Iain the trip. There was no reason to wait; Mr. Thomas wouldn't be back, and the afternoon would drag. She would rather spend the time helping Mrs. Fergusson, maybe reading to little Geordie.

She rocked back and forth, looking at the dog. Sigi lay beside her now, his narrow nose on his paws. He stared into the underbrush in front of him, in the direction of the house, his soft brown eyes seeming to watch, and wait.

After what felt like an eternity, she heard the second slam of the kitchen door. Rosetta lifted her head, and the dog jumped up and looked at her. When she made a lowering motion with her hand, Sigi sat down again immediately, his feathery tail spread on the ground behind him, motionless.

Rosetta waited much longer than the length of time she knew it would take Eli to get back to his fence-mending, then got to her feet and walked silently through the trees until she had a clear view of the farmyard.

The yard was still. No breeze ruffled the leaves of the morning glory or turned the creaking weathervane on the roof of the barn. The stillness was eerie, as if everything was holding its breath, was waiting for some unknown thing to happen.

When Rosetta came out of the woods and started walking across the yard, toward the house, her footsteps sounded unnaturally loud in her own ears. She wished she could see Eli, far out in the field, and run across the open yard when she saw his back turned. But he had moved so that he was blocked by the barn. Suddenly spooked, Rosetta took a deep breath and sprinted across the yard with Sigi beside her. Her heart pounded, and her feet seemed to thud with huge, slow steps.

She jumped up the stairs and opened the door. Sigi sat down on the porch, still watching Rosetta as she stepped inside and silently closed the door behind her. The kitchen was warm. Rosetta pushed open the window beside the door, propping it up with the thick stick that lay on the sill.

Eli had finished all the food. The cloth Rosetta had covered it with lay in a heap on the floor beside the bench. She scooped a dipper of water out of the bucket; it was warm and tasted woody, but it wet her parched lips and tongue and throat. She thought she would give Sigi one last treat before she left, and quickly started to cut a slice of bread. As she glanced toward the maple syrup can, she cut into the middle finger of her left hand with the sharp knife.

A tiny cry slipped out at the unexpected pain, and she put her finger to her mouth to suck away the bright beads of blood that sprang up in the flesh of her finger pad.

Standing at the table, her finger in her mouth, she heard Sigi give one hard, sharp bark. The knife dropped from her hand, clattering to the floor at the same time as she heard the door open. She whirled around.

All she could see in the sun-filled doorway was a dark form.

Rosetta stared hard, trying to make out the outline. For a second she thought it might be Mr. Thomas, but in the next instant she knew it wasn't. She took her bleeding finger away from her mouth and felt for the edge of the table behind her.

"So," said Eli's voice, slow and quiet, "the little Home girl decided to come in after all." He stepped inside. "It was real lonely, at dinnertime, with the mister and missus gone, and you nowhere in sight."

Rosetta felt her breath quicken. "Did you forget something?" she asked, trying to push the upward rush of air in her throat back down, keep her voice normal. She stooped and picked up the bread knife, holding it in front of her casually, but her loosely curled fingers were ready to grip it more tightly if she had to.

Eli stayed in the doorway, watching her. "What kinda sandwiches you makin' there?" he asked.

"Syrup. Just maple syrup sandwiches," Rosetta said, seeing the sweat-soaked front of his overalls, feeling the dull throbbing of her cut finger.

"I like maple syrup," Eli said. "I like sweet things."

The way he said "sweet" made a bitter flood of disgust rise in Rosetta's throat. She wanted to turn around, spread the syrup on the bread as if she didn't care that he was there, as if she weren't afraid of him. But she couldn't turn her back on him.

"So what did you say you came to the house for?" she said, the knife still held in front of her, blade pointing toward Eli.

He looked at her face, then at the knife. "Forgot to take some water with me after dinner," he said. "Sun's wicked hot today. Can't work all afternoon without no water." He held up an empty jar.

Rosetta felt a tiny prickle of relief. He *had* come back for a reason then. A reason she could stand to think about.

"You better get it then," she said, gesturing toward the pump with her head. "But you could have got some outside."

Eli looked again at the knife in her hand. Rosetta saw a long teardrop of sweat run from his temple down the side of his jaw.

"I know," he said, smiling and going to the kitchen pump.

Rosetta looked away from the sight of the brown stains on his teeth.

"See you at supper then," Eli said and left. Rosetta heard him whistling as he went down the steps.

She let her shoulders drop, and looked down at the knife in her hand. As she watched, her hand started shaking, just a tiny quiver at first, but quickly turning to a steady vibrating. The tremor went from her hand into her wrist and up her arm, and then her whole body was trembling. She clenched her jaw to keep her teeth still.

Only when the sound of Eli's whistling grew fainter and fainter, and finally faded away, only then did she turn back to the table and put the knife down. She felt for the back of one of the kitchen chairs, then let herself slide down onto it.

When she finally stopped shaking, and stood up, she noticed that her skirt was streaked with blood. Her finger was still bleeding, but she couldn't feel any pain. She couldn't feel anything, except the thump of her own heartbeat.

~

Rosetta ripped a strip of cloth from a clean piece of cotton in the rag bin and tied it around her finger. Then she tried to sponge the blood out of her skirt with cold water, but she couldn't get it all out. She went to the door and gave the bread and syrup to Sigi. He wolfed it down in two huge gulps, then settled down in the shade with a contented sigh.

She went upstairs and picked up her pillowcase, looking around the room one last time. From outside, she heard Sigi give a low bark, then another, and then the barking turned to hard, angry baying. Rosetta knew there was only one person he barked at like that. No, she told herself, not wanting to believe Sigi. No, he didn't come back.

But Eli was already inside the house and starting up the stairs, an expression on his face that wasn't quite a smile.

"Go away," Rosetta said. Then again, louder. "*No*! Go away, Eli, go away. I'll tell Mr. Thomas!" She thought of the knife, still lying on the table in the kitchen.

As Eli kept climbing the stairs slowly, with that strange, unsettling look on his face, Rosetta's eyes scanned the room. There was nothing in it, nothing but the bed and her empty trunk. Frantically, she threw down the pillowcase and kneeled on the bed and leaned out the window. It was far too small for her to squeeze through, and even if she could, it was a straight drop to the hard ground below.

When Eli reached the top of the stairs, Rosetta was still on her knees on the bed.

"You don't have to be scart of me, Rosie," he said.

"I'm not scared," Rosetta said, the skin just beside her mouth giving an odd pulling, a tiny dancing movement.

Eli took one step closer. "You know I always did fancy you."

Rosetta's eyes moved behind Eli, taking in the size of the stairway opening, trying to figure out how to get Eli away from it to give her room to get by.

"I never knowed anyone so pretty as you, Rosie," Eli said, taking another step into the room.

Rosetta scrambled to her feet. There was no way around Eli without being close enough for him to touch her. Outside, Sigi's frenzied barking went on and on.

Rosetta listened to the barking, thought about the kitchen, with its open window. "That silly dog," she said, parting her lips in what she hoped was a smile, and then, in one sudden movement, pursing them and whistling.

Eli stepped toward her, one hand outstretched. "What're you doing? Stop it."

Rosetta whistled again, backing away from Eli. "Sigi!" she screamed.

Eli sprang across the small room at her, grabbing her fore-arms in his huge hands. "I said stop it. Stop whistlin' for that dumb dog." He pulled her toward him.

As his face loomed above her, Rosetta smelled the sourness

of his breath, the stink of his sweat-soaked skin and clothes. She twisted her head away.

"One kiss won't hurt," Eli said. "You Home girls know how to kiss, don't you? I heared a thing or two about Home girls."

Rosetta kicked at his shins as hard as she could. She felt the toe of her boot connect with bone.

Eli dropped her wrists. "*Owww*," he cried. "You little . . ." he reached toward her and grabbed the collar of her dress, just under her chin. As Rosetta tried to pull away, she heard a ripping noise. She punched at the man's face with her fists and pushed one of her fingers into his eye. With a howl of pain he threw her against the wall. As she hit it, Rosetta felt as if a hot rod had been thrust into her lower back, just at the side under her ribs. Sigi raced up the stairs into the room.

"Sigi!" she screamed again. The dog flew at Eli's back, sinking his teeth into the bare skin of the man's upper arm.

The force of the dog's body and the shock of his bite threw Eli toward the bed. The little dog was too small to do any real damage, but he distracted Eli long enough for Rosetta to scramble down the stairway.

Behind her she could hear Sigi's growls and yips and Eli's curses. She sped through the kitchen and out the door, into the yard. Each time she tried to take a deep breath, the pain in her back grew fiercer and hotter, so she had to take small, shallow breaths.

There wasn't time to get to the woods. It would only be a minute before Eli had shaken off Sigi and got downstairs and outside, and he would see her running across the yard. And there were only the open road and fields – no other place to run where she couldn't be seen. Eli would jump on his horse and catch up to her in a matter of minutes.

There had to be some place to hide.

She raced past the barn. It would be the first place Eli would look, with its loft of hay bales.

She glanced at the henhouse, but knew the indignant squabbling and squawking of the roosting chickens would give her away if she tried to stay inside.

Then she saw the corn crib, off to one side of the henhouse. It was little more than a small bin, used for keeping the husked, dried corn-on-the-cob to feed the pigs and fatten the poultry. The crib's sides and ends were made of wooden slats, and the top was covered with a few old boards. The four posts that held it off the ground were wrapped with tin, to keep rats and mice from climbing in and feasting on the cobs.

Rosetta put her feet on the bottom slat and pulled back one of the top boards, gritting her teeth with the rush of pain the extra effort brought to the spot on her back. She climbed in onto what was left of the mushy, rotting corn from last fall's crop, then slid the board back in place. Holding her breath against the stench, she crawled to one far end, into a front corner, feeling the ooze of the soft cobs as she crushed them under her knees.

The cramped, stifling bin wasn't high enough for her to sit up, but Rosetta brought her knees up to her face and curled her upper body over them, trying to will away the hot, terrible pain in her back. She breathed into her skirted knees, partly to filter out the terrible moldy smell of the almost airless crib and partly to cover her gasps.

She heard the kitchen door bang, then Eli's voice.

"Rosie? Rosetta! You better get yerself over here."

Then there was silence. Rosetta kept her face buried between her knees.

Her head started to feel light and achy, and a far-away buzzing started in her ears. She thought of Sigi, and wondered what Eli had done to him.

Eli's voice suddenly rang out, so close she thought he'd found her. He must have been searching the barn all this time, and now had come out, and was right beside the corn crib.

"You can hide from me, Rosie, but you can't stay hidden forever. You have to come out sometime. And when you do, I'll be waitin' for you." One of the boards on the top of the crib was thrust back, and light flooded in. Rosetta pressed further into the corner and stopped breathing, waiting for Eli's shaggy head to come into view. But he must have looked straight down, not imagining that she could fit any farther in. The board dropped back in place. There was a sudden thump, and an odd, muffled sound that Rosetta couldn't figure out.

"I kilt your dog," Eli yelled. "He's dead."

Rosetta pressed her lips even tighter against her skirt.

"You better come out 'n bury him. He's lying here in the yard. Come have a look. The flies will be after him soon enough."

There was silence, then Eli started again. "I know you're around here somewheres, and you have to come out," he repeated, yelling louder this time. "And when you do, I'll be right here, waiting for you. You have to come out, Home girl."

Then there was only silence. Rosetta didn't know if he'd moved away and was looking for her somewhere else on the farm or was still there, leaning up against the fence near the crib.

She slowly put her trembling hand up to her front, feeling the torn material of her dress and petticoat. Her fingers touched her bare skin.

She thought of Eli's fingers there, on her clammy skin, then she pressed her mouth against her skirt again and whispered into it, so softly that even the rooster walking by the crib, neck bobbing proudly, didn't hear.

"No. I don't, Eli," she breathed. "I don't have to come out. Not for you. Not for anybody."

~

Time went by. It was hard to tell how much, but Rosetta felt like she was passing in and out of some strange, heavy sleep. At one point she thought she heard voices, and tried to clear her head. One voice was Eli's, but the other was too low for her to make out.

"Nope," Eli's voice said. "She run off, this morning. Took her things and was gone. I seen her go."

The other voice said something, and then Eli's again, sharper this time. "I told you. She's gone. You think I don't know what I seen?"

Iain, Rosetta thought. Iain's here for me. She lifted her head and tried to move from her bottom to her knees, but the same strange heaviness seemed to fill her head and body, and then blackness rushed in at her, covering her.

Chapter Twenty-Seven

Rosetta opened her eyes and lifted her head off the filthy floor of the corn crib. She remembered trying to get up, trying to – what had she been trying to do? Iain. Iain had been here, and she had tried to call him. But all she had managed to do was collapse on her side. She lay still for another moment, collecting her energy, and then pushed herself to her knees. She gasped as the movement awakened the pain in her back.

Licking her parched lips, she blinked in the darkness. The ugly thoughts of Eli, and of poor Sigi, rushed into her head, and dread wrapped her in fear as cold and binding as a wet sheet.

Stiffly, she moved enough to peer through the slats on the side of the crib facing the yard. The farmyard was flooded with bright moonlight.

She inched away the board over her head, holding her breath, and put her head up until her eyes were even with the top slat. She looked toward the house and, as she watched, saw the sudden flare of a match near the kitchen door. The flame moved upward, and Eli's face was illuminated. He was sitting on the top step. He lit the thin, rolled cigarette he held between his lips. Rosetta watched the arc of fire as he tossed the burning match onto the hard-packed dirt in front of the steps. The wooden match burned for a few seconds, then dimmed, and finally went out.

Rosetta watched the cigarette, following the red glow as it moved up to Eli's mouth and burned brighter as he inhaled; then, the fainter glow as it moved down when Eli rested his hand on his knee.

Rosetta carefully pulled in her head, but positioned herself so she could watch the step from inside the crib. She watched Eli smoke two more cigarettes and light a fourth, then flinched as he abruptly stood and flicked the still-lit cigarette onto the dirt. She noiselessly moved back a few inches from her watching place between the slats.

Eli stretched his arms over his head, then walked down the steps. The moon went behind a cloud, and Rosetta held her breath, wondering if he was walking toward the corn crib. But the cloud passed quickly, and when the moon's rays shone again, Rosetta could see Eli heading toward the shanty. Just before he ducked his head at the doorway, he took one long, slow look around the yard. Then he scratched under one arm, yawned, and went inside.

Rosetta waited. Her legs ached from kneeling so long, and she could feel one foot numbing. When the moonlight had moved down to the far end of the crib, she climbed out of the bin. She stood for a minute, steadying herself by hanging on to the side of the crib. She tried to reach around to the left side of her back with her right hand to feel what had happened, but it hurt too much. She tiptoed from the corn crib.

She had to leave as fast as she could, get to the Fergussons'. But before she left, she had to find Sigi. She couldn't whistle for him or call him. Eli could be lying awake, listening. Maybe even watching the yard, from his bed inside the doorway, just as she had done from inside the crib.

That thought made her freeze and glance toward the shanty. As she stood there, she heard a sound.

A tiny whimper, hardly louder than the chirping crickets. She strained, listening. It came again, the whimper, from the clump of long weeds a few yards to her left, just at the side of the main yard.

She knew the sound, and it made her heart leap. She moved toward the clump and, crouching on her haunches, carefully parted the weeds and made a circle with one hand. She put it to her mouth.

"Sigi?" she breathed into the circle of her thumb and fingers.

She was rewarded with the faintest of stirring from farther on in the weeds. Rosetta reached into the prickly green and felt the warm body she knew so well. But the normally soft hair was stiff and matted, and under her fingers the dog's body barely rose and fell.

"Sigi, Sigi," Rosetta whispered, making small kissing noises as she spread apart the weeds. When she saw the dark form of the little dog lying on his side, Rosetta shut her eyes. "Please be all right, Sigi, please," she whispered, then opened her eyes, straining to see him in the moonlight.

She pushed the weeds around Sigi down, then sat back on her heels. The dog's head and side seemed dark and strangely flat, and its back leg was twisted out behind at an unnatural angle.

"Sigi," she whispered once more. The dog's eyelids flickered and then slowly opened. Rosetta leaned forward and lay her forehead against Sigi's. "My poor, poor little dog," she murmured.

A strange sound came from the dog's throat, more of a gurgle than the whimper Rosetta had heard earlier. Rosetta lifted her head, and the gurgling stopped abruptly. Sigi lay still and silent.

Rosetta moved her head down to the dog's side, and gently lay her ear on it. It was damp and sticky, and Rosetta realized that the dark, flat look of Sigi's head and body was made by drying blood. She heard an irregular, weak flutter.

Sliding her hands underneath Sigi, biting her bottom lip with the effort not to hurt the dog even more, Rosetta lifted him so that he rested again her chest. The little creature lay limp in Rosetta's arms.

Looking over her shoulder at the shanty one last time, Rosetta rose, not allowing herself to think about her own injury, and, leaning protectively over the precious bundle, crept out of the yard.

~

Carrying Sigi, and with her own pain, it took Rosetta twice as long as it usually did to cross the fields to the Fergusson farm. Even though Sigi was small and light, Rosetta's arms began to ache. She longed to rest, but was afraid – afraid that Eli would come after her, and afraid that Sigi would die.

Rosetta thought of Mrs. Fergusson getting up with the dawn and baking a big batch of her fluffy biscuits, and realized how hungry she was. She thought of how wonderful it would be to wash her hands and face, and eat a still-warm biscuit, and crawl under one of Mrs. Fergusson's eiderdown quilts and sleep, just for a few hours.

As Rosetta stumbled through the newly turned earth of the fields, Sigi's blood caking on her own bare chest where her dress and petticoat had been torn by Eli, Rosetta finally saw the buildings on the Fergusson farm come into view. She allowed herself to stop for a moment, taking a few deep breaths. She leaned her head down against Sigi and, feeling the dog's tiny movement as he breathed, said a small prayer of thanks that he was still alive.

Rosetta staggered to the edge of the Fergussons' yard and had to stand still for a moment, swaying. Everything looked and sounded different. She turned her head at the swishing, almost galloping sound that came at her from the direction of the house, and then Bonnie was standing in front of her. The dog looked up, her usual friendly expression replaced by a worried wrinkling of the loose flesh on her muzzle.

"Quietly, Bonnie, quiet, there's a good girl," Rosetta said. She walked partway across the yard, to where an old children's wagon sat, piled with rags and a corn-husk doll. She bent down and pushed the doll aside with her elbow, gently placing Sigi on the soft rags.

Bonnie immediately moved in, her legs stiff and cautious, and began anxiously snuffling at her now-grown pup.

"That's right, Bonnie. You look after him," Rosetta said. "Look after him until Mrs. Fergusson gets up."

The old mother dog didn't glance at Rosetta, but began licking the smaller dog's side with long, slow caresses.

"Good, Bonnie," Rosetta said, then put her hand on Sigi's head. The pain in her back bit with a relentless gnawing. Rosetta managed to get her other hand up behind her back and feel, carefully. Her dress was ripped and, like Sigi's fur, stiff and matted with dried blood. Other than that, all Rosetta's fingers could make out was a crusty, tender area. She realized she must have punctured her back on one of the big nails that stuck out, here and there, of the rough walls of the bedroom. And if Mrs. Fergusson knew she was hurt, she would never let her go. She would make her stay until she was completely healed. She knew the way Mrs. Fergusson thought. She'd convince her to stay a few days, a week . . .

"No." Rosetta said. "No. I'm going. Now. Nothing can stop me this time. I'm going to be with Flora for her birthday." The pain in her back seemed to be lessening.

She looked around the yard. The clothesline that stretched between trees in the yard was strung with Mrs. Fergusson's never-ending wash. Rosetta went to the line and looked at the clothes hanging dry and still, attached to the rope with rough wooden pegs.

She unpegged a shirt and a pair of overalls that she recognized as Iain's, knowing she couldn't go on her way with her dress torn and bloodied. She felt badly about taking Iain's clothes, but felt worse that he would think she had run off without waiting for him, without saying good-bye. But this was the only way.

Before she slipped off her dress, she shoved her hands down into her dress pocket, hearing the crackle of paper and feeling the soft muslin of the doll.

She squeezed the little doll, then, setting it and the letter down on the grass, took off her dress and petticoat, wincing as the stuck, blood-stiffened cloth pulled free. She tore long strips from her petticoat, took a big handkerchief off the clothesline, and wrapped the strips around her body, holding the folded handkerchief in place over her wound. Then she put on the cotton shirt. It smelled clean and fresh, of laundry soap and summer night air. She stepped into the overalls and did up the straps. It felt strange to wear pants, but she was comforted, in a small way, by the fact that they were Iain's, that he had worn these clothes next to his body. She shoved the letter and doll into the overall pockets, then rolled her clothes up into a wad and pushed them down deep into the center of a prickly cranberry bush to one side of the clothesline.

Rosetta went back to the two dogs. Bonnie looked up at her, her patient eyes resting on Rosetta for a moment. Then she lowered her head again and continued her healing licks on Sigi.

"Good-bye, brave little Sigi," Rosetta said, bending down and kissing the dog on the narrow space between its ears. The dog's slanted eyes flickered again, opened, and looked at Rosetta. She saw that they no longer had the blank, dazed expression as when she had first found him in the weeds.

He blinked at Rosetta, as if trying to clear his vision.

"Good-bye, Sigi," Rosetta said again, wiping at her tears with the back of her hand. But when she started to straighten up again, the ground under her tilted and swayed, and suddenly raced up to meet her surprised eyes.

Chapter Twenty-Eight

She was moving. Strong arms were holding her. She turned her face and pressed against soft flannel, then opened her eyes and looked up.

It was Iain, carrying her. "Iain," she breathed. He looked down. She saw that his mouth was curved into a hard, straight line. She wondered if his face looked so different because of the weight of her, or surprise, or something else.

"My good Lord," Rosetta heard Mrs. Fergusson say, and in a moment Iain was cautiously lowering her into the rocking chair on the porch. "Oh my, oh Lordy," Mrs. Fergusson said again, then bent, looking into her face. "Where did you find her, Iain? And why is she dressed like that – isn't that your shirt, now?"

"She was just out in the yard. And Sigi's here, too, and he's hurt."

Mrs. Fergusson pulled a smaller chair up in front of Rosetta so that her knees touched the girl's. She brushed Rosetta's tangled hair off her forehead and looked into her eyes. "And are you hurt, too, lass?"

Rosetta let her upper back touch the curved wood of the rocking chair, fighting to keep her face blank, and shook her head slightly. "I'm all right," she said, but her mouth was so dry the words came out with a furry, distorted sound.

"Iain, get her some water." As Iain ran into the house, Mrs. Fergusson put Rosetta's two hands in hers. "Tell me what happened. Iain went over to get you, but that Eli said you'd run off. I couldn't believe it. There would be no good reason for you to do a thing like that. Iain wouldn't believe him either. He went back a second time, later on, but Eli stuck by his story. And Iain said there was no sign of you, or the wee dog, and he started to think there might be some strange truth to it. He even went into Magrath Corners, asking around if anyone had seen you."

"I was hiding," Rosetta said, barely above a whisper, and took the cup of water Iain held out to her. When she'd drained it, she licked her lips and said, "Hiding from Eli."

"Was it him that hurt Sigi?" Iain cried out.

Rosetta looked up at him and nodded. "He thought Sigi was dead, but I brought him here." She looked down at the overalls she was wearing. "My clothes were all torn."

A long, sad sigh escaped from Mrs. Fergusson.

"They were torn, and I . . . I needed something to wear, so I took these from the clothesline."

"And why were your clothes torn, lass?" Mrs. Fergusson asked, as if she already knew the answer. Her voice was gentle. She glanced in Iain's direction. "Go away with you, lad, for a few minutes. Let the girl tell me what happened."

Rosetta watched Iain's legs move down the porch steps and across the yard toward Bonnie and Sigi. She pressed her lips together.

"Was it Eli?"

Rosetta nodded, shutting her eyes and trying to blot out the sight of his mouth, so close to hers. Of his filth-covered fingers at her neck.

Mrs. Fergusson rubbed Rosetta's hands between her own. "Did he harm you? Tell me the truth, lass. It's no fault of yours, whatever did happen over there. You've nothing to be ashamed of."

Mrs. Fergusson's sad, kind voice and the warmth of her hands on Rosetta's were too much. Rosetta gave a single sob, and then the tears started. And once they started, she couldn't stop them. "No," she sobbed. "He tried to get at me, but I fought him off. Sigi helped me get . . .," she didn't even want the sound of his name on her tongue, "get him away from me. I kicked him, and scratched him, and I got him in the eye. A good one." She tried to laugh, but it came out watery and shrill.

"So you've not been hurt, then? You got yourself clear of him in time?" Mrs. Fergusson pulled a big white hanky from somewhere and mopped at Rosetta's eyes and then handed it to her. Rosetta blew her nose.

"Yes," Rosetta said. "Will you check if Sigi's all right?"

"Iain's just seeing to him. You come inside with me. You'll get cleaned up and have something to eat. A good cup of tea can do wonders. And then you go on to Shelagh's bed and try to close your eyes for a bit. There's something I have to do."

"But I'm still going to leave today."

Mrs. Fergusson tucked Rosetta's loose hair behind her ears and put her hands on both sides of the girl's face. "Are you sure you're up to it? A long journey right after such an upset?"

Rosetta nodded.

"Well, you know yourself. Come inside now, and have a wash. There's warm water ready and waiting. And then I'll make you some breakfast."

Rosetta didn't think she could eat a thing, or sleep at all, but she did both. As long as she moved very slowly, and kept her left arm close to her side, the pain stayed down. When she had finished the breakfast Mrs. Fergusson made, she lowered her head onto the little pillow on Shelagh's cot, and within minutes was fast asleep.

~

"Come lass. If you're to leave this morning, it's time you were up. You've been sleeping two hours now."

Rosetta waited until Mrs. Fergusson had left the room, then sat up. She reached around with her right hand and touched the soft padding of the folded handkerchief under Iain's shirt. It was still in place.

When she walked into the kitchen, Mr. Thomas was there. Her pillowcase was on the table in front of him. The man's eyes were bloodshot, and his cheeks were covered with stubble. Mrs. Fergusson, arms crossed, leaned against the sink.

"I went over with Iain, and he was just arriving home," she said. "I told him what happened while he was away."

Mr. Thomas glanced at Rosetta, his eyes widening at her clothing. "I brung your stuff over. It was spilled around your room, but I think everything's there."

Rosetta opened the pillowcase and looked inside, then nodded.

"I'll be outside, cutting some flowers," Mrs. Fergusson said. "All the kiddies are outside, too. Rosetta, you call when you're ready for Iain to drive you over to the Corners. He's got your first ride set up there."

Silence fell when Mrs. Fergusson left. There didn't seem to be anything for either of them to say. Finally, Rosetta said, "I'm glad you brought my things. I would have hated to leave without them."

Mr. Thomas rubbed at his eyes with his fingertips. "I went all the way over to Thomson's Landing. Slept it off there, then turned around and come back." He rubbed his hand over his head. "I never figured Eli for pulling a stunt like that."

Rosetta picked up the pillowcase. "I'll be on my way now."

Mr. Thomas looked up at her. "Do you believe she'll be back?"

"Runa? Of course."

"She told you that, for a fact? She said she and Soffia would come back to me?"

Rosetta sat down again. "She'll be back." The sound of the children's laughter came in through the windows. Bonnie barked as if joining the game. "Would you like . . . Mr. Thomas, would you like me to write a letter for you? To Runa?"

Mr. Thomas looked toward the open window. "What would I say?"

"Say what you're thinking. That's all. Tell her that you want her to be better, that you want Soffia to grow healthy. Tell her that you'll miss her. Isn't that what you're thinking?"

"That. And some."

Rosetta opened her sack and pulled out her last piece of paper. She went to Mrs. Fergusson's sideboard and took a pencil that was sitting on top of a book there. Then she sat down across from Mr. Thomas and they started the letter.

~

The ride to Magrath Corners was far too long, and far too short. All Rosetta could think of was that she was really, finally on her way to find Flora. And that this would be the last time she might ever see Iain Fergusson again. She had almost forgotten about the constant pain in her back, except for each time the wagon wheel hit a stone or hole in the road, and the jolt set her teeth on edge.

At the store, Iain introduced her to Mr. and Mrs. Jewell, traveling to a small town halfway to Cobourg. She would stay with them overnight, and then they would make sure she found another ride toward Cobourg. As the elderly couple were getting everything settled in their wagon, Iain and Rosetta stood to one side of the store steps.

"Thank you for all your kindness to me," Rosetta said, putting her hands into the pockets of Iain's overalls. Mrs. Fergusson had suggested she leave them on, for traveling, and keep her good navy dress clean.

"You don't know what you'll find when you get to Cobourg, and you'll want to make a good impression," the woman had said, as she fretted and clucked around Rosetta just before she got into the wagon. "And you'll write to us all, won't you, dear, when you get there? I'll have to know that you've found that sister of yours, and that you're all right."

"I'll write, Mrs. Fergusson," Rosetta had said, waving her thank-yous and good-byes to her and the children, who ran along behind the wagon all the way down the lane.

"And thank you for giving me your clothes," she added to Iain. He shrugged, then took off his wool cap and set it on her head. "Might as well have the whole outfit," he said, and she took off the hat and turned it round and round in her hands.

"Almost ready, young lady," Mr. Jewell called. Iain and Rosetta looked at each other.

"Good-bye," Rosetta said softly.

Iain put his arms around her, awkwardly at first, then firmly. Rosetta moved into them, nestling the top of her head under Iain's chin. She longed to move her head back, put her face up to his, but she was too afraid of what would happen if she did. Too afraid that it would make the leaving even more painful.

"Good-bye, Rosetta," Iain said, his chin still pressed onto Rosetta's hair, and Rosetta could hear his voice vibrate through the top of her head and travel down, all the length of her body. She took a deep breath of him, knowing she wouldn't forget his smell, then climbed into the wagon without looking at him again, but as they pulled away she couldn't resist. As she turned in the seat, he ran a few steps after the wagon, just a few, and called, "And I'll write back, I promise." She smiled and waved until he was out of sight, then pressed his hat to her face and kept it there for as long as she had to.

~

On the morning of the third day, Rosetta was jostling along in the back of a wagon, in between crates of flapping, alarmed chickens. Her legs, in the soft old denim that had grown stiff, caked with the dirt of the roads, hung over the back end of the wagon, and Rosetta watched the brilliant ricocheting of the sun through the emerald trees that rolled away from the wagon behind her. She shifted her weight, trying to get comfortable in the narrow space on the hard wooden floor of the wagon, putting her hands into her pockets and reassuring herself, for the hundredth time, that she still had the now-grimy letter with the address of the Forsythes in one pocket and the doll, also slightly dirty from Rosetta's constant handling, in the other.

Her back was worse today. The first night she had spent on the Jewells' parlor sofa, unable to find a position that didn't put pressure on her back. She had drifted in and out of a restless sleep, rising stiff and strangely warm. The next morning she had ridden on the back of another wagon, expecting to be in Cobourg late in the day, but one of the wheels had come off the wagon. She'd had to sit for most of the afternoon while the driver repaired it and got it back on, and by then he hadn't wanted to go the rest of the way that day. He'd taken her to a friend's farm, and after she'd been given a bowl of soup, she slept in the barn. By then she knew she had a fever. The puncture on her back wasn't bleeding any more, but when she explored the spot with her fingers, it seemed puffy and still very tender to the touch. Now, on this third day, she wondered if she could last on the wagon much longer, or if she would have to stop somewhere, in one of the soft-looking green fields, and just lie down, lie down and sleep and sleep. She was alternately burning hot, and then cold. Sometimes she almost fell asleep, but the constant clucking and squawks of the chickens kept her awake. Her eyes were gritty and sore.

Finally, she thought she couldn't stand it another moment and decided to ask the driver to stop and let her off. They must be close, and walking, even if it took twice as long, wouldn't be so hard on her. She half turned and called to the stooped, balding man holding the reins.

"Could you tell me how much farther you'll be going before you planned to stop?"

The man didn't turn his head. "No farther. Cobourg's just up ahead. I'll take you in as far as I'm going."

Rosetta turned and got to her knees on the rumbling floor and looked beyond the man's head. In the distance were buildings. The midday heat shimmered around the city like a magic cloud.

"You been to Cobourg before?" the man asked, again over his shoulder.

"No," Rosetta said.

"You visitin' folk there, then?" the man said.

"Yes," Rosetta said. "I'm visiting folk."

She couldn't stop herself from reaching into her pocket and fingering the soft muslin of the doll once more.

She was so close.

Chapter Twenty-Nine

Rosetta stood on a short street and looked at the houses that lined either side. They were small, but well-kept, the lawns trimmed and flowers blooming in the yards and window boxes.

Rosetta pulled out the letter again and looked up at the signpost. With the effort it took to raise her hands to her head, she tucked her hair up under Iain's cap more securely. She had worn the cap most of the time, but still, her hair was matted and filthy from the three days' travel, and she couldn't get her comb or brush through it. She had stopped at a horse trough on her journey through the city and washed her hands and face. Now she feebly slapped at the thighs of her overalls, seeing the puffs of dust rise out of them. She held her bag over one shoulder, knowing she should put on her navy dress, but the thought of finding a place to change, and the act itself, seemed a huge job. She just wanted to get to Flora, now. As she started up the street, the sidewalk under her feet felt uneven, twisted. She watched her feet shuffle along, wondering why it was such an effort to even pick them up.

Number Eighty was a two-storey red-brick house with gingerbread decorations around the roof and verandah. The front door had a long oval window with a sheer curtain over it. Before Rosetta knocked, she noticed that the front windows were closed, and the curtains over them tightly shut.

She took two deep breaths, then knocked.

She waited a few minutes and knocked again. After a third try, she realized, with a sinking heart, that no one was home. She sat down on a wicker chair on the verandah, telling herself that Mr. Forsythe would be at work and, likely, Mrs. Forsythe had taken Flora and gone to do her morning marketing. They would be home soon, she said to herself, sitting very still and looking out at the quiet street. She felt terribly thirsty, and at times her head felt like it was very light, so light that if she dared to close her eyes, for even a few seconds, to rest them, her head might float, float off her shoulders and into the air above. But she couldn't keep on fighting, and eventually her eyelids dropped over her eyes. With her eyes closed, everything started to become a dream, all of it, Eli and Sigi, saying good-bye to Iain, the trip to Cobourg. Maybe it was, Rosetta thought, and maybe it's a dream to think I'll ever find Flora.

She eventually opened her eyes and saw a woman walking heavily up the wooden sidewalk, carrying a basket over one arm. Rosetta leaned forward in her chair, trying to see if there was a child with her. But the woman appeared to be alone. Rosetta sat back.

The woman stopped at the gate of the house beside the Forsythes'. She was a middle-aged woman, heavyset, with a doughy face. Her eyes were like small, bright currants in the puffy flesh. As she started up the walk toward the house, she glanced in the direction of the Forsythes' house and stopped, staring at Rosetta.

"What are you doing there, boy?" she called, then, as Rosetta stood up and came to the edge of the verandah, her eyes widened. "Or are ye a girl? Which is it now?" Her voice was sharp and demanding, like she was used to asking many questions and getting the answers immediately.

"My name is Rosetta Westley, ma'am," Rosetta said. "I'm waiting for Mrs. Forsythe."

The woman shook her head. "You'll have a long wait, I'm afraid." She continued to stare at Rosetta's head, then asked, "And why, now, are ye dressed like a lad?"

Rosetta put her hand up to her head. "Do you know when the Forsythes will be home?"

"If you're looking for work, you'll find none there. The Forsythes are away, down to New York, to the United States. Off to help with Mr. Forsythe's brother. He fell from a roof, repairing some loose shingles, he was, and now he's paralyzed. Paralyzed, and will never walk." She shook her head again and made a whistling sound between her teeth. "Such a tragedy. And him with a young family. So no, there'll be no work for you there."

Rosetta came around the edge of the verandah and down the steps. The woman's eyes traveled over Rosetta's overalls, then rested on the cracked tips of her mud-encrusted boots. "If it's a job you're hoping for, you best clean yourself up a bit. Now I have ironing that needs doing, but I wouldn't let you near it, not in that state." She pursed her lips. "So you'd best be off with you. This is a decent neighborhood. We don't tolerate beggars or idlers here."

Rosetta came to the black wrought-iron fence that separated the two yards. "I've come to see my sister. The Forsythes adopted her. I'm looking for her." She fought to keep her bottom lip from quivering. "Did she go with them, to the United States?" A tremor ran through her voice. She wouldn't let her mind think about how far away from Cobourg that might be.

"The little girl the Forsythes took in last year? That was your sister?" The woman squinted suspiciously. "Don't see the resemblance."

"Do you know, ma'am, when they'll be back, exactly?" Her hands twisted at two of the pointed tops of the fence.

The woman sniffed. "Course I know. They would tell *me*, wouldn't they? I'm the one that's looking after their house while they're away, taking in any post and watering their plants. And I'm telling you, between my husband and myself, we keep the place up a lot tidier than it ever was." She looked at the house behind Rosetta.

Rosetta blinked her eyes rapidly. They felt scalded with held-back tears. "If you could tell me, ma'am," she said, "when they'll be back. Then I'd know how long I had to wait. Before I can see my sister."

The woman shifted the basket onto her other arm. "Oh, no need for you to wait," she said. "The little girl isn't with them any longer. She was always poorly. And Mrs. Forsythe," she leaned a bit closer to Rosetta, "well, I shouldn't be telling you this, but she didn't have the real mothering instinct. It was Mr. Forsythe that treated that little girl real well. I'd see them, out on the verandah, him reading to her and the two of them talking. Him taking her for walks, throwing a ball with her. Mrs. Forsythe always had some imagined ache or pain." She pursed her lips. "She was always complaining how she was sick herself, and couldn't be looking after a sick child."

Rosetta looked at her hands. Even though the skin of her hands was tough, blisters were starting along the fleshy pads under her fingers, where she'd been twisting them on the iron railings. "Isn't with them?" she said, still looking at her hands.

"No. She was took real bad, a few months ago, with some fever, something wrong with her throat. Even called the doctor in, which surprised me. Mrs. Forsythe is real tight with her purse strings. But the doctor couldn't do nothing for her either."

At the woman's words, it was as if the tears hovering at the back of Rosetta's eyes disappeared, dried up. Now her eyes felt as dry as her mouth. She felt dried out everywhere. She opened her mouth to speak, but her lips were stuck together. She tried to lick them, but she had no saliva. She looked away from her hands, into the woman's face.

The woman craned her neck forward, her eyes squinting again. "Now, you don't look too well yourself." She suddenly stepped back. "You don't have nothing, do you, nothing catching? Lots of strange diseases going around, with the hot weather."

Rosetta shook her head. "What . . ." her voice came out a croak. She tried to clear her throat. "What happened to her?" she asked, holding the woman's eyes with her own.

The woman's face softened. "Well, I don't rightly know," she said. "They could tell you over at the hospital. The hospital at the east end of town. That's where they ended up taking her. It's been a good two months since."

Rosetta drew in a ragged breath.

"It was Mr. Forsythe himself, bundled her up and took her over there. He never seemed the same, after. Mrs. Forsythe, she told me that even if the girl got better, they wouldn't have her back. Not the kind of girl they hoped for."

Rosetta curled her fingers into her palms, feeling the sting of the chaffed skin there. "The hospital is at the east end of town?" she said, looking up at the sky, to see the position of the sun.

"Go to the end of the street," the woman said, pointing over Rosetta's head. "Turn left, and walk, oh, a goodly mile or two. You'll come to a bridge, over a river. Go over the bridge and turn left again. Stay on that street, and ask someone to show you how to get to the hospital from there. It's only a short walk after you're over the bridge."

"Thank you," Rosetta said.

As she turned to leave, the woman called after her, "She was a nice little girl. Quiet, but real polite."

Rosetta didn't answer, or look back, but went through the gate, onto the sidewalk, and kept walking, walking toward the end of the street.

～

The hospital smelled of disinfectant and rubber. Rosetta walked to the front desk and waited while a young woman in a white uniform with a striped blue and white shirtwaist finished writing on a slip of paper.

"Yes?" the woman said, looking up. Her hair was a startling orange-red color, and freckles of the same color covered her face.

"I'm here to find my sister," Rosetta said.

"When was she admitted?" the woman asked, tapping the end of her pen on the desk in front of her.

"Two months ago," Rosetta said. She stared at the high white frill with the band of dark-blue ribbon that perched on the top of the woman's hair.

"Two *months* ago? And she's still here?" The nurse frowned.

Rosetta bit into her bottom lip. "I just found out that she was brought here then. I don't know anything more."

The woman sighed. "What's your sister's name?"

"Flora Westley," Rosetta said automatically, then corrected herself. "No, Flora Forsythe." She stopped. "I mean, Eliza Forsythe." A tiny bead of blood appeared on Rosetta's lip.

The woman rolled her eyes upward and crossed her arms over her starched bosom, shoving aside the small, round time-piece pinned onto the uniform. Rosetta noticed that even the woman's hands had the same bright freckles.

"Which is it then?" the nurse asked. "You've given me three names."

"I think you should try Eliza Forsythe," Rosetta answered, raising her index finger to her lip. When she pulled it away, she was shocked to see the smear of blood along the side of her finger. She wet her lips with her tongue.

"Wait here. I'll see," the woman answered. She walked down the hallway to where a tiny, bird-like woman, dressed in the same uniform, sat at another desk. Rosetta saw the first woman say something to the smaller one, turning and nodding at Rosetta as she spoke.

The bird-like woman looked at Rosetta, then stood and

went into a room to her left. Even from down the hall, Rosetta could read the word RECORDS painted on the door in square black letters.

The first woman came back to her post. "You'll have to wait," she said again, in a voice that meant she would have no more to do with Rosetta, then lowered her orange head over her work.

Eventually, the tiny woman came down the hall carrying a single sheet of paper. She approached Rosetta, and Rosetta saw that she was quite old, in spite of her black hair and quick walk. The woman's eyes were small and black, too, but had a gentleness.

"You're looking for a patient by the name of Eliza Forsythe?" she asked.

"Yes," Rosetta answered.

"Your sister, I'm told?"

"Yes," Rosetta answered again. She stared at the paper in the woman's fingers. Her heart hammered painfully against her ribs.

The woman looked down at the paper. "Well, she *was* here, last month." She looked back up, and a shadow passed over the dark gleam of her eyes. "She was hospitalized with quinsy. Badly infected, the throat was. She was treated, but . . ." she hesitated.

Time seemed to stand still. Rosetta watched the woman's mouth as if in a dream, as if she were underwater. Her own mouth filled with a heavy metallic taste. She wondered, briefly, if what she was tasting was more blood from her lip, or the taste of fear, fear at the next words she would hear.

Chapter Thirty

"But?" Rosetta whispered.

"But she's gone now," the woman said. "I'm sorry, but your sister's no longer here."

"No longer here," Rosetta repeated senselessly.

The woman stepped closer to Rosetta. The top of her head came to Rosetta's chin. "You should sit. There, behind you," she said, then put her hand on Rosetta's arm and pushed her toward one of the benches that lined the room.

When the hard edge hit the back of Rosetta's knees, she sat down. The woman lowered herself onto the bench beside her.

"I know it's a disappointment," she said. "You look as if you've traveled a very long way to find your sister." She touched Rosetta's dry, hot hand. "Would you like something to eat? There are always extra trays of food."

Rosetta's eyes were still fixed on a spot on the floor in front of her. "When did she die?" Her voice was not her own; it sounded as if it belonged to someone else, someone much older.

The woman's eyebrows lifted, and she put her small hand to her mouth. "Oh, *no*, my dear. Your sister isn't dead, not at all."

Rosetta finally raised her eyes. She opened her mouth to say "Not dead?" but no words would come. She just closed it again.

"I didn't mean to give you that impression. No, I just meant that she'd been discharged. She's no longer a patient, although she had a long and tedious recovery. She was taken away," she glanced down at the paper, "just over four weeks ago."

Rosetta's head gave a tiny shake, as if she were trying to clear her thoughts. "But the Forsythes didn't take her."

The woman looked down at the paper again. "I don't know, dear. The girl's name is listed under Forsythe, and a Mr. Harry Forsythe is the admitting name." She read further. "He paid for her stay, but under parents or guardians, only *orphan* is printed, with Marchmont Home written beside it." She turned over the paper. "Oh, here's something. Someone has written *See if Branmore Farm will take this one*. Then there's an address." She frowned at it. "It's a county road address, outside of the city. I know it's about five miles to the west."

She started as Rosetta jumped up. "Branmore Farm? To the west?" she said.

The woman nodded. "Well, yes, but surely you're not going to . . ." She stared after Rosetta as the girl turned and walked, as in a trance, toward the front doors of the hospital.

"Wait!" the woman called after her. "Wait. You don't know for sure if that's where she is. And you should have something to eat . . ."

But before she'd finished the sentence, Rosetta had already disappeared.

~

Rosetta hardly noticed the miles. The afternoon sun was directly in her face, but she pulled Iain's cap down low on her forehead, and the wide brim shaded her burning eyes. The main heat of the day seemed to have passed, and a cool, pleasant breeze started up. At one point Rosetta became aware of the smell of lilacs, and she breathed in the heavy, sweet scent as she traveled the government road that ran along the hilly land.

She looked at each farm she passed, and finally, when she met a couple walking up the road toward her, swinging their locked hands, Rosetta called out to them.

"Could you tell me how much farther to Branmore Farm?"

"Just up ahead," the young man answered from across the road. "The one with the orchard."

"Orchard?" Rosetta said.

"Apple orchard," the young woman answered. "The trees are beautiful right now. All in bloom."

"Thank you," Rosetta called, and suddenly her feet lost their weighted sensation, and she began to move faster, feeling lighter and lighter, as if wings had sprouted from the heels of her heavy, cracked leather boots.

~

The house stood on a slight rise at the end of a long, curving drive. Behind it was a barn and to the left of that, an area of short trees with dark, gnarled branches. But every branch was covered in breathtaking pink flowers.

Rosetta began trudging up the drive as the sun lowered, filling the sky with a soft pink that matched the apple blossoms. She realized she was saying "please, please, please, please" with each footstep, fingering the doll in her pocket as if it were a talisman.

As she tipped the brim of her cap back, so she could have a better look at the house, she could see the outline of several figures moving around the yard. Off to one side, there was a swing, suspended from a horizontal branch of a tall tree. Someone was swinging. The body was small, a child, and was little more than a dark silhouette against the pink sky.

As she climbed closer, Rosetta saw how effortlessly the little figure pumped. The child's legs vigorously worked back and forth under the skirt that Rosetta could now see was blue. The swing rose higher and higher. The child threw back her head, and Rosetta saw long curls fly out in a great crescent.

Rosetta stopped and took off her cap. Then, gripping the doll fiercely, she started her uphill climb again.

As if she'd been called, the little girl suddenly turned her head in Rosetta's direction, and her legs stopped. The swing slowed.

Rosetta kept on up the hill, silently, the only sound her own breath. She stared at the child, her eyes locked on her as if they could hold her in place, not let her disappear into a dream.

When at last she could see the child's face clearly, the little girl slid off the swing and lifted her hand in a hesitant wave. Then she waved harder and harder and, after a minute, began jumping up and down, the bright blue of her dress a beautiful stain against the clear pink behind her.

Rosetta raised her own hand, holding the doll, and waved back.